Stilled Life

Stilled Life

Mikel Dunham

St. Martin's Press • New York

STILLED LIFE. Copyright © 1989 by Mikel Dunham. All rights reserved. Printed in the United States of America. No part of this book may be used or reproduced in any manner whatsoever without written permission except in the case of brief quotations embodied in critical articles or reviews. For information, address St. Martin's Press, 175 Fifth Avenue, New York. N.Y. 10010.

Design by Joan Jacobus

Library of Congress Cataloging-in-Publication Data

Dunham, Mikel.
   Stilled life.

   "A Thomas Dunne book."
   I. Title
PS3554.U4684S7   1989   813'.54   88-29858
ISBN 0-312-02645-5

First Edition

10 9 8 7 6 5 4 3 2 1

for Margaret

To Rhea, waking up and getting up were synonymous. She opened her eyes, bopped the alarm, confirmed with the ceiling that she was mentally equipped for the upcoming day, tossed Crunch, her Jack Russell terrier, to the floor, and extracted herself from the bothersome mummy wrappings of her bed.

She didn't walk to the shower. She strode.

She didn't wait for the water to warm. Consolation wasn't what showers were about. Besides, it wasted water.

She took a towel to her skin like a squeegee, folded and poised the wet terry cloth over the bar so that there were equal chrome margins sticking out on each side and, realizing that vaporization had rendered her bathroom useless, abandoned it.

Only when she walked into her closet, where two full-length mirrors opposed one another, where a score of reflected Rheas conspired to distract, did she cease her self-propelled momentum.

Consultation in the mirror: base of operations looking good. Naked, shining, tall, dark and handsome if not actually pretty. Athletic and still great breasts at thirty-

1

ut the tallness, that was what was best. It made one's own lighthouse so much more appropriate to ʒve in.

She switched on the lights of the kitchen, gleaming white.

A fresh nutty smell emanated from the preset brewer. She poured coffee into a clean mug already waiting for her on the counter and booted up her IBM (her home unit was tied into the gallery's).

Over cereal, caffeine, and computer, she scrolled back last night's opening's guest list. From this she compiled a file of people potentially worth stalking for the next three and a half weeks, the length of the current show.

Out of forty-five guests, one art critic (noncommittal and probably not interested), two art-magazine publishers (one of whom was very enthusiastic but also very drunk), several artists who might be good for a few favorable SoHo grapevine reviews, assorted pretty people who, like the flower arrangements, were superfluous once the tables were cleared. Sales: one transaction completed, one major buyer who wanted to work a trade (unacceptable), two buyers who (as always) wanted insultingly bloated discounts, two definite "maybes," one maybe "maybe," one *under*whelmed Whitney representative, one American Craft Museum rep interested in showing a piece next spring (but who was rumored to be in the process of losing her job), one New Museum rep too stoned to accurately appraise.

She had her work cut out for her. There were twenty-four boxes in the show. Emil Orloff, her partner, couldn't be counted on for much assistance. He gave good, even sought-after opening night dinners and that was about it. For the duration of the present show he would more or less scud along on the basis of his reputation as one of the first dealers to leave Fifty-seventh Street for SoHo. The very thought of such lassitude was enough to make her light a Lucky Strike and suck to the butt.

She cleared the screen and went into a file listed DEADFALL, her euphemism for what Emil had become in the past several years: once a dense forest, now a mass of fallen timber and tangled brush through which she had been forced to bulldoze a path. What was the maximum she could get out of him for the show? A few telephone calls. A couple of late boozy lunches with die-hard clients known to be coming to town.

For a moment she daydreamed about murdering him.

She'd read somewhere that in the Middle Ages they would sew up criminals into bags of writhing snakes and hurl them into the Rhine.

The problem was that, even though he was a strutting paragon of discarded talent, he still retained one attribute that Rhea would never have: a natural, electric rapport with the artists. He was a chameleon with them. A magician. If they sulked, he encouraged. If they were dangerously overconfident, he joked them down to a more sturdy self-esteem. If they needed a drinking partner, he could bend elbows with the best of them. Ditto with illicit drugs.

Rhea wasn't the hand-holding type. Scratch the bag of serpents idea. Besides, she was virtually incapable of throwing anything away—a trait Crunch could well appreciate as she lowered her half-empty bowl of Cheerios to the floor.

She refilled her mug and chaperoned it to the bathroom, where she proceeded to shit like a German. (Her father was German and it was her deepest, if unverified, opinion that all Teutons could shit on cue with velocity, ferocity and entirety while Brazilians (her mother's side of the family) eliminated in an unacceptable bossa nova kind of dance-floor slackness.)

The telephone rang.

She knew with satisfaction and without consulting her watch that it was 10:00. She paid Catherine, her personal assistant, a damn hefty wage to be the first in the gallery each morning, exactly one hour before it opened its doors to the public, and to "punch in," via telephone, her arrival. It hardly mattered to Rhea that Catherine sometimes referred to her, behind her back, as "the human time clock." Catherine liked working for a machine. Their relationship, a strictly working one, was so exclusively pooled to gallery tasks that jocularity (at least the office banter variety) was trimmed down to what was not said.

Still enthroned, she picked up the phone in the bathroom.

There was silence on the other end.

"Catherine, is that you?"

Another hesitation on the other end before: "Yes."

More silence.

"What is it?"

"The gallery has been broken into."

"What?"

"When I put the key in the lock this morning," Catherine continued, "I realized that the gallery door was already unlocked. I thought you had maybe come early but when I opened the door . . ."

"We've been robbed?" Rhea interrupted.

"I don't know about that. I can't tell. But . . ."

"But what?"

Catherine took a deep breath. "The new show has been ruined, Rhea. Totally destroyed. Someone has taken all of Al's boxes off the walls and thrown them into two piles in the centers of the rooms. Wait. Let me correct that. They've taken the boxes off the walls and thrown them on the floor and then they've picked them up and carefully placed the ruined boxes in two neat piles, pyramid-like."

"Jesus Christ."

"Yeah, and get this. They even swept up afterward. All the debris has been swept up around the base of the piles. The broom is still leaning against one of them. The floors are ruined where they threw the boxes and—"

"What phone are you at?"

"I'm at my desk."

"Look around. Do you see anything gone?"

"The computer is still—"

"Yeah, I know that, I have it on in the kitchen. What about pictures?"

"Everything else seems to still be here."

"What about in my office?"

There was a pause while Catherine checked the next room.

"It doesn't look like anyone's been in there."

"God, I don't believe this. Have you checked downstairs yet?"

"No, the minute I got here I called you."

"And the alarm? It wasn't on?"

"No. It was off. That's why I thought you were already here."

Rhea paused before asking her next question. It concerned Emil and, although she had nothing but contempt for the man, she made it iron-clad policy never to share that contempt with her employees. Even with Catherine, who knew what was what. "Did Emil go back to the gallery after the dinner last night?"

"I left right after you, Rhea. I don't know. Hello? You still there?"

"Yeah," Rhea answered, "I'm trying to think. Poor Al Kheel. He's been working on that series for two years."

"OK, I'll be right there. Give me five minutes. I'm not dressed yet. Wait! You'd better call the police, I guess."

"What about Emil?"

"What *about* Emil? You know as well as I that his phone will be off the hook. If Simon gets there before me, give him the keys to Emil's loft and have him drag him out of bed. I'm on my way."

She banged the phone in its cradle without saying good-bye, already flushing, already heading for the closet.

She twisted into panties, yanked off the rack a linen suit that didn't require a bra or blouse underneath, found some low-heel shoes, grabbed her evening bag from the night before, extracted a clump of keys and stuffed them into her regular purse.

"Get out of the way, Crunch!" she yelled.

She stormed into the bathroom and brushed her teeth, flashed a dental smile into the defogged mirror, then, grabbing her purse, rushed down the hallway to the front of the loft.

The bolts on her door shot open. If Emil was in any way responsible for this. . . . She took a deep breath, assured herself that she was ready, and violently slammed the door on Crunch's rib cage. A piteous barrage of yelps ensued.

"God damn it to hell are you OK?"

Her concern sounded more like an accusation, and Crunch, sensing this, hunkered down accordingly and modified his complaint to a whimper.

"I'm sorry," she said, scooping him up into her arms and kissing him. "Brave the storm, Crunch," she said, "we've got a shitty day on our hands." And then, rejostling her shoulder bag in order to more tenderly accommodate the transportation of her pet, she ran down the stairs into a drizzling, warm September morning.

Her apartment was on Greene Street, just around the corner from the gallery on Prince. When she rounded the corner she saw Catherine, bleary-eyed, standing under the sodden red flag of the gallery. She was nervously pawing a piece of paper that she thrust at Rhea long before she was within proximity to take it. Even within the blur of these upsetting events, Rhea couldn't help being vaguely repulsed by Catherine's willowy figure. Man, woman or child, she liked a little meat on her humans.

As soon as she approached, Rhea dropped Crunch to the pavement and grabbed the proffered folded paper. She opened it. It was a hand-scrawled note in colored pencil and it read: "There is an exchange for all things, just as there are goods into fire and fire into gold."

"What's this?" Rhea demanded.

"I found it on top of the boxes in the big room."

"I can't believe this! Good God! This is like religious or something. 'Fire into gold.' Is that from the Bible?"

"How should I know?" Catherine snapped back.

"Are you crying?"

"No," Catherine lied.

"Yes you are."

"I'm sorry. It's just that it's so cruel and stupid, what they've done to Al's work. It's so sick."

Rhea stared at a pile of plastic garbage bags stacked against the brick wall next door. Even in the sickest of circumstances, what could have induced anyone to write this? Did she know anyone who would write this? The calligraphy, in red-orange pencil, was wobbly and cramped looking, almost spider-like.

"There's something else." Catherine said. "This note means that I'm incriminated."

"Why do you say that?"

"The police! Fingerprints. They told me to leave everything just as it was. So what do I do? I hang up, go back into the big room, find the note on top of the boxes and pick it up."

"Fingerprints," Rhea intoned while gazing down at the note, now in her hands.

She shot a glance at Catherine and they both began to laugh.

"Christ, the police," Rhea said in a self-sobering tone. "Have you ever dealt with them before?"

"Not really."

"Me either."

A ludicrous vision entered her mind in which cops chewing on crumbly doughnuts scratched their backs against an eighty-thousand-dollar bronze sculpture while asking her to explain what, exactly, was a box.

"Cops. Shit. Catherine, whatever happens, we can't

come off looking like a couple of ninnies. Please, Al or no Al, you have to can the tears. We've got to be on top of this.

"And as for this note," she said, realizing that it was now damp and beginning to stick to the palm of her hand, "well, I'll give it to the cops immediately so there won't be any embarrassment later on. Are you OK now?"

Catherine nodded her head.

"You sure? I hope so because I'm sure as hell going to need you today. Look at us! We're getting soaked. Let's go survey the battlefield. Crunch, come on! You can do that later."

The dog reluctantly abandoned a pee in progress and hobbled up onto the sidewalk.

"What happened to Crunch?" Catherine asked.

"Crunch? He's all right. Got caught in a door, that's all. Let's go."

They mounted the two steps that led into the gallery. Rhea stopped to examine the lock of the opened door. No evidence of tampering.

Once inside, what little levity had been mustered was instantly sucked up into the gallery's theatrical track lighting high above. Catherine had neither exaggerated nor imagined the weirdness of the scene.

As you walked in, there were two viewing areas divided by a non-supporting wall. To the right was the larger room, at the far end of which was a small opening that led into the outer office and, beyond, the more elegant office that Rhea and Emil shared. To the left of the wall was a smaller, L-shaped gallery that, when one entered and turned to the left, revealed a stairway, usually roped off. This led down to a private viewing room and a spacious area (always locked) for storing inventory.

It was to the left room that Rhea was instinctively attracted, perhaps because it was still dark.

"Catherine, throw on the lights in here."

Catherine obeyed. The spectacle was much the same as in the larger room.

Al Kheel's show, two years of labor, perhaps the best work of his career, had been lifted, piece by piece, off the walls, hurled to the floor (leaving indentations and gouges on her beautiful wooden floor), and placed in a heap in the center of the room. Precisely in the center of the room. It was this precision that gave her the creeps. The tidiness!

The boxes, approximately the size of portable televisions, were constructed of wood, but the interiors were comprised of mirror and glass and minutely carved architectural elements on a one-inch-to-one-foot scale. When they had been dashed to the floor, the mess, the shattering, the scattering must have been epidemic. Whoever had ruined the show had nevertheless abhorred the litter thus created. And then it struck her: what she was looking at was an installation in its own right. An aesthetic statement. A demolition created by an artist.

The series had been entitled the "Abandoned Hotel," each box representing one of the vacated rooms therein. "I wanted to register," Al had told her, "the reaction of a structure elaborately designed, then peopled for a long period of time, then forsaken and finally forgotten—an architect's ultimate nightmare." If it hadn't been that before, it certainly was that now.

But why? Who could have felt the need to do this?

She noticed that the thick velvet rope barring the public from the downstairs was off the hook. "Catherine! Did you go down after you talked to me?"

"No. I didn't want to stay in here. Especially after I saw the note."

Rhea descended. She had always hated these stairs. They twisted to the left, twice, before reaching the basement. The overhang was low and it made the transportation of art a tortuous process. How many nicked frames could attest to the fact? But as she went down this morning, her dislike was suffused with dread. Whoever had violated the upstairs had also been down here. All the lights were on and the storeroom door was wide open.

What if someone was still down here? The sudden thumps and clatter of Crunch's own loyal descent startled, then gave her new courage.

"Crunch!" she said, "go find the rats!"

Crunch wagged his tail and made a (still hobbling) beeline for the storeroom, disappearing behind a wall of crates. She waited by the door and looked to the right, where the private viewing area was reassuringly empty.

"Crunch?"

There was no answer, no barking. She ventured in. The first thing that caught her attention was an open bottle of Rémy Martin on the floor by a stack of large oil paintings.

Emil's favorite brandy.

Her self-assurance increased in direct proportion with her suspicion that Emil was somehow responsible for this chaos. She passed the crates around which Crunch had disappeared, turned to the right where a row of sculptures guarded a short aisle like sentinels, and approached a large workbench that Simon and Felix used to crate paintings for shipping. She walked up to it, looked over to the left, where there was another odd-job work area, and gulped a scream turned inside-out.

He was naked, face down, on the floor. One arm was stretched toward her with a syringe still stuck in the crook of his elbow. A rubber tube emerging from his rectum coiled over to a liver-colored enema bag. The back of Emil's head had been bashed in. His profile, once a source of self-adulation, looked pitifully surprised to be resting in a sticky pool of blackish blood.

Next to the body, covered in blood, was a steel branding iron with an electric cord attached to its handle. The branding iron Al Kheel had designed and with which he imprinted his monogram on the back of all of his boxes.

Crunch was sampling the goo.

Two

It was 10:30.

The other three employees of the gallery arrived before the police. First came Anne, the bookkeeper and secretary. Then Simon, who helped with installations and maintenance, and was a general handyman. Finally Felix, the most attractive of the lot, whom Rhea was preening for full-time sales. She led them and Catherine into her office. It was only after they were all seated that she told them of the murder.

She watched their reactions.

Anne looked frightened. Simon snickered, then, seeing that it wasn't a joke, fumbled with an apology that dwindled mid-sentence into "Oh, my God." Felix made no sound, and no movement other than a slight gaping of the mouth. Catherine began trembling and finally buried her head in her hands, sobbing. Again, crying from Catherine. Totally uncharacteristic and irksome. It was odd how people reacted to grizzly situations.

As for Rhea, the spectacle of Emil Orloff's grotesque body had annihilated all feeling, at least for the time being. Whatever his death (even the gore of his shattered head) meant to her emotionally, it would have to wait. Her determination to stay on top of the mounting chaos was more important; it put everything else on hold. This discovery in herself, in the midst of all this steeping dislocation, soothed her.

She *had* blanked out for a few moments, and that disturbed her. She didn't remember leaving the corpse. She didn't remember going back upstairs, and she certainly didn't remember picking up the bottle of brandy off the floor, although she must have since it was now before her on the desk.

She uncorked it, took a long slug, leaned over her desk and handed it to Anne with a gesture to pass it along. Everyone took a ritualistic taste, first the three on the couch.

Anne had a big drink with visible backwash.

Simon took a sip.

Catherine sucked on it like a baby bottle, then handed it across the coffee table to Felix, who was sitting in the chair in front of Rhea's desk.

Felix took a big German glug like a big German should.

Then back to Rhea, who said, "The cops should be here any moment. If there's anything any of you know that might shed some light on this, then for God's sake let's hear it. I expect everyone to be as helpful as possible to the police. And no condescension." She aimed this remark at Felix. "Just remember, they're cops, not sham potential buyers. It'll just add to your problems. I shouldn't wonder that we'll all be suspects, so try not to piss them off. I want them to want to help us, OK?"

She took another hit from the bottle and again passed it to Anne. "Which one of you was the last to leave Emil's loft last night?"

Simon shot up an index finger. "I left around one o'clock. There were still a few people left."

"What's a few?"

"Four, five, maybe six. I don't know."

"Well, you better know." Rhea straightened up in her chair and scorched the group with her look.

"That's exactly what I'm talking about. There's information in every head in this room and I expect it organized and immediately offerable to the police. Now think, Simon. Who was still there when you left the party?"

But before he could answer, she said, "This is ridiculous. Where are the cops? Catherine, stop that incessant sniveling and go call nine-one-one. Tell them there's been a murder on top of the robbery and if they don't get here soon your boss is going to kill you."

"Maybe I should do it," Felix offered as Catherine lurched from the couch.

"No, let her. Her voice will have the ring of authenticity. She needs something to keep her busy. Besides, it's probably best if you three stay in here. If you haven't been wandering around, they can't suspect you of messing around with evidence, right?"

"Right," Anne and Simon eagerly agreed.

"But I'll tell you what *you* could do," Rhea said, handing her phone to Felix, "Get on another line and call Becker. He should be here." Becker was an old friend of Emil's and the gallery's lawyer.

"Hello? This is the Orloff Gallery calling for Mr. Becker. Is he in please? I see. Can he be reached? This is urgent. Where? Oh. Is this his answering service? Will you please have him call as soon as possible? His client, Emil Orloff, has been murdered. Murdered. Yes. Yes, he has the number."

"Where the hell is he?" Rhea asked before Felix could hang up.

"Sea-kayaking somewhere off the coast of Washington. Won't be back till Monday."

"Great. Anne, don't Bogart the brandy. You're not getting drunk, are you? Better not be." Anne vigorously shook her head.

Rhea's face suddenly went white. She stood up, her hands gripping the edge of the desk.

"What is it?" Felix asked.

"Crunch! He's still down there! Having fucking brunch. Don't anybody move."

She charged out of the room, ran through the office, and banged into the uniformed shoulders of two policemen just arriving. "Whoa, lady. Calm down."

"You don't understand! My dog—"

"Calm down! Now just relax."

She closed her eyes.

Great beginning for her Ms. Together act.

By noon, Rhea no longer had a gallery. At least one that felt like hers.

They were all over the place: forensic people, doctors, photographers, detective types, assorted cops and, for all she knew, cops' cousins who had decided to come along for the ride. If a crowd like this had invaded her gallery on a normal day, she would have called the police.

The flurry of short interviews (usually the same questions) with various people from various offices exasperated her. Just how many different investigations were being conducted, anyway?

At one point she was approached by a representative from the DA's office, a woman by the name of Shears. Shears edged by her, then spun around dramatically and said:

"You're Ms. Boo-erk-lind?"

"Ms. Who?" Rhea looked her straight in the eye.

Rhea had noticed her earlier and decided she didn't like her. She stalked the gallery as if in conquered territory. She was Rhea's junior by ten years, took herself seriously in a way only short people can, and was in urgent need of a lesson in high-heel walking and appropriate dress.

Shears consulted her pad: "Your name *e-r-k-l-i-n*?"

"That's right, pronounced like it's spelled, no bles, no *d* at the end. First name, Rhea. What's your—"

"Let me advise you, Ms. Buerklin, that it will be your advantage to help the DA's office in any way—"

"I can assure you, Ms. Shears, that correcting you when you are incorrect can only be of the utmost help. My," Rhea added, "what a charming dress."

The dress under attack was a pitiful attempt to achieve femininity and, really, it was beneath Rhea to ridicule it but she couldn't help herself. Shears had on such a ludicrous creation: a flowing, mid-calf flower-print tea-party number that made a mockery of her blatant bitchiness and, well, the lawyer needed to be brought down a notch or two before things went any further. Rhea was aware that she was doing precisely what she had warned, Felix not to do—snubbing—but too bad. Besides, the comment had its desired effect: after a few questions Shears got the hell away from her.

The fingerprinting was kind of fun. All five gallery workers were herded into the outer office, corralled and besmudged with ink. Branded, really, which, given the corpse in the basement, was a creepy reminder.

Speaking of creepy reminders, Crunch, who was having the time of his life making up to every idle cop in the gallery and reaping more pets per minute than he had in years, was trotting about with little black socks of blood, something Rhea intended to remedy at the earliest possible moment.

As it stood, they weren't allowed to use the toilet until the forensic mob had finished powdering the toilet bowl, a condition that didn't improve group disposition.

The outer office where they were confined was split-level: as you walked in from the main gallery there was Felix's desk to the left, adjacent to Rhea's office, and to the right, Simon's area, which had a window that looked back

gallery. Behind and above, joined by four steep
was the upper platform for Catherine's and Anne's
. The architect had called it Post Modern. Rhea
ied it JAN (Judgment at Nuremberg), and the acronym
ad stuck; the entire staff referred to the outer office as
JAN. Two cops were on sentry duty at the short staircase, unidentified officials milled about, the rain had turned the day into soup, the overhead fans churned to no avail.

Still, things began to settle down a bit. She was finally introduced, briefly, to the detective in charge of the police investigation, who appeared to know what he was doing.

His name was Tennyson, presumably no relation to the lord, and though his name struck her as funny, his looks had a slightly unsettling effect on her. She couldn't say why, nor did she have time to pursue this sensation, because he was suddenly besieged by assistants who needed him downstairs.

When he returned he announced his intention of asking a few questions of the employees, separately. "I hope you don't mind me using your office?" he asked her.

"No, not at all," Rhea answered, again slightly unnerved by his appearance. He was well groomed though not expensively dressed. He had jug ears and yet he wasn't unattractive. He spoke in a gravelly inner-city baritone and yet with a softness that belied his largeness. But there was something else, something familiar, not vaguely familiar but familiar in a way that was so close to her everyday experiences she was incapable of disentangling it from her confusion.

"Let's see. Catherine Miller . . ." he said, turning away from her.

"Yes?" Catherine responded weakly.

"You were the first to enter the gallery this morning, right?"

"Yes."

"Will you come with me please?" He [...] rine into Rhea's office and closed the door b[...]

Whatever it was about him that bugged [...] could see that Tennyson clearly represented orde[...] underlings. She relaxed a little and, following his e[...] ple, began some coordination of her own. She delegate[...] Felix and Simon to the long-overdue job of sorting 35 mm slides. She busied Anne with some correspondence. Finally she gathered a stack of trade magazines, plopped them down on Catherine's vacated desk, took a seat and settled down to the tricky task of not drawing attention to herself by feigning an interest in the competition's ads.

No one said much. With all the cops around, and given the severity of the situation, even the most innocuous comments sounded amplified, charged with surreptitious meaning, phony.

Lunch was brought in. Sandwiches from a local deli. She was ravenous, but halfway through her ham on rye she caught a glimpse of Emil's shrouded body being carted away. Her sandwich was carefully returned to its paper plate and swiped to the side of the desk.

"Stay, Crunch."

When they opened the outside door, the rain was pouring on another drama in progress: modular barricades wobbled in front a group of shoving TV reporters. Jesus, she hadn't thought about the news media. She supposed, sooner or later, she was going to have to deal with them, too.

The door closed, and Emil was gone. What did that mean? What was it supposed to mean to her? She was weighed down by so many thoughts that no single thought would rise up and announce itself. And the sitting around, the waiting sharpened her mental impotence.

Catherine finally came out looking worse than when she'd gone in, brushing away copious tears.

"Rhea Buerklin," Tennyson called.

Rhea relinquished her chair to Catherine.

"...e's some Valium in my purse, Catherine," she ... giving a damn who heard her. "Why don't you try ...aful."

"Ah, Ms. Miller," Tennyson called out, "you can go ...me now, but stay where you can be reached. Jones, get ...er address and phone number."

Rhea told Catherine to call her later and walked out of JAN, into her office.

She started toward her desk, only to see that Tennyson was already taking *her* seat at *her* desk. No time to get territorial, she cautioned herself. Tennyson, as if reading her mind, countered with a gesture of hands and eyebrows that silently asked, "Would you prefer to sit here?"

"Please, go ahead," she said.

"Well, if you don't mind, I think I will."

Sighing, she sat down in the chair in front of the desk.

"You see," he continued, "this is quite a treat for me."

"What is?"

"Sitting at a desk made by the hands of Wendell Castle."

Rhea tried to disguise her disbelief. "You know Wendell Castle?"

The detective laughed. "I don't know him. I know his work. My ex-wife teaches at Pratt. Sculptor. We used to do the gallery rounds and this was one of them."

"I see."

"What's a desk like that worth? Fifty thousand dollars? Seventy-five?"

"More," Rhea said, lighting a Lucky.

Tennyson shook his head with admiration. Then he picked up a piece of paper and handed it to her. "This note that Ms. Miller found."

But Rhea waved him off, explaining, "I've already made several copies of it. I don't need to see it again. And I've never, to my knowledge, seen that handwriting before. As for the content, I don't know what it's supposed to mean. I have a feeling it's biblical. I have a friend in publishing who could find out with ~~haven't been allowed to use the phone.~~

Tennyson seemed amused. "She's a Bib~~but I~~

"No. Her sister works in Reference at the" library."

Rhea gave him the phone number, and he motioned for one of his assistants to go to the outer office and make the call. Then he changed the subject to Al Kheel. "You said earlier that he would be here today."

"He'll be here, poor guy. This is his opening."

"I thought last night was his opening."

"Today's the opening for the public. Last night was for, oh, I guess you'd say friends."

"What sort of man is he?"

"Al? Well, he's a nice guy. He's about my age."

"And what's that?"

"My age? Thirty-seven."

"Do you know him well?"

"He's been with the gallery for about three years. This was to be his second solo for the Orloff Gallery."

"Solo?"

"One-man show."

"Does his work sell well?"

"Well enough. We were getting the price up there."

"How much for one of his boxes?"

"For this series, four to five thousand dollars, depending on the size."

"That's not much compared to Wendell Castle."

"Castle's our star. He's been around a long time. Kheel is just getting his feet wet. But you're right. He's on the low end of our price list."

"What do you know about his private life?"

"He lives in Connecticut. With his son. He has a sweet kid, I don't know, six or seven years old."

"His wife?"

"Divorced. Horrible woman."

"You've met her?"

or twice when we first took him on. I don't know her."

"You said she was horrible."

"She dumped Al for another man and left him with a kid. Where I come from, that's inexcusable."

"You consider yourself a woman of traditional values."

"Certainly on that issue."

"Do you have children?"

"Nope. Physically incapable."

"Married?"

Rhea laughed. "Divorced."

"What's so funny?"

"I don't know, everyone seems to be divorced around here. That's all."

"Would Al Kheel make enough money on his art to support himself and a kid?"

"No. He's a carpenter. It's a vocation pretty common for artists. I mean to keep food on the table."

"The branding iron he uses: is that a common way to sign pieces of art?"

"As far as I know it's unique. He comes from the West. Grew up on a cattle ranch. I guess that's where he got the idea. We had a little problem with it in the beginning."

"How's that?"

"Well, Al wanted to use *just* the branding iron. Emil and I had to convince him to sign the fronts as well."

"Would you describe him as stubborn?"

"No. I would describe him as the most pliant, the most self-effacing artist in our stable. In fact, I would describe him as the most stable in our stable. Reliable. He's always managed to come through, especially with commission work, which can be very tricky, problematic."

"If he doesn't show up today . . ."

"If he doesn't show up today, you'll have to go to Connecticut. He doesn't have a phone."

Rhea caught Tennyson staring at her breasts. Or was

he just thinking? Again, that familiarity. And then it struck her. Tennyson's nose! It was a dead ringer for Emil's. That same finely chiseled nose, the kind of nose women in this town would kill for or at least pay their plastic surgeon five thousand dollars for. Suddenly she saw other similarities: the strong jawline, the conservatively cut brown hair. Of course this guy was a rougher version of Emil, but . . .

"Ms. Buerklin, you don't seem to be very upset by your partner's death."

"Neither do you."

Tennyson answered with another stare, this time eye to eye.

"Sorry. Look, I know how I come off. I wish I could cast an atmosphere around me that seemed more appropriate for the, the situation— "

"Situation. Not tragedy?"

"No, Mr. Tennyson, not tragedy. Just a waste."

"What was your relationship with Emil Orloff?"

"We were business partners."

"That's all?"

"Yes."

"How old was he?"

"Forty-eight. Would have been forty-nine this month. About your age, I would say. And by the way, there is a resemblance between you two."

"Yeah, Ms. Miller said the same thing. What was his background?"

"He came from what I guess you would call a privileged upbringing. European, though the family was originally from Russia."

"White Russia."

"Yes," she admitted, aware that she was having a rather good time of the cross-examination. Still, she cautioned herself, he had a trick of bringing out the chumminess in her, which might or might not be in her best interest. "After the revolution, Berlin was a major dumping ground for exiles. That's where he was born, right before the war. Later, his family moved to Paris."

"How did he end up in New York?"

"He moved here in the fifties. To study art. There's a slew of gallery owners in this town who are frustrated artists."

"Interesting. Did he have family?"

"Not here. He has a sister in Paris. Véra Vertbois—that's her married name. Bitch of bitches. As far as I know, that's it."

"Were they close?"

"No. They kept in touch. That's about it."

"Did he have any enemies?"

Rhea shrugged. "Sure. There were a lot of people in this town who disliked him. He was successful, outspoken. There's no asshole like a successful one. I'm not saying that people were standing in line for the honor of murdering him but he pissed a lot of people off. Especially in the last couple of years."

"How do you mean?"

"I mean that in the last few years his swing grew wider. He was a very bitter man. Toward the end he didn't give a damn about anything. I bet the autopsy will confirm that."

"Why do you say that?"

"His liver was shot. His doctor warned him but he didn't care."

"He was an alcoholic."

"Of herculean proportions, Mr. Tennyson. He was also into pills. Barbiturates."

"Cocaine?"

"Cocaine too. Sniffing. No crack that I'm aware of, though I could be wrong. And . . ."

"And?"

"Heroin."

"How could he run a gallery?"

"He didn't. He ran *away* from the gallery. In fact, his

presence here was almost nonexistent. I ran the gallery. Me and my crew."

"Did you hate him?"

"I despised what he was doing to himself. Before he started sliding, he was the best. And *that's* the tragedy."

"It couldn't have been easy for you."

"What do you mean?"

"Running the business by yourself."

"Lots of women have galleries in this town. I like running the show."

Tennyson flicked a little smile as if to say, "I bet you do." Then he asked, "Was he suicidal?"

"I don't know about that. His drug intake was certainly suicidal but I don't . . . I can't see him just sitting down and taking his own life, if you know what I mean. In spite of everything, there was a level on which he was having a good time. I think he saw himself almost godlike in his cynicism. He even bragged that his life had become the embodiment of what the art world has become."

"And what would that be?"

"Pointless. At least to his way of thinking."

"And what do you think?"

"About art? Not pointless."

Tennyson laughed. "Why the hesitation? It sounds like you're dodging an accusation."

Rhea laughed, too. "I am, in a way. For the last decade, the dynamics of art have been in the hands of a few trendsetters. After abstract expressionism became a dead issue—"

"*Is* it a dead issue? My ex will be mighty disappointed to hear that."

"I didn't say the abstract expressionists were dead. Still, it's increasingly difficult to unload their work. Anyway, since then, all sorts of sputtering movements have had their little moments."

"Like what?"

"Oh, you know. Neo-expressionism. The East Village

scene, graffiti art. That's certainly a dead issue. The East Village, gallery-wise, is beginning to look like a ghost town."

"I didn't know that."

"Yeah, well . . ." Again Rhea observed that chatty charm about Tennyson that was there one second and gone the next. "Anyway, last year came the arrival of neo-geo—"

"What's neo-geo?"

"Technically? Who knows? It's also known as simulationism, which is just a fancy way of saying fraud, in my book. Making something new by redoing something that's already been done. Recycled work. It's called a lot of things; simulationism will really get into full swing this year, I'm afraid. And the prices for this crap—"

"You call it crap?"

"Most of it, yes. The prices for the latest trend are bloated beyond all comprehension and have no relationship to their real value."

"You don't like that?"

"I'd be a fool not to. I'm running a business, and art has become very lucrative because of these various trends. In any case, I don't see what this has to do with Emil's—"

"Perhaps nothing. About Emil: you say that yours was merely a business relationship. Why don't I believe that? In fact, it doesn't sound like that at all."

"No, I suppose it doesn't. I knew, always knew a great deal more about Emil's private life than I ever cared to. Often, in our business, transactions are done on a social level, untold quantities of egos are involved—the artist's, the buyer's, the critic's . . ."

"The gallery owner's?" Tennyson inserted.

"Yes," Rhea admitted, "exactly. You must understand that sales in this business are conducted, often as not, *after* business hours. We do, did, a great deal of entertaining in Emil's loft, in restaurants, in other cities, even in clients' homes. There was a lot of traveling and bantering and, well, we were together most of the time. In some ways we were closer than most married couples."

"Was Orloff straight?"

"Very, when it came to sex."

"And you are a very attractive woman. In all that time you spent together, he never tried to— "

"There was something he needed in me that was more important than sex. I came to this gallery equipped with a private income. You may as well know. You'll probably find out anyway. My husband was an extremely successful investment banker in Munich. When he dumped me I didn't leave exactly empty-handed."

"I see. And you came to New York."

"That's right."

"When was that?"

"About ten years ago. I've been with the gallery for the last six."

"How did you meet Emil?"

"Years ago, when Emil still had his gallery on Fifty-seventh, my father bought work from him. They became friends. There's also a family connection that goes way back, somehow, but I've forgotten precisely . . . anyway, I met Emil through my father. I came to him just at a time when he needed a substantial amount of liquid capital and, well, I bought in."

"I see."

"Well, now that you see, I might as well set the record straight. As a matter of fact, I *did* rock and roll with the idiot. Once. No pyrotechnics. It was mainly just to get him off my back. Emil wanted to conquer, that's all. I let him have his little victory and, believe me, it was one of the more effective moves of my life."

"He didn't bother you after that."

"Not in that way, no."

"But you were still stuck with him?"

It was a leading question and Rhea decided it was time for a little defending. "Emil made this gallery. It was

Emil who put together our stable of artists. It was his baby, his inspiration. Even toward the end, I could learn from him."

"But you indicated that he had long lost his inspiration."

"Yes."

"And you were stuck with him."

"If you insist. Yes. More or less. Especially in the last two years."

"Enough to want to kill him?"

"Endlessly."

"*Did* you kill him?"

"No. If Emil walked through the door right now, I would blow his fucking brains out. But I did not kill him. Would you mind if I had a sip of that brandy?"

He handed her the Rémy Martin. She turned it upside down and killed the contents.

"When you discovered the body . . ."

"Yes?"

"The enema bag. Can you explain that?"

"I have no earthly idea."

She felt her stomach restrict. Was it the rich shock of the alcohol or was it the horror of Emil's ultimate degradation? What *had* he been doing down there? Naked and with an enema bag . . .

"No idea," she repeated softly.

"Where did he get his drugs?"

"I don't know. I didn't want to know. And I made sure Emil knew I didn't want to know. It would have been easy enough for him. Artists do their share of the drug intake in this town. There would have been an untold number of SoHo-ese willing to place his order. But I can look you straight in the eye and assure you that there were never any drug deals transacted in this gallery. I wouldn't have stood for that."

"You don't do drugs?"

"I suppose there's a time and place for everything,

though, its been my observation that it's no longer as fashionable as it once was. In fact, among my friends, it's almost anachronistic."

Tennyson sighed. "You know, Ms. Buerklin, it wouldn't be difficult to construct a case against you."

"Why? What's the motive? Emil's and my lawyer—"

"Yes, I'm a little surprised you don't have one here."

It was Rhea's turn to sigh. "At this moment he's flailing away in a canoe somewhere in the direction of Russia. He's supposed to return Monday. When he comes back, you'll be able to see for yourself that I was in the process of buying Emil out, the papers were drawn up, the deal to be closed by the end of the year."

"What is the present arrangement?"

"What do you mean?"

"Present contracts, wills. What will happen now that he has died?"

"It was an equal distribution of partnership. I got, I get everything. I am automatic owner of everything except for Emil's personal property."

"A lot cheaper than buying him out."

"And a lot more dangerous. You are free to examine my financial statement."

"I am aware of that, Ms. Buerklin."

"You'll see that I am not exactly hard-pressed for money."

"You mentioned personal property. What did he have besides the gallery?"

"Well, there was his loft; maybe a million there. And there was his obligatory house in the Hamptons. His art collection. I wouldn't be surprised if he were worth, apart from the gallery, four or five million."

"Stocks?"

"I really couldn't say."

"Beneficiaries?"

"I suppose his sister."

"You?"

"Given the circumstances, I hope not. I haven't read the will."

"But there is one."

"Yes, Becker, our lawyer, drew one up. He drew one up for me at the same time."

For a moment his eyes met hers refocusing toward the sofa, where Tennyson's assistant (partner?) sat taking notes. Rhea had forgotten all about him.

"Am I going to be arrested?"

"No."

"Not for the time being," Rhea said.

Tennyson changed the subject. "According to your assistant, Ms. Miller— "

"Catherine."

"Yes. According to Catherine, you left the party early last night. Any particular reason for that?"

"I usually do. After Emil's dinners, things degenerate into a lot of boozy promises, et cetera. A waste of time. Besides, I wanted to catch the end of the Mets-Cardinals game. Total disaster in the ninth, did you see it? Ron Darling's out for the season."

"I'm a Yankees fan. So you went home. Where's that?"

"Greene Street?"

"Alone?"

"Yes."

"Anyone to verify that?"

"I doubt it. I don't remember seeing anyone on the streets I knew."

"Neighbors?"

"I live in a reconstructed warehouse. There are only four lofts in the building. Mine is on the top floor. The floors are very thick, practically soundproof."

"So the person below you would not have heard anything."

"Not likely."

She looked up at Tennyson. "About last night, I have a guest list if you would like to see it."

"Very much."

"Simon can help you there. He was the last one of the employees to leave."

"Sounds like you're conducting a counterinvestigation."

Unselfconsciously, Rhea nodded. "Why not? I don't know when Felix left. Anne didn't attend. Catherine left right after me."

Tennyson looked up. "Why do you say that?"

"Because she told me this morning. I asked her. Why?"

"Your staff—were they your employees or Emil's?"

"I don't follow."

"Who hired them?"

"Anne's been with Emil forever. She was with Emil on Fifty-seventh. Simon, well, he came along just when we needed another hand. He sort of fell into our laps. He's an artist and plans to quit next spring. I personally hired Felix and Catherine."

"So you would describe them as yours?"

"Very much so. They came after Emil had already started to fall apart."

"They didn't answer to Emil?"

"Sure they did, but the occasion didn't arise all that often."

"Did they like him?"

"I doubt it. But I never gave them any opportunity to display their feelings. Emil really just wasn't any of their business."

"Does it strike you as odd that Catherine is taking all of this so hard, or would you describe her as the emotional type?"

Rhea shook her head. "I've never seen her like this and I find it odd as hell. In fact, I hired her and have been very pleased with her precisely because she wasn't apt to be emotional."

"You didn't know she was having an affair with your partner?"

"Catherine and Emil?" Rhea laughed. "Where did you get *that* idea?"

"Ms. Miller told us just before you came in."

Rhea stopped laughing. "I don't believe it."

"You think Ms. Miller is lying."

"Either that or I don't have any idea who she is."

"Thank you for your help, Ms. Buerklin. That'll be all for now."

"But— "

"And please don't leave the gallery just yet. I may need you again." Turning to his assistant, he said, "Let's have Simon Golden in here next."

She was ushered out the door.

Three

When Rhea reemerged she was immediately struck by the evacuated look of JAN. Her employees (all but Catherine, who had already left) and a couple of cops were still there, but everyone else was gone. "Where'd everybody go?"

Orders had been given to a group of Tennyson's men to go search Emil's loft, and Anne had produced a key to facilitate their hunt. Rhea wished she could have gone with them just to see Inez give them hell.

Inez had been Orloff's housekeeper since year one. She came each morning at eleven o'clock to put the phone back on the hook and cook her boss a late breakfast, served to him in bed with a crankiness that superceded his own. Emil savored this ritual. It inevitably put him in a jaunty mood. After she kicked him out, her remaining duties consisted of light cleaning, heavy eating, laundry and ironing, ordering untold amounts of expensive food to be delivered from Jefferson Market, talking to all of her relatives on the phone, nursing a bottle of Pinot Noir (acquired taste) and, above all, staying on top of at least a half dozen soap operas. Barging into "her" home, cops or no cops, would approach the insurmountable.

Rhea peeked out the doorway and noticed that the forensic people and other assorted experts had left as well, taking with them their equipment and leaving in their wake a mud-tracked, debris-strewn gallery. Al's boxes had been pawed over and were no longer in their two neat piles. She couldn't say why, but the messy exodus made her feel violated and forgotten.

Shears hadn't forgotten.

She waylaid Rhea in the main gallery, pad and pencil poised, fresh lipstick applied. The questions started all over again—generally along the same lines as Tennyson's—but what a difference! Shears's interrogative method, if you could call it that, was far less natural, far more quizzy. She drew attention to herself rather than to the case. She had this banal habit of puncturing the air with her pencil every time she posed a new question. Rhea resigned herself to the onslaught and was forthright—she was too exhausted to be otherwise—but Christ! Shears took so long to get to the point and extracted a lot less information in the bargain.

In the meantime, Anne, Simon, and Felix had their separate turns with Tennyson. They emerged bedraggled, if relieved. They were free to go, but not before Rhea made them promise to avoid the press and to call her later at her loft.

There were a few new developments, which Rhea was allowed in on. Her friend's sister had called from the library. The "fire into gold" message was *not* biblical but rather, ancient Greek, 500 B.C., written by a man called Heracleitus of Ephesus. "Say who?" was the general response. Rhea had never heard of him, either. No bells rang, though she did recall that at one time Emil had been somewhat of a Greek buff. She felt duty-bound to mention this to Tennyson. He wasn't terribly impressed by the weak connection, and neither was she.

Without exactly being invited, she followed Tennyson about as he rummaged through the remains of the show.

She silently repeated the message: "There is an exchange for all things, just as there are goods into fire and fire into gold." Fire into gold? What fire? What gold? Something of value? The wreckage she was shuffling through . . . what *was* she looking at? An installation that no longer existed. Or rather an installation that had been radically altered, twice, in a matter of hours. First the tidy piles, now the scattered remains.

"Whoever was here last night," Tennyson grumbled as if reading her thoughts, "whoever did this wanted someone, either you or me or someone, to be impressed by all this destruction. Is it a statement about art? In which case we can assume the person or persons were closely involved with the art world. Or is it a fancy invention to divert suspicion? In which case it could *still* be someone connected to the art world."

Tennyson was thinking out loud in Rhea's presence, and she found it very attractive. This unreliability of evidence was an entirely new idea for her, a stimulating one. He was the source of that revelation and she wanted more of it. On top of the whirlpool in her head, she knew she was growing to like Tennyson or, at least, she sensed a need to attach herself to him, to grab onto him like onto a sturdy piece of buoyant wood. She vowed to cultivate a complicity with him even if it meant submitting her will to his expertise.

He turned to her. "Do you think Al Kheel could have done this to his own work?"

"No!" she said. "We're looking at two years of his life."

"What if it were two years of a *bad* life?"

"No," she repeated. "Artists take it out on themselves, not their work. No matter how wretched their existence may be, their vanity would prohibit the destruction of the work . . . you know, just in case, a hundred years down the line, someone decided to proclaim them a genius."

Then she added: "Of course, what do I know? I would have bet my life that Catherine and Emil never . . ."

"Emil could have done this," Tennyson continued. "If what you say about him is true, his disillusionment with art . . ."

"Emil *could* have done this," she agreed. "But that doesn't explain his murder."

"The two don't necessarily have to be related."

"No, well, no, I guess not."

"OK." Tennyson took a sizable breath. "Emil has had enough. He's loaded to the gills. After everyone leaves the party he comes back to the gallery, looks around the walls, sees what a mockery his life has become, sees, *on exhibition*, the very thing he can no longer believe in. For some reason it puts him over the edge, he goes on a rampage and destroys the show. Then, still trembling, he stumbles downstairs, gets out his trusty syringe and takes a further step into oblivion."

"OK, that's possible. Then what?"

"Then. Then Al Kheel, out of vanity or nostalgia or for whatever reason, comes back to the gallery, sees the carnage, finds Emil downstairs and bashes his head in."

"Jesus Christ."

"Or," Tennyson continued, "Catherine Miller, the discarded lover—"

"*Had* she been discarded?"

Tennyson shot her a look. "You sound hopeful," he observed.

Rhea met his gaze. "I don't like people who fuck around in their own backyard."

"OK," Tennyson said, chuckling. "OK, so Catherine Miller, the discarded lover comes back to the gallery, doesn't give a damn about the destruction of the show, she's too impassioned, she sees red, finds Emil and bashes his head in."

Unconvinced, Rhea did a couple of pendulum swings with her head.

He continued, "OK, what about this: Rhea Buerklin, ever the watchdog, comes back to the gallery, sees the carnage, finds Emil downstairs and, in a fit of rage and disgust, bashes his head in."

She was less amused by this last hypothesis. "I hope you don't believe that."

"Ms. Shears does."

"I shouldn't have mentioned her dress."

"What?"

"Never mind her. What do you believe, Tennyson? Do you see yourself right now walking around with a disgruntled business partner driven to murder? Is that who I am?"

"I'll tell you this much, Ms. Buerklin. If you *did* kill Orloff, you're a good actress."

"Why?"

"Because, the way I see it, your curiosity is genuine."

"Some defense."

"By the way," Tennyson calmly changed the subject, "it's still unofficial but it was heroin in the syringe and coffee in the enema bag."

"Coffee!"

"Narcotics constipate."

"That is disgusting. Why not take a pill, a laxative?"

"Immediate results."

Rhea swallowed hard, then looked up. "Then why was Emil in the basement?"

"What do you mean?"

"The bathroom is up here, right next to the stairwell. If you're treating yourself to an enema and the effect is immediate, wouldn't you want to be right next to the toilet?"

Tennyson grinned. Well flossed but uneven teeth. She liked that. She didn't trust people whose teeth were too straight.

"You're right," he said. "It doesn't make sense."

She patted her jacket pockets for cigarettes. She was out. Tennyson offered her one of his, a menthol.

"Thanks," she said, ripping off the filter. "So, do you think Shears will have me arrested?"

"Not yet. She's not that stupid."

"Ah! But you *do* think she's stupid."

"I didn't say that and you shouldn't think that."

"She's a power-hungry envious little . . . person . . . who could put me away, at least temporarily. Look, as long as we're going to be playing this cat-and-mouse game, could we at least be on a first-name basis?"

"Sure. My name's Emil."

"You're kidding!"

"You're right. My name's not Emil."

"God! You had me—"

"Real name is John."

He struck a match to light her cigarette. Just as she leaned toward the flame, the main door of the gallery swung open. Silhouetted against the outside commotion, Al Kheel entered, drenched and holding his little boy's hand.

Four

The cash register read $235.65, and Rhea nearly dropped dead. Two hundred and thirty-five dollars for toys? It was just a few items. Barely filled one bag. Was she just being naive? How long had it been since she had purchased a toy? Or was this just another SoHo yuppie consumer rip-off? Probably both, she concluded as she fished out her plastic (her *gallery* plastic, not her personal; her tax lawyer would have to justify it somehow) and relinquished it to the salestwerp behind the counter, who wore Japanese designer clothes (solid black) and an asymmetrical blocky haircut that must have cost *him* a fortune. She glanced over at Jack, Al's kid. He was respectfully fondling a giant inflatable tyrannosaurus rex in the corner of the store.

"Are you mad at me?" Jack asked her once they were back outside on Spring Street, where a cop car was waiting for them.

"Why should I be mad at you?"

"My dad always gets mad at me when we leave toy stores."

Toy store? She had just left a toy store? She was obviously still in a daze from the initial shock of the murder. Displaced. Disjointed. As Rhea and the boy got into the back seat of the cop car with all their loot, she forced herself to play back the events that had placed her in such a non-sequitur situation.

———

Al's reaction, when he entered the gallery, was as meager as it was sovereign. He stopped. He stared. He dropped his son's hand. He sank to the floor in an Indian-style sitting position. He said nothing.

The kid's reaction was to go have a better look.

Rhea rushed to Al and sank down by him. John Tennyson held back. (Was it decency or curiosity that held him back? From where he stood, he could scrutinize all of them.)

Her condolences sounded stupid, even strangely impudent as they came out of her mouth. They didn't seem to stir him. He remained motionless. He barely blinked. His silent resistance to everything but the obvious destruction looming around him was absolute and harrowing to observe. Finally, Tennyson approached and sat down beside him. Al turned to him and said, "Where's Jack? Where's my boy? He shouldn't be here."

"Jack's right over there," Rhea pointed. "See? He's fine. He's playing with the dog."

"I don't want Jack here. I don't want him to see me."

Rhea looked at Tennyson. "I could take him to my place," she offered, although babysitting was the last thing she felt capable of doing.

Tennyson immediately agreed. "Sergeant Lipski can go with you."

"Is that really necessary?"

"I'm afraid so. Anyway, he'll be of help."

"Oh? How?"

He motioned to the front door. "There's a wall of reporters out there you are going to have to get through. Look, I'm not going to hound Al. Not now. As soon as I get a few things cleared up I'll personally bring him over to your loft, how's that?"

"So you can personally have a snoop around my place? You're a very efficient man."

"Thanks. Lipski, you got a car handy?" The sergeant nodded.

"We don't need a car. I'm just around the block."

"You want the whole world to follow you home? Would you let me help you please? Lipski, take them off like you were going downtown and then circle back to her place."

"Toys," Rhea thought out loud.

"What?"

"I have a grown-up loft. There's a toy store on Spring. Could we stop there first?"

By the time they got to her place, the rain had let up. Her enormous living room looked down over the corner of Greene and Spring. Usually at this time of day, the late afternoon sun would be bathing her minimal decor in almost uninhabitable brightness. Today the room looked blue and streaked. She poured herself a glass of scotch; Lipski morosely abstained. Jack dumped $235.65 worth of junk on her floor.

"I'm going to take a shower," she announced. No one answered her.

It was funny: she had always told herself that, if she had been able to have kids, she wouldn't spoil them with a lot of crap. And yet at the first opportunity to put this policy to a test . . .

After her shower, she put on blue jeans, a light sweater and heavy socks. She padded into the kitchen to feed Crunch only to realize that the dog was still wearing his black blood boots and that the computer had been left on from this morning. DEADFALL was still on the screen.

"Shears would love to see this!"

She pressed the delete button and watched her incriminating file on Emil vanish into the cosmos. Was that what death was like? One great big delete button up in the sky?

The telephone rang. Lipski answered it from the other room. She stuffed Crunch into the sink and scrubbed away Emil. She was drying him on the floor with a dish towel when Jack ran in. He gave her a quick bear hug and ran back out.

She froze for a moment in her squatting position. She could still feel the imprint of his small arms around her neck.

She went over to the sink and turned on the water full blast. She dropped her head close to the rushing faucet. The resinoid smell of Crunch's flea shampoo clung to the porcelain. For the first time in years, she cried. It wasn't much of a cry. Three big heaving sobs and it was over. More like throwing up, really.

She went to the refrigerator. She pulled out everything in sight. She opened the pantry door, yanked things off the shelves and lined them up on the counter. She pulled out pots and pans and proceeded, barely aware of what she was doing, to bang out a dinner of unprecedented volume.

"Goddamn it!"

She thrust the lasagna into the oven. Then she peeled asparagus. Then she made pesto. Then she made a fruit salad.

Then she made a call to Paris.

After her call (Lipski standing in the doorway) she returned to the counter, where there were eight unused and accusatory limes. She got out the flour. She made a Key lime pie. There were two limes left, so she switched from scotch to vodka tonics.

She'd just begun what was intended to be an enormous and very angry tossed salad when she remembered the Mets-Cardinals game. She switched on the TV next to the oven. Through the downstage clutter of mixing bowls and lime rinds, she saw that the game had just ended. They'd lost again, goddamn it, 8 to 1! Dwight Gooden had pitched the worst two innings of his career, allowing six Cardinal runs before Davey Johnson benched him.

"Figures." She snapped off the TV.

The buzzer-intercom sounded. She started for the door but Lipski beat her to it. She returned to the kitchen. A few minutes later, she could hear Tennyson and Al being let in. Al went straight into the living room to be with Jack. Lots of laughing. Tennyson was mumbling to Lipski in the hallway. Finally she heard Lipski being dismissed and let out of her apartment. A few moments later, Tennyson came into the kitchen.

"How is he?" she asked him without turning around.

"He's doing all right. He seems more concerned about his boy than his show or Emil. It may be that it really hasn't hit him yet. It's hard to tell."

"That's right, his shock is probably just playacting."

Tennyson shrugged off her sarcasm. "Lipski says you made a call, in French. You want to tell me about it?"

Rhea turned around with a dripping head of lettuce in her hands.

"I called Emil's sister in Paris."

"She doesn't speak English?"

"As a matter of fact, she speaks perfect English. Just like me. You'll be able to interrogate her tomorrow night at the Carlyle Hotel. That's where she stays when she comes to town."

"What did she say?"

"I just told you. She's going to get on the earliest possible flight and come over."

"No, I mean how did she react?"

"It was very odd. She acted like her brother had just been killed."

"Who's the big dinner for?"

"I don't fucking know," she said, slam-dunking the

lettuce into the sink. "Maybe I'll throw a wake. That is, if I'm ever allowed to call my friends without police scrutiny."

"Do you have any friends?"

"Of course I have friends."

"Lipski told me that there have been no incoming calls."

"So?"

"Everybody in SoHo must know by now. It strikes me as odd that no one has tried to get ahold of you. Especially the press."

"My phone is unlisted. Two weeks ago I had it re-unlisted. I despise chitchat. My employees have the number and that's it. If they give the number to the press, it'll be their jobs."

"What about your friends?"

"They can reach me in the daytime at the gallery. Speaking of which—when do I get it back? The gallery is closed on Sundays and Mondays. By Tuesday I want to be open again."

"With what?"

"I don't know. I haven't had a lot of time to think about it, have I? I guess I'll throw together some sort of group show for the next three weeks. That is, *if* the city of New York will give me my gallery back."

"We should be out of there by tomorrow sometime. I'd like to do a little research on your other artists."

"Why?"

"Did they all love Emil?"

Before she could respond, the phone rang. They looked at each other. "That'll be for me," he said as he reached for the receiver. "Tennyson here, who's this? Yep. Good. What'd you find? Right. Right. Hunh. You're sure? Hunh. And what time was that? OK, send the report over to Crabb's office and I'll talk to you in the morning. No, there's no point in me coming back tonight. I'll call you before I leave here. Right."

He picked up her bottle of scotch and, to her surprise, took a long drink.

"Let me guess," she said, "Emil's not dead after all."

"Oh he's dead, all right. It's how he's dead."

"What do you mean?"

"It seems we have a set of unidentified fingerprints."

"Unidentified?"

"Uh-hunh. On the branding iron. On every box. All over the walls where the boxes had been hanging. And on the note. There's a set of fingerprints that don't match up with anyone connected with the gallery. That includes Al. My man checked with Records and they didn't come up with a matching set there either."

"Then that means . . . someone else killed Emil."

"No. It means that there is an unidentified set of fingerprints, and that's *all* it means until we have some way to make use of them."

"Oh, come on, Tennyson—"

"I thought we were on a first-name basis."

"As long as you're in my house, drinking my booze, answering my phone, I'll call you any goddamn thing I want."

But this new information had instantly cooled her anger and, in spite of herself, she couldn't make herself sound angry. "Someone else killed Emil. It's obvious."

"I don't know. He was doing a pretty good job of it himself. He may not have needed a murderer."

"Why do you say that?"

He exhaled and set the bottle on the counter.

"According to the coroner's report, Emil *should* have died of an overdose of heroin. He was practically embalmed with the drug. Someone got to him first. The first blow to the head—which was the blow that killed him— occurred around two-thirty last night. The other blows occurred sometime *after* his death."

"How can they tell that?"

"By the amount of blood, the conformation of the

bruising . . . when the heart stops pumping, wounds stop bleeding. There are blows to Emil's head that are not accompanied by the appropriate bruises."

"And if he hadn't been struck by the branding iron . . . the coroner thinks he might have died of an overdose?"

"Apparently it was nip and tuck."

"A mixed-media death . . . Emil would have liked that. Jesus," she said rubbing her forehead with a wet hand. "And he was struck on the head after he died. Why would anyone kill a dead man? Maybe they didn't know he was dead."

"Something else: you remember the broom leaning against the pile?"

"Yes."

"There are no fingerprints on it at all."

"I don't understand."

"Well, it would appear that whoever swept up all the crap around the boxes *considered* fingerprints and did a damn thorough job of removing them from the broom handle."

For Rhea, it was one too many complications. It made absolutely no sense. From the living room came barking, then laughter. "What about Al?" she asked. "Does he have an alibi?"

"Yes, he does. Pretty good one. He spent the night with the Tompkinses, on Ninety-fifth and Fifth."

"The Tompkinses," she repeated. "Of course! I knew that. They came with him to the party. They were kind of late. Some problem with the baby-sitter."

"That's right. The baby-sitter for Jack was late. It all checks out. We've talked to her and Karl Tompkins as well. Do you know them?"

"The Tompkinses? They were one of Al's first buyers. He's a big firecracker down on Wall Street. Serious art collector. Al did a commission for their house in Southampton. Emil knew them from out there. I haven't spent any time with them but I know their crowd. Oh, that's great! They're so straight. It couldn't be better."

Tennyson nodded in agreement. "The three of them left Emil's around one-fifteen. A hired car took them back, directly to their apartment. The limo service confirms it. Then . . ."

"Then?"

"Then the baby-sitter is paid, tipped, sent on her way. They have a celebratory shot of cognac, go immediately to bed. The Tompkinses to their bedroom, Al to the guest bedroom where Jack is already asleep. He waits until everything is quiet. Al puts his clothes back on, sneaks out, hails a cab, goes to the gallery—"

"Oh, bullshit," Rhea said, squeezing lime into a new drink. "Why do you want Al to be the one?"

"I don't want anyone to be the one. Right now everything is fantasyland as far as I'm concerned."

"I'll drink to that."

"But I can tell you one thing. When I showed Al the note . . ."

"Yes?"

"I would swear, on a stack of Wendell Castles, or whatever is holy to you, that Al knew what that message meant."

"What did he say?"

"It wasn't what he said. He didn't say anything at first. It was just a look, a moment. Eventually he *said* it didn't mean anything to him but you could tell that he was lying, that he *wasn't* saying something that he could have said."

Rhea thought for a moment. A kind of happy flush came to her face.

"Well, John, if he was genuinely caught off guard . . ."

"What?"

"Then that means he didn't know anything about it. That he wasn't at the gallery last night."

"No. It means that he hadn't seen the message before, that's all."

"I don't believe you! You're doing everything you can to twist this around to Al. You're obsessed with him. You know what your problem is, John? I just figured it out. You're jealous of artists. That's what it is. I bet that's why you got divorced. You got tired of being dragged around to all the galleries while your wife swooned at the talent."

"You know what your problem is, Rhea?" Tennyson smiled.

"What?"

His smile grew broader. "Never mind."

"*What?*"

"Never mind."

"Why, you asshole. Is this where you take me in your arms and I surrender, is that it?"

"You might be flattering yourself."

"Christ, you remind me of Emil. Just when I begin to get my hooks into this mess, I take a look at you and . . . skid." She laughed and made a sweeping gesture toward all the food around her. "You know, while I was creating this groaning board, it occurred to me that Emil, in death, managed to do something that he never succeeded to do in life, though he sure as hell tried often enough—to fluster me, to make me lose control. I've been going in and out of a daydream that none of this is real, that Emil is still alive, that it's all an elaborate joke Emil is playing on me and that *you* are in on the joke. I don't know. You're some long-lost bastard brother who nobody knew about and Emil has hired you to . . . it's all so stupid. I feel like Dwight Gooden must have felt today. I'm pitching but I'm not there and neither is the catcher and neither is home plate."

Tennyson took another swig. Almost apologetically he said, "I'm not off duty."

"Do you think I give a shit? Do you want a glass?"

Al walked in. "Here's the guy who needs a drink," she

said, walking over to him, taking him by the hand and hacking him over to Tennyson like a recently raced horse. She suddenly had an overwhelming desire to exploit (explode?) the weird intimacy springing up between her and the detective. She gave Al a big hug. Al seemed embarrassed. Tennyson pretended not to watch.

"Let's eat," she said. "Or do you have to go?" she asked Tennyson.

"I can stay."

Five

But Tennyson didn't stay. Just as Rhea was dealing out the plates, the telephone rang. It was another one of those "uh-hunh, nope, maybe" conversations with an unidentified colleague, and when he hung up, "I've got to go" was all he offered as an explanation.

Al didn't bother to disguise his relief. Rhea walked him to the door. "Am I free to go to the gallery tomorrow?"

"Monday," he said, shaking his head.

His exhausted expression reminded her of how devitalized *she* was. She felt absurdly close to him. Fatigue-induced camaraderie? She'd known him for only one day. Did she like him? Or was he merely her new software, her state-of-the-art data acquisition and control adapter? Her reluctance to answer any question regarding Tennyson seemed to match his own toward her.

"Will you at least call me if anything interesting happens?"

Again he ignored her question and asked, "Will they be staying here for the night?"

"I don't know. I have an extra room. What are you smirking about?" She sighed. "I'll call *you* if anything interesting happens, how's that?"

"It was an in-the-line-of-duty question."

"Hum. Then why do I feel like this is the end of a one-night stand?"

For a moment Tennyson considered his hand, which was holding the edge of the open door. Then he looked at her. "Maybe because this is where you conclude your one-night stands."

"You're a rough . . ."

He nodded and walked out the door. She stormed into the kitchen and grabbed the vodka. Al and Jack were sitting, politely waiting for her. "Go ahead without me, boys, I'm not eating."

The "boys" ate with abandon. Rhea was content to sit close by and watch . . . and drink . . . and feel like she'd just rolled into camp with the chuck wagon.

Al insisted on cleaning up afterward. There was nothing superficial about his housekeeping techniques and, to her approval, Jack fell right in line with understood duties of his own. There was a self-sufficiency being enacted that both impressed her and made her feel unconsciously jealous. It was obvious that if Al had a woman in Connecticut, she wasn't the apron type. She also concluded from the way Jack loaded the dishwasher that their home was not without amenities.

It was eight-thirty. The rain was coming down hard. She couldn't get back into the gallery until Monday. She excused herself and went into her bedroom to call her staff. They would have to forget about taking Monday off. If there was any way in hell she could mount a group show and have it ready for Tuesday, even if it meant repainting the gallery walls herself . . .

Also, what were the alibis they had given to Tennyson? She intended to find out and, in quick succession, she accomplished just that.

Anne: She lived with her mother in Queens, had spent the entire night at home watching back-to-back coverage of the pope's arrival in the States.

Felix: After leaving Emil's, he had taken his date and met with friends at Nell's, the current "in" nightclub and social conduit for hip Manhattanites. They had stayed until nearly dawn.

Simon: He left the party at one o'clock, went straight back to his apartment on Fourteenth and Ninth Avenue and passed out. The guests remaining at Emil's? Simon could recall Al, the Tompkinses, James Drummond (uptown gallery owner), Drummond's boyfriend, and Arlene Brice, an aging albeit ever-horny and every-hopeful art consultant who was always the last to give up.

She saved the worst for last. Catherine.

"Do you hate me?" Catherine whined.

"Why should I hate you?"

"I mean about me and Emil."

"Let's get something straight, Catherine. I'm not interested in your shabby love life. I don't care if you're playing touch-tag with Leo Castelli, Mayor Koch and Francesco Clementé. But I do care if it gets in the way of business and I especially care if I'm the last to know. Where were you last night?"

"I told you, I went home after the party."

"You told me you left right after I did. You told Tennyson that you stayed a while. Which is it?"

"I guess I stayed a while."

"And when you got home, was your roommate there?"

"Yes."

"So what the fuck do you bring up your little fling with Emil for?"

"It wasn't a little fling."

"Well it couldn't have been a big fling. What with Emil's drug habit, erections per session couldn't have been exactly Olympian, could they? Were you scoring drugs for him, too?"

"I despise you and so does everybody else in the gallery. Emil needed me."

"And I counted on you, Catherine, and you've proven to be nothing but a . . . you're fired."

"I quit, you bitch."

"Super. You can pick up your stuff on Monday."

The minute she hung up she wondered if she had behaved rashly. She liked things to move fast but this was ridiculous. There were so many scattered details, so many questions . . . was she sabotaging her own effort to reconquer order?

When she returned to the kitchen, Al was bent over the sink scouring one last pan with a thoroughness indicative of his art. "Nice job," she said, admiring his butt. "Very anal retentive. Like all my artists."

She laughed at her own joke, which wasn't a joke at all. It was one of the few things she and Emil had never argued about: the artists they represented must excel in technique and self-discipline—criteria looked down upon as passé by many of the trendier galleries in town. "The idea is all, the technique is secondary." None of that bullshit for her and Emil. Detractors used this to argue that the Orloff Gallery was fuddy-duddy, out of touch. "Oh, yeah?" Emil would respond. "You go ahead and pay forty thousand dollars for the latest trend, hang it above your sofa, don't worry about the fact that it's ugly, that it has no technical expertise; the important thing is that everyone will know that you are *up to the moment*. And then, ten years down the road, when your statement-painting is no longer up to the moment, when all that's left is an ugly crappily executed painting, just try to get your money back."

Mutual anger—had that been the basis of their relationship? Was she surrounded by people who hated her? Could she afford to care?

"Where's Jack?" she asked.

"Guess."

"Playing with his new toys. He's a nice kid."

"Yeah," he said, folding up the dish towel. He suddenly looked totally lost. It was as if without the busywork, he might fly apart. She couldn't have handled that.

"I'll tell you what let's do. Let's get drunk."

Al laughed. "I thought that's what we *were* doing."

"No, I mean really drunk."

She pulled a bottle of champagne out of the refrigerator. The cork hit the ceiling. She overpoured two wine glasses and handed one to him.

"What do you think about Tennyson?"

Al took a sip. "Tasty. I think he'd like to nail me."

"He might want to nail me."

"Yeah, but not in the same way he wants to nail me."

"Well, at least someone likes me."

"What do you mean?"

"Skip it."

They walked into the living room. Jack was sound asleep on the floor. Al set down his glass, picked him up in his arms and took him off to the guest bedroom. When he came back he said, "Crunch jumped up in bed with him. Is that OK?"

"Sure."

She did and she didn't want Al and the kid to be there. She did because she was insufficiently sure that she could handle the night alone. She didn't because they saddened her and brought out a pathos in her that made her feel vulnerable . . . perhaps more vulnerable than if she had been left to herself.

They finished the bottle. She immediately got up and fetched another. In the meantime, Al had turned on the TV.

"Do we have to have that on?" she groaned.

Al pointed to his watch. "It's almost ten. I wanted to see if we're on the news."

The pope was the lead story. Then something about a corrupt New York official on trial. Then, before their eyes, was an exterior shot of the Orloff Gallery. In the foreground, a woman holding an umbrella with one hand, a mike with the other, was being very at-the-scene-ish. "Apparent suicide," she said, "though foul play has not been ruled out."

Where had they got the suicide idea? It was an odd sensation, to watch something on the news about which you knew more than the newscaster. In spite of everything, it was exhilarating.

And then it was over. The screen cut to another story. They appraised each other's reactions.

"It's like make-believe," she shuddered.

"They didn't even mention my name," Al muttered. "Two years down the tubes and they didn't even mention my fucking name."

Without asking, Al went into her bathroom and took a long shower. He came back out with a towel wrapped around his waist. He was shorter without his boots on. His shoulder-length hair clung to his neck in wet tangles. He sat next to her. It was odd, smelling her soap on a man.

"Feel any better?"

"That depends."

"On what?"

"You're going to think I'm crazy. Do you remember how the gallery looked when you walked in this morning?"

"Yes."

"No, I mean do you remember *exactly* how it was. The neat piles, the—"

"The neat piles," she nodded, "the broom against the pile in the larger room. I told you, I remember everything."

"Enough to reconstruct it?"

"Absolutely."

"You're going to think I'm crazy."

"What is it? What are you smiling about"

He took a deep breath. "Let's show it."

"Show what?"

"The ruins. Let's show the installation of our unknown madman to the public. Rhea, don't you see? Fuck a group show. You've already got the hottest show in town."

Rhea's eyes widened. The blatant opportunism of the suggestion was shocking. The further suspicion it would cast on both her and Al was too dangerous to contemplate.

"You're right. I think you're crazy."

"I am crazy. It makes me crazy just to think about it."

"It's crazy," she repeated.

"So?"

She slung her arms around him and buzzed his cheek. "Let's do it!"

"You're serious?"

She giggled in the affirmative.

"No take-backs in the morning?"

"Waste not, want not."

They clinked glasses with a sloppiness that cinched the deal.

Six

It was eight in the morning but the sky was quite dark. The rain on the roof was in collusion with the pounding in her head. Rhea declared war on the hangover in which she was imprisoned.

She forced herself into the medicine cabinet. She chewed four aspirins before swallowing them and, thus fortified, took two 600 mg Motrins and chased them down with a double Alka-Seltzer. Woolly and throbbing, she ducked her head into the sauna to make sure there were no towels still in there. She closed the door and turned on the timer. She regretted that it would take thirty minutes to heat up. The waiting would be intolerable.

She groped her way down the hall, past the guest bedroom, past the opening into the living room where scrolls of rain curled down the large windows, past the laundry room and into the kitchen, which she prudently left unlighted. She found a church key and opened some tomato juice. She drank it from the can. It slid down her throat, thick and nourishing as blood. She opened and drained a second can. She pulled out a large garbage bag from the under-sink cabinet.

She walked back down the hallway. She felt the tomato juice taking liberties with her stomach. She steadied herself at the doorway of the guest bedroom and peered in.

Still life: "Man and Boy with Dog." Two naked torsos cut off by a single sheet. If she could have left her head at the door, she would have gladly included herself in the composition. A tail thumped twice and then went back to sleep. Crunch was a whore.

She put on a jogging outfit and running shoes. Bending over while manipulating four laces was a particularly shaky affair. She stuffed her key clump and a fistful of quarters into one pocket, the plastic bag in the other and sneaked—if bumping into walls could be called sneaking—out of the apartment, quietly closing the door behind her.

The street was always empty on Sunday mornings. But today it was unnaturally dark, the innumerable potholes and collapsed gutters were overflowing with rain, and the scene reminded her of some demented urbane version of a lake district.

She charged into the downpour and instantly felt like a part of it, drenched from head to foot. Her headache turned sumptuous in the purge.

She ran over to Sixth Avenue and all the way up to Eighth Street (though she needn't have gone so far), where a tarp-enclosed newsstand was open. She purchased the Sunday *Times* and two lighter tabloids. Sorry Emil, no banner headlines.

She had two alternatives: to run back to Greene Street or to drop dead. She coerced the three papers into the plastic garbage bag and sloshed-jogged back to SoHo.

She took the stairs instead of the elevator as one last punishment. Once inside her door, she stripped, walked her ball of wet clothes to the laundry room, threw them inside, grabbed a towel and retreated to the sauna.

She spread out the towel and reclined in a supine

position. Within seconds the heat announced itself. Her breathing began to slow down, the trembling began to abate. She stared at the low cedar ceiling and listed, out loud, the poisons she had so willing introduced into her body the day before. "Brandy, scotch, vodka, champagne."

For some reason, the womblike acoustics of the paneled enclosure reminded her of her lonely adolescence spent in a Swiss private girl's school.

The oppressive heat made her turn over on her side. Rivulets of sweat tickled her breasts, her stomach, the small of her back. *"There is an exchange for all things . . . gold into fire . . ."*

I would swear that Al knew what the message meant, Tennyson had told her.

The audacity of Al's idea the night before—was it incriminating or merely brilliant? And either way, drunk or not, how could he sleep?

She had always seen the unrolling of her life as a series of easily characterized events and she had always confronted those events with crystal-clear motives and plans of action.

If Al *had* gone back to the gallery . . . it meant that she didn't know people as well as she thought. God knows, she'd misjudged Catherine. Were people really capable of such convolutions? And if Al was guilty, how would that tally with her ineluctable desire to climb into bed with him? She couldn't remember having gone to bed last night. Had he carried to her bed? Sex was definitely becoming an issue. With whom? With Al? With Tennyson? With Emil and Catherine?

The truth was she was happiest when she didn't have to think about sex. Looking back, it hadn't been all that edifying. In her early twenties, she had been promiscuous, especially while living in Europe. From Denmark to Greece, she'd sampled the local wares—right up to the back door of Asia—and she was glad she had had so many men, because it gave her a basis for analytically dismissing what was not worth repeating. Then the marriage. Then the accident. Then the divorce . . .

She sometimes still needed sex, had no particular difficulty procuring a willing partner, did it (though with increasing selectivity since the plague of AIDS), and got on with her life. Did she have sex so that she wouldn't have to think about sex? That was a pretty dreary notion. And pretty convoluted. Or was it simple?

Was Emil's death complicated or simple? Why had someone wanted it to appear complicated? Why was Emil in the basement? No, there was no point in thinking about that now.

She quit the sauna and went directly into an ice-cold shower. She emerged flushed, radiant, artificially revived for the day ahead. It would have to do. She brushed her teeth, flossed, and brushed again. She dressed and made a pot of double-strength coffee. She checked the *Times* obituary first. One column, seven paragraphs. She didn't even bother to read the copy. The idea of his life being reduced to seven puny paragraphs . . .

"Well, what did you expect?" she said out loud.

"Who are you talking to?" Jack asked, standing in the doorway and rubbing one eye with his knuckles.

"Morning, Jack. I was talking to myself. Do you ever do that?"

"Just to HoHo."

"Who's HoHo?"

"A ghost. He's really my grandfather but he's dead. He died a long time ago. Dad doesn't like it when I tell him about HoHo and HoHo doesn't like it either. So I have to talk to him all by myself and it makes me look like I'm talking to myself but I'm not."

"Ghosts are only make-believe."

"Yeah, I know."

"Let me cook some breakfast. What would you like?"

"Some of that lasagna."

"Really?"

"I liked it."

"You got it, kid. Lasagna comin' right up."

Father and son were into leftovers, was that why she felt so at home with them?

The phone rang. It was Becker calling from Seattle. He'd just heard the news and would arrive at LaGuardia by late afternoon. The reading of the will would be at ten o'clock tomorrow. Anne and Inez were apparently beneficiaries because he asked Rhea to make sure they were there.

She had no sooner hung up when the phone rang again. It was a reporter. Who had given him her number? Catherine Miller? He wasn't saying. Rhea told him she had no comment at the present time and slammed down the receiver. Abusing her phone was becoming a regular habit. What did people do before they could slam phones?

Before the lasagna had been heated up, another reporter called. She unplugged the phone in the kitchen and turned on the answering machine in the bedroom.

"Hey," a voice called as she passed the guest bedroom.

"Morning, Al. We're getting ready to eat lasagna. Want some?" No answer. "Well, there's an arsenal of retaliatory drugs in my bathroom if you prefer. And the sauna's on, which I strongly recommend. It brought me back to life."

He nodded and asked, "No take-backs?"

She breathed in. "No, no take-backs. We're about to raise some eyebrows in this town. By the way, how did I get to bed last night?"

Al pointed at his chest twice.

"You didn't do anything naughty?"

"Don't remember."

"Thanks."

The intercom buzzed. She went to the front door. It was Tennyson asking to come up.

There was a pair of sunglasses on the hall table below

the intercom. She picked them up and gingerly slid them past her temples. There was a knock, and she opened the door.

"Been keeping busy, John?" she asked, helping him with his raincoat.

"How about yourself?" he asked, pointing to the sunglasses.

"We kept the orgy down to a minimum."

"What did you think of the newspapers?"

"What makes you think I've read the newspapers?"

There was a small window in the foyer. Tennyson motioned for Rhea to look outside. Down, across on the other side of the street, was an umbrella with two feet sticking out from under it.

"You've got a stakeout on my place?" she asked with a laugh. "Wonder if he's into jogging?"

"He is now," he said, following her into the kitchen.

"Would you like some coffee? How about a side order of lasagna?"

Tennyson greeted Jack, whose expression went somber. He backed out and ran into the living room.

"You have a way with kids, John," she said.

He shrugged, then, noticing that only the Sunday *Times* had been disembowled, said:

"Then you haven't seen yet."

"Seen what?"

"The mix-up."

He picked up one of the other papers, turned to page four and handed it to her. There was a large photograph of Tennyson.

"Oh look," she mused, "you got your picture in the paper. Isn't that nice."

Tennyson smiled. "Now read the caption."

"'Emil Orloff, shortly before his death.'"

Seven

The reason for Tennyson's visit was not to amuse Rhea with newspaper gaffes.

"How hard would it be to round up all the artists you represent?" he asked her.

"Hard. There's only five who live in or around Manhattan. The rest are spread all over. Florida, California, Santa Fe . . . Berlin, one in Barcelona, one is on a fellowship in Japan . . . and then there's a few other artists, artists we no longer represent and a few we're considering but haven't made any commitment to."

"But you have samples of their work in the gallery, right?"

"Probably. I can check inventory with the computer. What's on your mind, John?"

"I'd like you to go to the gallery with me."

"This morning?"

"I need you to identify samples of each artist's work so that my men can take fingerprints. I keep coming back to the way Al's show was wrecked. You called it an installation. So did Al. That would point the finger at an artist."

She agreed, typing a command into the computer. Then she dropped her hands. "The problem is that . . ."

"What?"

"I've been thinking about this all morning. I don't want this to sound condescending. Practically everyone I meet is an artist of some variety. Either they wanted to be artists when they were younger and gave up or they're still clinging to the hope. Maybe being a gallery owner brings out this latency. I go to the dentist with a racking toothache and before he'll give me novocaine I have to look at his mobiles. Don't laugh, it's a true story. Even Emil's housekeeper, Inez, draws . . . her specialty is assorted kittens with balls of yarn."

"I know all about her drawings," Tennyson said, chuckling. "They almost got her thrown in the slammer yesterday."

"Why?"

"Your friend Shears and Inez locked horns."

"Shears went over to Emil's?"

"Um-hum. She picked up a batch of Inez's artwork, there was a tug-of-war, shoving, kicking, a regular Mexican hat dance the way I heard it. Anyway, Shears almost booked her for obstructing justice."

"Shoving?" Rhea grinned. "Shears got off easy. Anyway, Inez is going to have the last laugh. Becker called me this morning and . . ."

When she mentioned Becker's name, Tennyson averted his eyes.

"And he wants Inez there for the reading of the will. Ten o'clock tomorrow morning in his office."

She could have sworn that Tennyson already knew about it. Had the son of a bitch tapped her phone? Lipski could have done it yesterday . . .

Tennyson pensively sipped his coffee. About that time, Al entered naked save for a pair of blue jeans. It pissed her off. He knew Tennyson was there. What was he thinking about? Was the bare chest a deliberate ploy to provoke Tennyson? On the other hand, so what? Nothing had happened between them. Still, it annoyed her. For some reason it was his bare feet that made her most uncomfortable.

"Morning."

"Morning."

The men greeted each other as if they were finalists in a bass voice contest.

Tennyson scratched his jaw. "Rhea and I were just talking about frustrated artists. Anyone got a personal grudge against you?"

Al stretched and shook his head.

"How about your work?"

"A grudge against my work? Unfortunately, my work hasn't caused that kind of stir in New York."

"But you wouldn't mind if it did, would you."

It was a statement, not a question. Rhea shoved the sunglasses back up onto the bridge of her nose. "Lay off, John. Let him have his coffee first."

"It's all right," Al said, sitting down next to Tennyson.

Without looking at her, Al accepted the proffered coffee as if she were a short-order cook. On the other hand, when he pulled out a cigarette and Tennyson lighted it for him, there was an intimacy, an immediacy, an intensity between them that made Rhea feel quite excluded. There was definitely some mutual dick-waving going on in her kitchen and there was nothing she could do but hold her tongue.

"Do you have any personal enemies?" Tennyson asked, blowing out the match.

"Present company excluded? No."

"You're sure?"

"I'm a carpenter. I work like a dog all day, I come home and work on my boxes. I don't have time for friends, let alone enemies. There's my boy, my work and that's about it."

"What about your wife?"

"Ex-wife."

"Ex-wife."

"She doesn't give a fuck. I mean she's not there. Period." And then in a softer, more natural tone: "She didn't even call Jack on his birthday."

"Where is she?"

"Ever heard of the Van Gogh-Goghs? No reason why you should have. It's a rock band. Her boyfriend is the drummer. You find the band, you can probably find her."

"Any other family?"

"My parents are gone."

"Brothers? Sisters?"

"Nope."

"Aunts? Uncles?"

"I guess I have some relatives still around but my dad was a loner. He never saw much of them and I never kept up after I left Missouri."

"He was a cattle rancher?"

"That's right," Al nodded. "He was also an artist."

"What did I tell you?" Rhea sneered while taking the lasagna out of the oven.

"Do you know any of the other artists with the gallery?"

"I've met several of them. I'm not friends with any of them. I don't have time to hang out."

Tennyson turned to Rhea. "Would you describe any of your artists as unbalanced?"

She pivoted, twiddling her spatula. "Were you speaking to me?"

"Yes, Rhea. Any borderlines in your stable?"

"You've got to be kidding."

"Let me put it this way. Are there any crazier than the others . . . Rhea, if you're going to roll your eyes at me, why don't you at least take off those sunglasses."

"I'll nurse my hangover any goddamn way I want."

The men exchanged a sidelong glance. She plopped down two plates of steaming lasagna in front of them, content that it was the last thing they wanted staring up at them.

She took a third plate into the living room, where Jack was watching cartoons. She sat down beside him and contemplated the universal nuisance of testosterone. On the TV screen, a cigar-smoking raven was strangling Woody Woodpecker.

———

Rhea and Tennyson went to the gallery around ten-thirty. As they entered, Tennyson cautioned her. "We'll have to go downstairs. Can you handle that?"

"Return to the scene of the crime? I'm not looking forward to it. Fuck it. You get thrown from a horse, you get back on, right?"

"Are you a horsewoman too?"

"Used to be."

The gruesome business of returning to the gallery, of going back downstairs and into the storeroom, wasn't as bad as she had expected. In fact, like getting back on a horse, it was cathartic. The tedious two hours of going through the inventory, sidestepping from one carpeted bin to the next, sliding out paintings, sliding them back in again, bad-mouthing cops who mishandled the merchandise, seeing and remembering works that she had totally forgotten about—all of this helped to destigmatize the scene of the murder, or at least *transfer* the horror of Emil's corpse to the melancholy of unviewed, dust-gathering art. It *was* a diverting depression: art on ice. What was a gallery's storeroom but a kind of aesthetic morgue? There were lots of corpses down here.

It was an idea no doubt instigated by the chalk outline where Emil Orloff had enjoyed his last enema. At one point it was even necessary to step across the phantom. She took special care to avoid the dark stain with the puppy-dog tracks.

Once the ordeal was over and she was back upstairs, she again asked John when she would get her gallery back.

"We'll be out of here sometime today."

"Promise?"

"Promise. Which reminds me. You need to call a locksmith."

"Why? The lock wasn't tampered with."

"Emil's keys are missing. The only things in his pockets were his wallet, cigarettes, and three dime bags of heroin. There weren't any keys found in his apartment either. Did anyone have keys besides you and Catherine?"

"Nobody. Of course, I'm beginning to think I don't know anything around here." She sighed. "Where am I going to find a locksmith on Sunday?"

"Don't worry, I'll have the place watched tonight."

Rhea scanned the ruins of the gallery. "It's odd," she said. "When I'm downstairs, everything centers around Emil's death. But when I'm upstairs, Emil is almost superfluous. Does that make any sense? It's like two unconnected crimes. What do you think?"

"I don't want to sound condescending but everybody I meet sees themselves as detectives."

"Saving that one up for me, John? All right, Mr. Expert. Do you have any real leads or are you just dog-paddling like the rest of us?"

"We've been doing some leg work."

"Like what?"

"We have a pretty clear picture of the party after you left. By most accounts, your partner was in rare form that night. Arlene Brice was the last to leave, and she said he grew more belligerent as the evening wore on. He was very democratic with his rudeness. He insulted Al, Simon, James Drummond's boyfriend, several others." Tennyson pulled out a notepad, flipped back the pages until he said, "According to Mr. Drummond, at one point Emil told Catherine that her legs were the clutchiest contraptions since the invention of the waffle iron." Then, looking up, he asked, "Does that sound like something Orloff would have said?"

"Waffle iron?" Rhea checked a smile by looking up at the ceiling. "So what have you done? Fingerprinted everybody who came to the party?"

Tennyson ignored her. Like a cat he began to walk along the perimeters of the larger gallery room, speaking over his shoulder as he did. "We've got one or more people who came in here after *or* with Emil. We don't know who. We don't know why. Did Emil tear up Al's show? Or was it someone else? And why? Why was Emil having an enema in the place where it would be most difficult to get to the bathroom?"

"That was *my* detective work," she called out to him.

He pretended not to hear. "Why did someone wipe down the broom handle? Why strike Emil again, thirty minutes after he was dead? Are we looking for a sicko or does someone want us to think it was a sicko? Why go to the trouble of putting a message on top of the boxes? And who was the message for? Incidentally," said Tennyson, coming back up to her, "the handwriting doesn't match up with any of your staff's, including Emil's. The thing that most bothers me about this case is that there's too goddamn much going on. Whoever was here the night before last was a very busy person. So what's the motive? And I'm not talking about the murder motive. What's the motive for all the busywork? I don't know anything, Rhea, except that this whole case smells of overcompensation. Bogus."

"Tell that to Emil."

Tennyson pulled a small opalescent ball out of his pocket and handed it to Rhea. "Do you recognize this?"

"It's an Austrian hand-blown marble. Al used them in several of his boxes."

"Was it just decoration or did they have some symbolic significance?"

"Definitely symbolic. He sees spheres as private universes."

Tennyson nodded. "Emil was clutching it in his hand when he died."

Rhea handed the ball back to him. "Thanks so much for sharing that with me."

"What about funeral arrangements?"

"Jesus Christ, throw on the brakes, would you? First you tell me I need a locksmith. Then you show me how Emil finally lost his marbles. Now you want me to throw a funeral. That's his sister's problem."

"Come on, you must have some idea."

"He wanted to be cremated . . . you know, gold into fire, that sort of thing."

"What about a memorial service?"

"What about it?"

"Don't you art hotdogs have memorial services?"

"I guess so."

"Well?"

Rhea nudged one of the broken boxes with her toe. "As far as I'm concerned, you're looking at it."

Eight

It was half past noon when she left the gallery. The sky had brightened but it was still drizzling. Maybe the Mets game wouldn't be rained out after all. The rain felt comforting on her upturned face. She decided not to go straight home. A taxi came bumping down Prince Street. She hailed it.

"Fourteenth and Ninth Avenue."

She got in, well aware that her umbrella man was scrambling toward an unmarked car. She consulted the address book in her purse because she'd never been to the place she was looking for.

The taxi pulled up to a large, uninviting apartment building. She got out and waved to the car pulling up behind her. She went inside, located Simon Golden's nameplate, and buzzed up.

"Who is it," came a voice over the intercom.

"Rhea. I need to talk to you."

There was a long pause before: "I'll be right down."

"Simon, that won't do. I need to come up."

Could a buzzer sound reluctant? Simon's did as the door clicked open.

His place was on the second floor. Simon opened the

door in a paint-smeared kimono. She walked in without waiting to be invited.

"I realize I have no business barging in like this, but I'm kind of locked into a situation. My phone is tapped, I think. Catherine quit last night. Anne's in Queens. Felix is God only knows. I've got to be at the lawyer's first thing in the morning so you're going to have to toe the line for the gallery until I can get back downtown. I need you to make quite a few phone calls for me today. Now here's what's going on."

She filled him in on Al's idea for the installation.

"Al will open up the gallery at nine o'clock tomorrow morning. You need to get there as early as possible. Whatever he wants in lighting, in paint, whatever, you're to get for him. Come to think of it, we'll probably need Bill Whitehead too."

Bill Whitehead was a friend of Simon's, a sculptor. The gallery sometimes employed him for odd jobs.

"Aren't you usually the one who gets ahold of him? Good. Do you think you could get him on a Sunday?"

Simon nodded.

"But the most important thing—and this goes for Anne and Felix too—is to keep this secret until we're ready to open to the public. Keep the door locked at all times. Oh . . . and Catherine. She's not allowed inside. Can I use your phone?"

She called a locksmith in the yellow pages and made arrangements for a change the following morning.

"Where was I?"

"Catherine is not to come in."

"Yeah, that's not a problem for you, is it? Or were you sleeping with her too?"

"What do you mean?"

"Don't tell me she hasn't called. I don't have time to worry about affronting people's sensibilities right now. Besides, according to Catherine, you all hate me anyway.

Let's just hope there's a little respect that goes along with the hate."

"I don't hate you."

"Glad to hear it. What was I saying? Bill Whitehead, Catherine . . . oh, yeah. Empty the contents of her desk, put them in a box and have it ready for her in case she comes by. I think she's been talking to the press so I don't want her to know what's going on. That's extremely important."

All this time, Simon had barely uttered a word.

"Can you do this for me, Simon? You think the installation idea is distasteful, don't you?"

"Why should I think it's distasteful?"

"Why *shouldn't* you think it's distasteful? It is."

"Then why are you doing it?"

"Call it a hunch. It's the kind of flaunting that this town will fall for. It's exciting. That's it. It's exciting and my gallery is boring."

Simon smiled.

"You agree with me, don't you? It is kind of boring, isn't it? The same artists, show after show, year after year."

For the first time, she allowed herself to focus upon the contents of Simon's studio. It was on the backside of the building, so on the brightest of days there would have been little light. Today it was . . . well . . . add a few stalactites and you would have had a great cave. It wasn't his fault, of course. She supposed that his salary wouldn't have allowed for any place nicer than this, which rather put her in the position of Scrooge visiting the Cratchets.

"If we can pull this off by Tuesday . . . secretly . . . I'll make it up to you, all of you. Big bonus from bitch Rhea."

Simon made no comment. He looked self-consciously around his room. Then she understood. Except for the bare necessities, Simon's studio was entirely devoted to his painting. She'd never seen his work before and wasted no time in getting up and perusing what was on view. He followed her around.

The technique struck her as interesting. Large canvases had been crosscut into quarter-inch squares; there must have been tens of thousands of squares on each canvas. At first glance the pieces were nonrepresentational, but on closer examination one could detect architectural elements: a staircase here, a flying buttress there, all composed of enlarged matrix dots. It was like having your head shoved up against a television screen.

She turned around to him. His face was flushed with apprehension.

"Why didn't you ever show me any of this?"

"I showed it to Emil."

"Emil never told me. What did he think?"

"He said it was shit."

"Everything was shit to Emil. Emil thought that the last good painting was completed in the quattrocento. You should have shown this to me, Simon. I'm beginning to like it."

"Really?"

"The grids that are only partially colored in—is that on purpose or are they just not finished yet?"

Simon was apologetic. "It takes so long to complete one painting that I usually go on to another idea before I have time to—"

"Don't worry about it. The unfinished ones are better than the finished ones."

"Really?"

"Quit saying 'really.' It's just my opinion."

She walked over to an easel that cradled a three-by-five canvas. "What's this one?"

"Don't look at that one. I've only been working on that for a couple of weeks."

"What's it going to be?" It had a strong horizontal line slicing through the top third of the painting. Hanging down from this was a V-shaped valley. On one side of the incline was a blurry bristled slash.

"Looks like an upside-down volcano with an antenna."

Simon shook his head and grinned while gnawing on a thumbnail. (Such slender, feminine wrists! Definitely not the branding iron–wielding type.)

"So what is it? You're not going to tell me? It doesn't matter. Do you have any plastic?"

"Why?"

"I'd like to take it home with me. Come on. Let me live with it for a while."

"Why don't you take home something that's finished?"

"I told you, I like the unfinished ones."

She bullied him into letting her borrow it.

When she got back to her apartment, she unwrapped it and asked for Al's opinion. Al stared at it for a moment and then made a noncommittal gesture. "What's it supposed to be?"

"The truth? It's supposed to be a way to confuse the asshole cop who is following me around New York in the rain."

Al was appalled. "God, Rhea. You shouldn't mess around with Simon's head like that. That's shitty."

"I'm just kidding. I *do* like it. It intrigues me."

"Then why did you say that?"

"Look, on the way home in the taxi . . . I was thinking about the cop following me, what his report would say. It was just a joke. Forget it. I like it, OK?"

"Why?"

"I don't know yet. It reminds me of something I know about but something I don't particularly want to know about. That doesn't make any sense, does it?"

She looked at her watch. "God! Turn on the TV! It's time for the game!"

The Mets-Cardinals game got off to a jerky start.

There were two rain delays before the game really built up steam. During these unwanted intermissions, Rhea moved her new painting around the room. Al sketched ideas to enhance the installation. Rhea categorically agreed to everything he showed her, but Al finally complained. "You're not even looking."

"Yes I am."

"No you're not. You're agreeing because the Mets are winning."

David Cone pitched a 4 to 2 victory. Rhea was delighted. In spite of everything, a smooth satisfaction overcame her. She was tempted to call Tennyson just to rub it in, but thought better of it. Instead she rang up the Carlyle Hotel. The receptionist told her that Véra Orloff Vertbois had just checked in. She connected her to her room.

Rhea asked Véra if it would be all right to speak in German *and* French because she suspected her phone was tapped.

"Don't Americans have translators?" Véra asked.

"Véra, we're talking inconvenience, here."

"*Pas de problème.*"

"*Alors* . . ."

Rhea filled her in on the sordid details. Véra listened quietly, passively, almost as if she weren't interested. It wasn't until Rhea mentioned the reading of the will that Véra seemed to come to life. "I do hope he's been generous to me."

"I wouldn't set my hopes too high, Véra."

"Of course not, dear. Emil was always a little twit. He loved to embarrass me and my friends. It seems that I've spent half my life avoiding him. Still, one can hope that one can replace one's eight-year-old lynx in the very near future."

Al and Jack prepared bacon and eggs and home-fried potatoes for dinner. Rhea relished its simplicity and washed it down with ample quantities of beer. Crunch was given his own generous helping, which he promptly regurgitated all over Jack's Lego blocks. Tears, reproachful cursing and threats resulted in Crunch's retreat to the nether regions of a chest of drawers where even six-year-old arms couldn't reach.

Once again Rhea had cause to marvel at Al's sense of economy. He turned the upheaval into a game. He scooped the goopy blocks into a colander, made faces and throw-up sounds that made Jack giggle in spite of himself, ran the abused cargo into the kitchen, dropped it in the sink, turned on the water, pulled up a chair and offered his son the pullout nozzle. No further explanation was necessary from Dad. Jack scrambled up to the sink, grabbed the makeshift water pistol and squirted away happily until it was time for bed.

Did Al economize in the same way with a woman? They drank scotch and watched TV.

"You're a good father."

"Yeah."

"How come your wife left you?"

"There was reason enough. I don't make a very good husband. Not unfaithful, but not attentive either. There was my work, and when Jack came there was Jack. That put her in third place. Moving to Connecticut also had something to do with it. I was burned out with New York. And when she got pregnant, that was the last straw. I didn't want to raise a kid here. She hated the country from the first. She missed her friends and the nightclub scene. She wanted me to be hipper than I was. She was convinced that in order to make it big as an artist in New York, I had to be part of the night crowd. She hated being a mother, and I hated her for not wanting to be a mother . . . you know how that shit goes on . . . building up . . ."

"Why did you get married in the first place?"

"I guess because I loved her. Why did you get married?"

She held her glass up to eye level. "To be rid of the need to be married."

"Um, that's a good reason. Why'd you break up?"

"Variation on a theme. My husband was always traveling. I was having problems getting pregnant which we both wanted. So to keep me company, his father—not him—his father bought me a beautiful Arabian."

Al lighted her cigarette. "He bought you a Moslem?"

"A horse, asshole. A magnificent horse named Jazzanova. God, I loved that horse. I was jumping him one day, over a wall, not much of an obstacle, a wall we'd jumped a hundred times before, and bam. It was all over. I went first. The horse came last and landed on top of me. My pelvis was crushed, there was extensive internal bleeding—"

"Good lord—"

"Oh, I didn't feel any of it. I was out cold. When I came to I was in traction, with a crushed pelvis, two broken femur bones, minus half my bladder . . . not to mention my womanly hardware . . . on morphine and, in general, in outer space. I was in traction for three months. It was the hysterectomy that killed the marriage. The family I had married into . . . let's just say it was a long line of filthy rich Bavarians keen on continuing the dynasty ad infinitum."

"That's awful. I'm sorry."

"No reason to be. I was well rid of *them*. All that time in traction and casts and drugs—it was like being in a cocoon. I was baking inside, turning into . . . well, *not* a butterfly . . . but certainly something different. There's one thing, though, that will never change. Several years later I was told by an eminent gynecologist associated with Cornell University that he could see no reason for the hysterectomy. It was highly unlikely, he said, not impossible, but highly unlikely, that it was a necessary operation. I'll go to my grave wondering about that one."

They drank in silence.

Al started laughing.

"What's so funny?"

"My life is more depressing than yours is. No, it's not. Yes, it is. Is not. Is. Is not. Is."

"Yeah, well . . ."

"Do you have any scars?" Al asked a little later.

"What," Rhea said, laughing, "don't tell me you're into scars."

"I'll show you mine if you show me yours."

"You've been prancing around here all day half naked. I haven't seen any scars."

He looked at her, did push-ups with his eyebrows, stood, and pulled down his blue jeans. On his left side, from mid-thigh going right up and disappearing into his underwear, were the irrefutable, inimitable corrugations of a third-degree burn.

"Very impressive," she said, shuddering. "How did you get that?"

He shook his head, pulling his jeans back up over his hips.

"Not until you show me yours."

"OK, cowboy." Rhea set her drink on the coffee table and got up.

He took her by the hand and led her into her bedroom.

Nine

Becker's office was on Fifth Avenue, two blocks downtown from the Flatiron Building. Architecturally, it was not a glamorous area of New York. Six-story, prewar office buildings of modest, though sometimes detailed facades offered many a small business person the kind of space he or she could afford—two rest rooms per floor, bare echoing hallways, that sort of thing. In the last ten years, however, an impressive number of prominent commercial photographers had infiltrated the area, so that (among the tailors, secretaries and one-room entrepreneurs) Rhea might be obliged to share the elevator with a ravishing, bubble-gum-snapping, portfolio-toting model from an illustrious uptown agency.

To be fair, Rhea couldn't rule out the possibility that this was why she hated going to Becker's. (On more than one occasion, Emil had rubbed her face in this idea.) But there was a more apparent reason, readily apparent once you entered Becker's office.

He was a watercolorist of the seashore variety, as mediocre as he was prolific, and it was this latter qualification that so irritated her. He must have been supporting half the frame shops in lower Manhattan. There wasn't one place in the reception room where your eyes could take a break. Every available square inch was decorated with beached canoes, sunny bungalows and sensitively tangled driftwood. It wasn't a law office. It was a spider web to which a lawyer lured his clients so that they would be forced to "admire" his talent. Nor was there any relief when you were ushered into his consultation room. Pass the sun block and sign on the dotted line.

Rhea wore tight corduroy pants and cowboy boots. Anne, as always, was dressed sensibly. Véra Orloff Vertbois was sensational in a suit that smacked of the Plaza Athénée. But it was Inez, the last to enter, who stole the show: black shoes, black hose, black dress, black gloves, black sunglasses and a voluminous, rustling mourning veil that (save the hue) could have been easily mistaken for bridal.

"Who's the swarm of flies?" whispered Véra.

Becker pulled a folder from a drawer and set it down on his desk. Every eye in the room pounced on it.

"Ladies," Becker began, "before I read the will, I would just like to say that Emil insisted upon the overwrought wording of the document. We all knew him. You will have to bear with me, just as I had to bear with him. I would like to emphasize that what I am about to read in no way reflects my own sentiments."

He cleared his voice and opened the folder.

"'To my faithful and regrettably self-effacing secretary, Anne Barlow, I bequeath my David Hockney photocollage. Hang onto it until your mother dies and then go have yourself a party.

"'To my clock-watching and otherwise imperturbable sister, Véra Vertbois, I bequeath all my earthly belongings—save my real estate—including my art collection, which, if sold properly, should keep her in younger boyfriends for the rest of her inconsequential life.

"'To my imperious bulldozer of a partner, Rhea

Buerklin, I bequeath my property on Prince Street, provided that she first have her pet, Crunch Buerklin, put to sleep. In the event that she is unable to comply with this stipulation, the property shall be sold and the proceeds donated to the ASPCA.

"'To my Bambi-disposition housekeeper, Inez Borges, I bequeath my property in East Hampton, Long Island, so that she can at long last fulfill her dream to consolidate her large family under one roof. I feel confident that the broad-minded and neighborly folk of the Hamptons will accommodate her inheritance by redefining the word *hospitality*.'"

Anne and Rhea shared a cab downtown. Neither one mentioned the will, but it was clear that Anne was brimming with excitement.

It was nearly eleven when they got back to the gallery. Activity abounded. The locksmith had already come and gone. Al was sweeping debris up against the piles of boxes. Tarp was spread along two white walls of the larger room, where Felix and Bill Whitehead (the extra hand Simon had contacted the day before) were rolling on coats of dark gray paint.

"Somber color for somber occasion," she mused as she strolled by.

"Rhea," Bill called, hopping off the stepladder and carefully balancing the roller on the edge of the paint tray. The tall young man approached her with a steadfast gaze. "Do you have a minute? I need to talk to you."

Reluctantly, she stopped. Bill was a nice guy; good, dependable help when you needed him, but he always moved with such slow deliberation and spoke with such chronic anxiety that she was inevitably reduced to irritation. There was also this: she was prejudiced against his physical appearance. Running down from the top of his forehead to the bridge of his nose was a deep crease, an unnatural indentation that turned his brow into a double bulge. One got the unfortunate impression one was staring directly at the hemispheric conformation of his brain. He looked as if he had a permanent headache and, for Rhea, it was contagious.

"It's about my show," he said with a perturbed expression.

"Show? You got a show? Well, congratulations. What gallery?"

He blinked his eyes. The crease in his brow grew deeper. "I was afraid of that." He paused as if to gather strength. "Emil promised me a show. Next spring."

"You don't mean . . . here?"

Bill nodded.

"Emil never talked to me about it."

An undulating image of one of Whitehead's large steel sculptures—a silver fire hose gone amok—looped back through her memory. He had a frenzied, curlicue style that had attracted some attention in the late seventies, but few sales and fewer new ideas had ushered his career to a premature dead end. His peers, SoHo's answer to Hollywood's Brat Pack (and the critics who courted them) had left him behind.

"Jeez." she tried to smile. "I don't know what to say. When did all this happen?"

"Several months ago. Emil said next spring. He said the April slot was still open."

"Well that's true but . . . Bill, he would have had to consult me before . . . I mean it wasn't just his decision." She was furious.

It served to remind her that, though dead, Emil could still, at any time, drop a bomb on her organizational powers. She had no intention of showing Bill's work, of course. Several years earlier, she had rejected it out of hand. At its best, sculpture was the most difficult of art markets, and Bill's work had struck her as mediocre, derivative and, in spite of its large-scaled flourishes, forgettable.

Bill could be lying?

It didn't seem very likely. Anyway, it was his word against a dead man's . . . a dead man who had been perfectly capable of saying or promising anything for the flimsiest of reasons.

As if reading her thoughts, Bill offered, "I wouldn't make something like this up. Simon was there. And so was Al, for that matter."

"Al?"

"Yes. It was during the installation of the Spring Group Show. Remember? You guys called me up because, at the last minute, Emil wasn't happy with the color of the walls. And the day I was repainting them, Al came into town with some of his new boxes. I helped him bring them in from his van. Anyway, at one point I was showing Al some slides of my work. Emil came over and had a look for himself. He really got excited about them. He said he'd never seen such 'well-intended sincerity in steel.' Those were his very words."

"Sounds just like Emil," Rhea said with a shudder.

Emil broke out in hives at the mere mention of the word *sincerity*. She suddenly saw the real picture: amusement springing from idle meanness and at the expense of another human being—that's what this was all about—setting up an unrealistic hope in Bill for the perverse pleasure of being able to thwart it later on.

"Hey, Al!" Bill called. "You remember that day last spring when you were in town and Emil looked at my slides?"

Al stopped his sweeping and looked up, nonplussed.

"You remember! He talked about doing a show of my work."

Al seemed unenlightened.

"You know you heard. And after the show was

mounted, we all went over to Fanelli's and had drinks. He talked about it there, too."

"I'm sorry, Bill. I don't." Al shrugged. "Mainly what I remember at Fanelli's was having to help Emil out of the place." He returned to his sweeping.

Bill remained motionless, staring down at her with his earnest, bulging brow. She had two choices. Either she could be a downpour and immediately dash Bill's hopes (and risk him quitting on the spot), or she could postpone the bad news by going through the motions of reconsidering his unsalable work.

"I'll tell you what. Bring in slides and we'll talk."

"I gave Emil some."

"Those could be anywhere. Bring in some more and I'll look at them."

"Tomorrow?" he suggested.

Just then, Al called to her.

"Can you come here a moment?"

"Whenever . . ." she said over her shoulder and walked to the heap of boxes where Al was standing.

"Did you say that, in the original piles, some of the boxes were upside down?"

"Every which way. By the way, where's Simon?"

"He left right after the locksmith left. Went to get some red paint."

"Any sign of Catherine?"

"Nope. The phone's been ringing off the hook, though. I told the guys to let it ring." Lowering his voice, he added, "I figured you needed a little rescuing just now."

"Yeah. You sure you don't remember anything Emil might have said?"

"I remember Bill showing *me* his slides. I remember Emil walking up and, the minute Bill's back was turned, I remember Emil flaring his nostrils and whispering, 'Not in a zillion years.'"

He wiped his hands on his jeans.

"About last night," he said, grinning.

"Not now, Al." Suddenly his rescue became less of a relief. Was it possible she had gone to bed with him the night before? He still hadn't told her how he got the scars on his thighs. "Definitely not now. Anne!" she called, using the opportunity to escape from Al *and* Bill. There were too many things forcing themselves upon her already. She walked into JAN and approached Anne's desk.

"We've got a minor dilemma. With Bill. He claims Emil offered him a show for next spring. Did Emil say anything to you about it?"

Anne shook her head. Then her chin jerked to the side as if remembering something. She got up, crossed over to the slide files and rifled through a drawer. "It was late last spring. Emil handed me a few slides of Bill's work and told me to file them. I remember I asked him if we were now representing Bill and he said, 'No, no, no. Just hold them for a while.' Here! I found them."

"Pull them," Rhea ordered in a distressed whisper, as if the slides' proximity to her other artists' slides might somehow be contaminating.

Anne handed them over. One by one, she held them up to the light in much the same way she would have scrutinized samples of an alien virus. The slides were all dated 1986–1987.

"Oh dear," she murmured. "It's the same old stuff he was doing eight years ago. You want to take a look?"

Anne closed the file drawer and shook her head.

"Damn it," Rhea said, seething, silently wishing she could have yanked Emil's file this easily. "Anne, tell me the truth. Did you hate the bastard as much as I did?"

Anne put on an apologetic expression. "What can I say? He just willed me a David Hockney."

"Right."

She stormed into her office. Jack and Crunch were on the floor playing with plastic building blocks. The sight stopped her dead in her tracks.

Rhea, the baby-sitter.

What had her partner done to her? To pick up a branding iron, to swing it with all of one's might . . . what a satisfying moment that must have been for someone.

Véra arrived around noon. "Let's go have lunch!" she sang. "Somewhere new and exciting."

"Oh, brother," Rhea replied.

"Yes, my poor darling brother."

"You'll have to celebrate on your own, Véra. I've got work to do."

"But it's such a gorgeous day, after all that rain. Besides, I have work for you too, dear."

"What's that?"

"A big fat commission for selling Emil's art collection."

Rhea stubbed her cigarette. "OK, let's go."

She walked into JAN and told Anne that they'd be at Central Falls if anybody needed her. As she and Véra passed through the main gallery, Rhea stopped at two tall stepladders positioned beneath a colony of spotlights. Al, Felix, and Bill, in various positions on the ladders, had peeled off their shirts and were wrestling with a contrary fixture that wouldn't go into the track. They paused while Rhea introduced them to Véra. "We'll be back in an hour," she said. "Where's Simon?"

"He had to go get some pin lights," Felix offered.

"I thought he had to go to the hardware store."

"That too."

She shrugged. "Well, keep the doors locked. Where are the new keys, by the way?"

"You'll have to ask Simon."

"Come on, Véra. Véra?"

"Yes, dear?"

"Are you ready?

"Jesus," she added, as they hit the sidewalk, "why

didn't you just grab Felix by the crotch while you were at it?"

"Was I that obvious? It's little wonder that you like the gallery business. All that living art. Your new boyfriend's not bad, either. Very well packaged. I thought artists were supposed to be emaciated."

Rhea stopped. "Are you talking about Al?"

"You know I am."

"What makes you think . . ."

"Just as I was getting ready to go out last night, a Mr. John Tennyson paid me a visit."

"That son of a bitch—"

"You really should have warned me."

"About what?"

"The family resemblance. It was like Emil had come back to haunt me, which we both know he is perfectly capable of doing. I nearly tinkled in my beaded Givenchy. Anyway, Mr. Tennyson was very interested in knowing all about *you*. I couldn't decide whether he wanted to put you under arrest or just put you under, if you know what I mean. He's not without charm, even if he is a little on the old side."

"He's younger than you."

"Oh, so you *are* interested. Well, I'm not. It would be too utterly incestuous."

"What did he want to know?"

"Very odd questions, now that I think about it."

"Like what?"

"Well, like where you acquired your American accent. 'How could that possibly be significant?' I asked him. 'I don't know,' he answered. So anyway, I told him how your mother died when you were a little girl and how your father dumped you here in Manhattan in that waspy girl's school—Brearley, wasn't it? Then how you were shipped off to the Alps—"

"God, I bet you were a wealth of information."

"I tried to be. It's everyone for themselves when it

comes to the police. Don't be angry. I was very supportive of you. I assured him that your father left you in a very handsome state of orphandom and that, given your background, a branding iron simply wasn't your style."

They sat down in the back of the restaurant. The place had just opened, and they were the first to be seated. Véra ordered champagne. Rhea ordered a Bloody Bull.

"What in heaven's name is a Bloody Bull?" Véra asked.

"A Bloody Mary with bouillon."

"You've been in the States too long. So tell me, did you really kill Emil?"

"No, did you?"

"I was in Paris."

"You could have hired someone."

"True."

"And nobody would doubt your potential for greed."

"True again. Of course, munificence isn't exactly your strong point, either."

The waiter pulled up a stand with a bucket of champagne. Véra tasted and approved. (Of the cup or the cupbearer? It was hard to tell).

"My God," she continued, "when I think of all the times I wished there was something I could do to make Emil's life miserable . . . when all along, he had you to do for me."

"Don't bite the hand that feeds you, Véra. If it weren't for me these last few years, there probably wouldn't be anything for you now."

"I'm eternally grateful. And I won't deny that I can use the money . . . I may as well confess. The fact is, I'm out of pocket . . . stone bloody broke."

"I never loan money."

"I'm not begging, dear. Isn't there something you could sell for me right away?"

"Véra, where were you this morning? Becker said that it could be months before the will goes through probate. And if the state suspects foul play, and we know that the state does, if could be—"

"Don't even say it."

Rhea called for another Bloody Bull. "In any case, it'll take a while to get rid of his collection. It may be years before some of it's sold . . . unless you want to put it on the block and auction it off."

"What I want has nothing to do with it. I need some money right away."

"What have you got yourself into?"

"Life on a scale I can no longer afford. Nothing very extraordinary, but distressing all the same."

"There is something," Rhea said after a long bout of silence.

"Tell me."

"Emil was an early collector of Claudio Bravo. He has three pieces tucked away in the gallery that I would buy from you."

"Splendid!"

"At," Rhea held up one hand, "the prices he originally paid for them."

"I believe you're trying to take advantage of me."

"Then you'll just have to wait, won't you? And if you take your paintings somewhere else, how long do you think it will be before you see any hard currency? There'll be an outlandish commission . . . I don't see anything wrong in both of us getting what we want. I could write you out a check today."

"Is what you're suggesting illegal?"

"Do you know what kind of records your brother kept? Nonexistent ones. Since the paintings aren't sequestered in his loft . . . I can work around the legalities. You would be selling me paintings from your own, previous collection. I can work it out."

"It would be too good of you."

"Goodness has nothing to do with it."

"How much?"

Rhea took out a pen from her purse, wrote down the price on a cocktail napkin and slid it over to Véra's side of the table. Without touching it, Véra peered over her champagne glass. Her eyes widened. "How much are they really worth?"

Rhea shrugged.

"I really do need the money." She heaved a sigh in Rhea's direction. "You win. Well, here's to Emil Orloff, whose body, as we speak, is on its way to a New Jersey crematorium."

"You're not going out there with him?"

"Would you?"

"He put a contract out on my dog. Why should I? He's your brother."

"Yes, but he was always kind of a loner. And I didn't think he'd mind if I had this little chat with you instead. Besides, I've been told, warned really, that New Jersey is terribly foreign."

Ten

The boy was curled up on the couch in her office, sound asleep. She halted Véra at the doorway and motioned for her to stay put while she slipped around quietly to her desk and wrote a check from her personal bank account. She tucked it into a blank envelope.

Two new keys twinkled on the surface of her desk. Simon must have put them there, though she hadn't noticed them before lunch. She tucked them into a side pocket of her purse (from now on she would be the only one with keys) and came back out to Véra, who seemed hard-pressed not to drool on the proffered envelope.

"Good-bye, Véra."

Véra understood immediately. Anne was above them at her desk, and there was no reason to make her privy to their underhanded transaction.

"Good-bye, dear. I'll never forget how supportive you've been in my time of need."

Rhea arched a decorous eyebrow.

"Too bad," Véra continued, "I can't be here for tomorrow night's memorial service."

"But you said at lunch—"

"Oh, I know. I can't imagine how I could have overlooked . . . I really do have to get back. I can catch the Concorde at one, tomorrow afternoon. Be sure and look me up whenever you're in Paris. It's been such a comfort to see you again. We have so much in common."

She pecked Rhea on both cheeks and glided out of JAN.

Rhea dropped to the chair by Felix's desk. Her face was infested with Véra's implacable perfume.

"Eau de Enema Bag," Rhea muttered.

"Excuse me?" Anne asked from her perch behind her.

"Nothing."

Like Emil, Véra wallowed in her own base values, paraded her sweet-smelling fraudulence as if it were a seductive commodity. But that wasn't what enraged her.

We have so much in common.

Like a mongoose and a cobra.

Still . . . the idea that she, on any level, could be compared to Véra . . . Both women had suffered a violent dislocation of their lives, and yet the violence had not seemed to emotionally affect them; it had certainly not crippled them.

She couldn't deny it: Emil's death still felt like nothing. Hadn't she meant it to be that way? In order to stay on top of the crisis, she had instinctively inaugurated a policy of doing everything possible *not* to emote. Now that that policy was so successful (and now that she stank of Véra's perfume), her basic humanity seemed to be in question.

What was the spiritual consequence of making oneself shatterproof? Had it really been the conquest of mind over matter, or, like Véra, was it merely a manifestation of inherent callousness?

The Monday sports section lay open on Felix's desk. She picked up the paper, snapped it to attention and scanned the Mets situation: two and a half games behind the first-place Cardinals, with only twenty games left in the season. Darryl Strawberry was quoted in the article:

"We gave some games away here. We can't afford to lose any ball games. We can't afford to keep making mistakes."

She put down the paper. Wasn't that a fairly accurate description of what Rhea's life had been reduced to: urgency and self-reliance, without any "higher order" to fall back upon?

The truth was that, spiritually, she felt closer to the Mets' dilemma than to Emil's death, or to Al's lovemaking, or to John's unnerving omnipresence, and yet there was a deeper truth: Jack's little arms around her neck . . .

"Memorial service?" Anne's voice came from behind and dissolved the daydream.

Rhea inhaled deeply and wheeled around. "Killing two birds with one stone, so to speak."

Anne seemed angry. There was no reason why she shouldn't have been. It was a tasteless remark. But it suddenly occurred to Rhea that Anne had already been mad. She sensed a complete mood swing since the taxi ride that morning. She decided to tack the conversation.

"Anne, do you have the guest list for the original opening night? I have about twenty names, maybe thirty, to add to it. But first, ring up Matt for me, would you?" Matt was the man the gallery used for printing. Anne worked her fingers through the Roladex, stopped and blurted, "Catherine came while you were out."

"Good," Rhea responded, then added, "she didn't see what was going on, did she?"

"No. Simon barred the door just like you told him to."

"I didn't exactly tell him to bar the door. I suppose you've all been in contact with her."

"We worked together, side by side for over two years."

"I understand. I just want you to know that, whatever she's told you, I had to fire her. She really gave me no choice."

Anne tucked her chin guiltily. She said nothing. She held her breath. Then, suddenly, she banged her fist on the desk. Rhea was astonished. She had never seen Anne demonstrate any kind of physical aggression.

"I just can't believe Simon told her," Anne said, seething and trying to get a hold on her emotions.

"Told her what?"

"About my getting the David Hockney."

"Simon told her about your inheritance? Why would he do that?"

"He had no right to tell her," Anne moaned. "Now she has it in for me, too."

"Obviously you shouldn't have told Simon. Anyway, what do you mean 'has it in for you'?"

"Don't you see? Now she hates me. She hates all of us."

"Guilt by association with Rhea Buerklin."

Anne made no attempt to deny it. "Don't make light of it. You haven't seen her. I have."

Rhea crinkled her brow. "What could Catherine possibly do to—?"

"Do you remember on Saturday, when all the cops were here and you told her to take a handful of Valium? She took the whole bottle with her."

Rhea seized her purse and ravaged the contents. The bottle was missing.

"Anyway, she called me up that night. Crying and totally hysterical. She was threatening to kill herself . . . with your drugs so that everyone would know what a murderess you really were. I ended up going over to her place. I don't think she was really serious but . . . here." Anne extracted the bottle from her desk drawer and, leaning over, handed it down to Rhea who was now on her feet. Rhea stared at the bottle, rattled it and swallowed hard.

"She says I killed him?"

"Not in so many words."

"Not in so many words?" Rhea exploded. "What have I done to this wretched bitch? I paid her an exorbitant salary. I treated her with great respect. I thought her work here was exemplary and gave her increasing power as a reward. And what does she do? She returns the compliment by hopping in the sack with bloody fucking Emil—though I still find that unfathomable. What possible reason does she have to hate me?"

"Right, Rhea. Why would any woman hate you? Just because you're beautiful and smart and rich. Just because you're in a position to do anything you please. Just because you've always been in that position . . ." Anne caught herself and averted her eyes.

"Go on, let's have the complete inventory."

Anne shook her head, trembling from her own audacity.

"Come on, let's hear it," Rhea insisted.

"You live in a different world, that's all," Anne offered in a much lower voice. "You and women like Emil's sister—"

"Don't you ever, *ever* compare me to that bum."

"I'm sorry."

"What do you know about it, anyway?" Rhea's breath quickened.

"I said I'm sorry."

"I've worked goddamn hard for what I've got!"

Al poked his head through the doorway. "Is everything all right in here?"

"Fine. Go on. We're fine . . . just doing a little character analysis."

Al shrugged and went back into the main gallery.

Rhea used the interruption to catch her breath. The fact that the men were getting an earful automatically helped her to calm herself. She mounted the stairs and sat down at Catherine's vacated desk.

Anne looked over and asked, "Are you going to fire me too?"

Rhea sighed. "Everybody's nerves are shot. Let's just drop it. Forget it."

"You never forget anything," Anne said simply, looking her straight in the eye. She was smiling. The smile was not unkind. She added: "It's just that Catherine has . . . she's really out of her mind with jealousy. She kept repeating over and over again how much Emil adored you."

Rhea let out a cheerless laugh. "You're right. She *is* out of her mind—"

"He did adore you, Rhea. Everybody could see it."

"Quit saying that. Emil was consumed with hatred. And that included me. Jesus. What else did she say?"

"How you beat Emil into his grave with your superiority."

"If that's true, then how the hell could Catherine think that he adored me?"

"I don't know."

It was a standoff. The mere idea of continuing the argument was exhausting.

"Would you please get me Matt on the phone?"

"There's one more thing, Rhea."

"What?"

"She called me last night. She was bragging about how some reporter from *Manhattanite* was going to do a story on Emil's death . . . Catherine's story."

It took some time for Rhea to absorb this new information. *Manhattanite* magazine was yellow journalism at its yuppiest, favoring cover stories about the sordid and often violent endings of successful New Yorkers' lives.

"I see," she concluded her thought aloud, "free publicity. Do you know the reporter's name?"

"Joan McCabe. Taylor McCabe's sister."

"Taylor McCabe? The ad luminary? Christ, do you realize that he was at the party the other night at Emil's? Well, well, well. McCabe's sister. That *will* be an inside story. Listen. By all means, put this Joan McCabe on the guest list."

"You mean, invite her for tomorrow night?"

"Absolutely. Now will you please get Matt on the phone?"

Anne willingly obeyed, relieved to be back on a professional footing. "Line two, Rhea."

Rhea picked up. "Hello, Matt? Yeah. Thanks, it's been tough. Listen, I've got a rush job for you. I need a memorial card printed for tomorrow night. No later than six. A hundred copies for tomorrow but I'd like the usual number you print up for our mailing list. Can you do it? Yeah, well, *everything* costs me extra these days. I'd like it on the thickest card available. Very simple and very heavy. Black border? I'll let you decide. But be sure to use the same font we use for all our advertising. Just a few lines. You have a pencil? Let me think:

> *In Memoriam*
> *Emil Vladimir Orloff*
> *1938–1987*
> *Death Exhibition*
> *September 14–October 1*
> *Emil V. Orloff Inc.*

"And include the address and phone number, et cetera, under the gallery's name in smaller print. Yeah. Of course you're invited. Thanks." She turned back around to Anne, whose mouth was slightly agape.

"'Death Exhibition'?"

"What would you call it? Just keep telling yourself that Emil would have wanted it this way. I want you to start calling everyone on the list and invite them to a memorial service to be held at the gallery tomorrow night, say from seven to nine, no, that's no good . . . makes it sound too much like an opening—"

"Which it is," Anne inserted.

"Just say memorial service for Emil at seven. But make sure you get in touch with all the press I add to the list. And don't forget Ms. McCabe."

"Catering?"

"No. We'll just get some red and white wine and have it available in JAN. Nothing elaborate."

Rhea scribbled the names to be added, handed the list to Anne who was already on the phone, and, with a sigh, walked into the main gallery.

Everyone was hard at work. The industry and the dramatic change in the look of the gallery slightly lifted Rhea's spirits. Felix was just finishing the larger room. Bill was setting up a ladder in the second room. Tensing under his earnest gaze, she walked over to him. "About those slides," she said. "I found the ones you gave Emil."

"And?"

"I really haven't had time to . . . you'll have to give me a few days until everything else . . ."

Bill peeled a flake of latex off his thumbnail. His double brow wrinkled. "Emil thought they were very good," he said simply. "And so did Al."

"Look." She touched his shoulder, lousy at deception. "What Al or Emil thought isn't relevant. That was then and this is now, and it's what *I* think that matters. But just for the record, Al got the distinct impression that Emil *didn't* much care for your work."

"But—"

"Let me finish. I have every intention of giving your work a fair shake, OK? The way I feel about Emil right now, it would be to your detriment if he *had* liked your work. Sit tight, Bill. Forget about Al and forget about Emil. I'll do what I can as soon as I can."

She rounded the corner and entered the larger gallery. The heap of boxes now shone in an intense light that seemed to emanate from the boxes themselves. Here and there on the higher regions of the walls, shards of light were reflected from the broken mirrors. Felix was painting yellow-orange dotted lines to indicate where the boxes had originally hung: phantoms on the wall. Even Crunch was earning his keep. There was a flat pan of burgundy paint on the floor in which Crunch's paws were being submerged. Holding him under the chest at arm's length, Simon was using the dog like a stamp, stamping the dark walls with red paw prints. Rhea approached.

"So Catherine came by."

"That's right," Simon answered, avoiding eye contact.

"Why did you tell her about the will?"

"She asked."

"What did she say when you told her?"

His face reddened. "She spat in my face."

"Good God."

Carefully avoiding the four extended paws aimed at her stomach, Rhea patted Simon on the shoulder. "Big bonus on the horizon, Simon. Oh, and Simon, just to clear the air, I think you should apologize to Anne."

Rhea walked to the far end, where Al was working. Using as a reference a grid photocopy of the anonymous note, Al was painting on the charcoal wall, in deep orange, an extravagantly enlarged version of the crabbed calligraphy.

There is an exchange for all things,
just as there are goods into fire
and fire into gold.

"And now we're fanning the fire," she said.

"How's it look from back there?" he asked.

"Crazy, like the work of a crazy, chicken-shit son of a bitch."

"Are you OK?"

"If you're going to push things to the edge, you have to get to the edge. Isn't that the daily prescription for all artists?"

Al kept working. "I know why I'm doing all this," he said, "What about you?"

"Whoever did this to my gallery, to Emil—"

"And to me—"

"And to you, will be here tomorrow night. At least

that's what I'm hoping. I'd like to think that, somehow, some way, this will flush the son of a bitch out."

"That's assuming that the son of a bitch isn't one of us here, now, in the gallery."

"Did you have anyone in mind?"

Al put down his brush. "You know what I'd like to do?" he whispered. "I'd like to rip off your clothes and make love."

"The staff would enjoy that."

"We could go downstairs."

A chill ran down her spine. "No thanks. There's a painting downstairs counterinductive to lovemaking."

"What painting?"

"'Still Life with Branding Iron,' by Emil Vladimir Orloff."

Somewhere in New Jersey, a crematory was roaring.

Eleven

It was a quarter past ten when they sped across the Connecticut border. The Merritt Parkway was dark. Few cars were making use of it and the heavy overhang of foliage gave each curve and hollow a tunnel effect.

The ride was uncomfortable. The back of Al's van was laden with every conceivable appendage of the carpentry trade. Tools and hardware rattled in drawers. The heavy van listed on the turns, and whenever they hit a bump Rhea, who was holding Jack in her lap, would incur the full weight of his body.

She couldn't have cared less.

The loneliness of the road accentuated the coziness of the interior. Crunch at her feet, Jack on her lap, a bottle of Dewar's scotch at her side, the glowing dashboard, Al's broad blue-collar hands gripping the steering wheel, the Mets game on the radio (they were beating the Cubs), the contentment of having completed the installation in one day—there was no place she would have rather been.

She almost hadn't come. If it hadn't been for Tennyson . . .

Tennyson arrived at the gallery around seven, just as they were cleaning up upstairs. He walked through the installation scratching his neck at this, scratching his neck at that. Everyone stopped what they were doing to watch. He nodded to each member of the staff as he passed them, greeted Al vocally, and finally walked over to Rhea.

"Who's the guy with the weird forehead?" he grumbled.

"Oh. Bill. We use him occasionally when we're in a jam."

"Another artist?"

"Yeah. A disgruntled one at the moment."

She told him about the alleged show promised by Emil.

"Why would Emil . . ."

Rhea shrugged, but the weight and ballast of her anger was resurfacing. "Leading people on was one of Emil's specialties. Shit. I wonder what the average cruelty quotient is per human being? You know, the number of malicious deeds divided by the number of years a person lives . . . or something like that. I bet Emil was way up there on the chart. God, I'd like to shake his hand."

"Emil's hand?"

"No, the murderer's hand."

"Or her hand," Tennyson mused.

"Or, in Emil's case, the entire legation's hands. So," she changed the subject, rubbing the back of her neck, "what do you think of the new show?"

"You're shooting dice all over the place."

"I don't know. With the cynicism in this town?"

"Hmm."

"To my way of thinking, there's not much of a gamble here. Besides, I thought you'd be pleased. I've set the stage for a very interesting gathering tomorrow night. Everyone who came to the original opening has been reinvited.

Whoever *doesn't* show up will be just as revealing as who does."

"Wake up. I'm not talking about cynicism. I'm talking about violence. Emil had his head bashed in, remember?"

"I remember."

"You don't act like it. You've just doubled the danger to your own life. Or don't you care? There's still an unidentified set of fingerprints walking around and—"

"The fingerprints of a chicken-shit," she raised her voice. "Bashing in his head *after* he's dead? I'm supposed to be afraid of that?"

"Ninety-nine percent of the violent crimes in this town are perpetrated by chicken-shits. The jails are overflowing with chicken-shits."

"Great. Now tell me where there aren't chicken-shits, John. This is a chicken-shit world we're living in. You wake up."

Everyone in the room was staring at her. With thumb and forefinger, Rhea tweezed a piece of lint from Tennyson's lapel. "You think I'm a fool," she said in a lower voice. "Well, I'm not going to deny that. But I'm not going to cower under a table and worry about it either. Nobody else does. And I'm not shooting dice all over the place. Damn it, I've turned a disaster into a gold mine. And I'm also facilitating your investigation."

"You're facilitating naked ambition."

"Anne!" she called to JAN. "Is the guest book ready?"

"Yes!"

"Bring it in here, would you?"

A moment later, Anne lugged in an impressive leather tome. She handed it to Rhea. Rhea hefted it into the crook of one arm and opened it toward the back. "See what we've done?" she said, turning away slightly so that Tennyson could look over her shoulder.

At the top of each page, in alphabetical order, was the name of one of the invitees. As she flipped through, the heavy paper released a musty aroma that, mixed with

Tennyson's clean scent, slightly disturbed her. She glanced at his neck and the side of his jaw and noticed a red splotch where he had been scratching. Had a razor chafed his skin in the morning? Then she realized that he was watching her. Quickly she stepped away to dispel the unintentional intimacy. She lost her train of thought. He darted a smile at her and a shocking idea deposited itself in her mind. John's face had erased Emil's face . . . or rather, had taken the place of Emil's face. It all amounted to the same thing. She couldn't remember what her dead partner looked like, and it frightened her. To add to her confusion, she realized that Al was suspiciously eyeing her from the sideline, and then, quite inexplicably, she remembered Simon's painting and wondered anew what had attracted her to it.

She carefully set the guest book on the floor and stayed in a bent position.

"What's wrong?" Tennyson asked.

"Nothing. I felt dizzy for a moment. I'm tired, that's all."

Tennyson wasn't satisfied. He picked up the guest book and then helped her straighten up at the waist. "Take some deep breaths. Why did you show this to me?"

She rubbed her wrist, where the book had rested and which was now tingling. "What did you say?" She couldn't concentrate with him looking at her like that, with that splotch, with Simon's painting hovering in the back of her mind.

"The book. What's so important about it?"

"Oh. Well, you'll notice that there's an entire page for each name."

"Yeah. So?"

"So, we're going to fingerprint everyone."

"You're joking."

"No, I'm not. We'll have a table over there, right by the front door. As the guests come in, Simon will open the page to their name and fingerprint them."

Tennyson laughed derisively. "You can't make them do that."

"I don't have to. Most of them will jump at the chance. Don't give me that face, John. I'm speaking from experience."

"Fingerprinting experience?" he sneered.

"When you're innocent and unaccustomed to detective work, *as I am*, getting fingerprinted can be quite exhilarating."

"So? And presuming you're innocent, a possibility that doesn't exactly lend itself to this . . ." He made a sweeping gesture toward the installation.

"That's precisely one of the reasons, a minor reason, that they'll submit. Deep down inside, everybody thinks I did it, right? I'm not saying they won't balk at first. But once they get the idea, they'll dive right in."

"I don't see why."

"This guest list is like a thesis on snobbery and boredom. For some of these people, *life* is one opening night after another. Do you have any idea what that's like? Getting their attention is a major ordeal. You have to do something to jolt them. It's just the right kind of unusual, distasteful snag that will make their silly hyphenated names squirm and stand up."

Tennyson squinted at the track lighting, shifting the book from one hand to the other.

"So what do you think?" she persisted. "Admit it. It's a great idea. And the press will love it."

"You should have gone into PR."

"At the very least, we'll know who *doesn't* match the prints."

"True."

"There's one problem. It has to look authentic."

"What problem?"

"If I'm going to do it, it should be done right. I was wondering if I could get Forensic to loan me a fingerprint kit?"

"Get out of here."

"Why not?"

He shook his head. But he didn't say no, and she somehow sensed that he was warming to the idea and would come up with a kit.

"How about it, John? There's no reason why you shouldn't want to help me on this."

"You'll owe me one," he warned.

She took another deep breath. Had he read her mind? She'd been thinking the same thing and she didn't like the possibility. Why? Because she couldn't quite gauge the consequences of owing him something? "Maybe," she said, bristling. "But if I get the fingerprints, you'll owe *me* one. Look, do I get the kit or not?"

He narrowed his eyes and nodded.

"Thanks. I assume you'll be here."

"Are you going to fingerprint me too?"

"Absolutely. Oh, and why don't you bring Lipski with you?"

"Why?"

"I don't know. A uniformed cop milling about would add a certain—"

"Jesus, you don't let up, do you? Is all this what you call simulationism? I thought you said it was fraudulent."

"What isn't, John? And what do I have to lose? The way I figure it, the only reason for your compliance is that you're beginning to think that I *did* do it."

"Maybe I always have."

He started to leave and then turned around. "Here's your fancy guest book."

He didn't let go when she grabbed it. She looked up at him.

"Watch yourself," he whispered.

"I thought the NYPD was doing that for me."

"Somebody needs to."

She shrugged.

He turned his back on her and walked out the front door without saying good-bye.

Felix clapped.

"Oh, shut up," she told him. "He's onto something. If that man ever decides to strike . . ."

Bill Whitehead was finished and seemed anxious to go. She thanked him and he left. Felix sat down on the floor and smoked a cigarette in unspoken approval of the reinstallation. Al and Simon hurried to clean up the last bit of clutter. It was unbelievable what they had accomplished in one day's time. They felt very much like a team, even if there might be a murderer among them. Anne intuitively came in with Rhea's bottle of scotch.

Jack and Crunch came up from downstairs. They watched while the grown-ups drank in silence.

She tried with little success to assess what had just transpired. For now, she'd got what she wanted from Tennyson but it didn't feel like a victory. He'd come at her like a spurned lover. Or was that just her imagination? Was there something else?

Having her way with Al was a different story. She had assumed he would be staying in town for the night. She was wrong. "Jack and I have been in the same clothes for three days," he explained. "He's already missed a day of school. He shouldn't miss any more. We're heading back tonight. Why don't you come with us?" She had immediately dismissed the idea.

But later, as they were closing up and as she watched the staff leave one by one, and as she started turning out the lights, a feeling began to build—the disturbing feeling of stopped activity, of being left behind.

Watch yourself, Tennyson had warned.

At the last minute, she changed her mind.

A car zoomed by and she saw Jack and herself reflected in the windshield. New York and the ice-cold-red-hot reality of Tennyson's visit seemed far behind them. With each toll booth passed, she felt more secure, less troubled. The stars were twinkling through the branches, a quarter moon was shining, a kid-encumbered Rhea was bouncing to the humbling, delicious rhythm of familial intimacy. She gave Jack a squeeze.

"What's that for?" he asked, looking up.

What, indeed? She answered with another hug. What right did she have to think of family units? Her life made a mockery of the family unit, just as Al's art was now making a mockery of a crime . . .

The Mets got another run. Al passed her the bottle of scotch, and she took a sip. Crunch nuzzled her ankle, which had fallen asleep.

It was crazy, but somehow she knew that this moment would be one of those few in which she would remember herself as happy. She may as well have been on an eiderdown cloud. Or on drugs. Or on some motherly alien planet. What had she ever done, in her entire life, to deserve this homelike calm?

A temporary calm, of course.

She didn't care. It was enough to treasure it and to make believe that, like the road and the glittering sky, this recumbent feeling would go on and on. They turned up a country road. Every quarter of a mile or so a house would come into view. They were working their way into a forest. Suddenly, to the right, a lake appeared that they began to circumvent. The moon shone down and scattered quicksilver ripples across the surface. A mile past the lake they turned off onto another, narrower road.

"Here we are," Al announced.

He turned into a lane guarded by two stone pillars. Beyond, on the crest of a broad, inclining lawn stood an enormous white Colonial house, now blue under the moon.

She straightened up. "That's your house?" she exclaimed.

"No," he said, laughing. "That's the owners' house."
"What do they do?"
"Commodities. They're in Bali right now."

They drove by it and turned onto yet another lane to the left. Ahead stood what once must have been the carriage house. "This is home," he said, turning off the engine and headlamps. "Rent free in exchange for work around the estate."

They got out. She could barely move her legs, they were so stiff. Jack and Crunch raced on ahead. She and Al met in front of the van and converged in an awkward embrace. Suddenly she felt his body stiffen. He looked in horror at the house. Lights were coming on inside as the boy and dog raced back and forth.

"Jack doesn't have a key," he said. He broke into a run.

"Somebody's broken into the house?" she called.

But her voice was lost in the darkness.

Twelve

There was nothing to be done about it. Before going in, Rhea had to trot over to the side of the yard and pee like a dog. Though she was loath to be left behind, she had no choice. Having half of her bladder removed had often made travel an incapacitating experience. Her legs were still partially numb from the ride, her feet still tingling, and by the time she hobbled up to the front door, everything was still. "Al? Jack? Crunch?"

There was no answer. The silence and the unfamiliar surroundings made her feel more like an intruder than someone in search of an intruder. The first area she entered was a tiny low-ceiling living room (couch, two chairs, table, rickety upright piano, cross-country ski gear) connected to a cramped kitchen from which it was divided by a long, ill-proportionated, roughly hewn counter. In contrast, the two windows were miserly. Apart from Jack's artwork, which had been taped along the walls, the space was pure lumberjack. To the left of the kitchen was a long, open flight of stairs.

"Anybody up there?"

Again, no answer. Groping the banister, craning her

neck, she went up. At the top of the stairs, she caught her breath.

There were no light on, but she could see perfectly. The spacious windows, above tree level, brought in the moonlight in great blue slanting quadrangles. It was magical: an enormous loft inexplicably paneled in bird's-eye maple and of beautiful proportions. The ultimate tree house. Walking up into it was like suddenly being protected by a giant wooden umbrella. From the center of the ceiling, beams radiated down in all directions to gabled French doors. The central "rod" was a debarked maple tree. Rhea couldn't help imagining that if you knew the right knot to press, the whole ceiling would fold down.

The only furnishings were a platform bed, a low chest of drawers, a telephone, and a portable TV—all shoved together in the far corner of the room. Entranced, Rhea did one of the most bizarre, uncharacteristic things of her entire life.

She walked over to the bed and lay down.

The intruder could still be here. What was she doing? Why wasn't she frightened? Where was everybody? And why was she consciously acting out the role of Goldilocks? Why wasn't she looking?

Because something horrible had happened here and nothing horrible should have happened here and she was going to have to learn exactly what it was and she wasn't ready and for a few minutes she was not going to know about it and she was going to make those few minutes last a lifetime.

No more break-ins. Please, no more break-ins. Maybe it was a mistake. Someone's been sleeping in my bed.

She remembered Al's lovemaking. Scar against scar—there had been no need for words between them and no need for searching. There had been no intrusion . . .

"I must be losing my fucking mind," she said aloud.

She propped herself up on her elbows. Where was everybody?

"Is there anybody here!" she yelled as hard as she could.

No answer.

For the first time she noticed, at the opposite end of the room, the darkened rectangle of a doorway. She got up. If anybody was going to suddenly jump her, she knew she had the strength to kill them with her bare hands.

She walked across the room to the door. Just inside the opening was a light switch. She flipped it on. To the right was a bathroom: toothbrushes, an old shaver. To the left was Jack's bedroom: a single bed, a few toys, a poster of the solar system.

She sat on Jack's bed and exhaled. Even though she had never been here before, she was certain nothing had been disturbed. What was to disturb? There was such a paucity of home amenities, a thorough search could be done almost instantaneously. What impressed her about this stark environment was that she wasn't looking at a conscious attempt at minimalist decor (like her own loft). She had invaded the space of two males who didn't much think about it, who just didn't need much, who probably regarded it as a comfortable shelter when they couldn't be where they really wanted to be—outdoors.

A door slammed downstairs.

She spun around. She heard Jack wailing for his dad, and then a sudden silence. She jumped up and tore down the stairs.

"Jack? Jack?!"

Back down in the kitchen, behind the open stairwell was a door that she had mistaken earlier for a closet. Now it was open, savagely illuminated and proving to be no such thing. It was a huge studio that made up the rest of the ground floor.

She walked in.

Tears spilled out of her eyes. A different universe.

Only this time it was overflowing with the secrets of material possessions. It was like stepping carefully among the unabashed inner ravings of an artist's mind. A cram-packed room of tortured alleyways, storage racks, workbenches, bins of tools, paints, books, and itemized containers of clutter—marbles, glass beads, croquet balls, clay pipes. One false move and Rhea might send some precariously balanced shoe box to the floor. A human pack rat worked here, where fantasy lurked from every nook and sawdust reigned supreme.

This was the backdrop she would remember in retrospect. But that wasn't why she was crying.

All of Al's boxes (pieces from past series that had never been sold and works in progress) had been hurled to the floor and broken.

"I hate him I hate him I hate him!" The little voice came from the back, where Jack was leaning against a table saw wiping angrily at his streaked face. "Why would he do this?" he whimpered.

"Jack, where's your dad?"

"Went to the big house to see if he broke in there too. I hate him!"

She paused for a moment. She didn't understand who Jack was talking about.

"Who do you hate?"

He shook his head furiously and clinched his lips until they turned white.

"Who are you talking about?"

"I hate you too!" he screamed and ran out of the room,

She turned to follow him. He ran out the front door. "Jack, come back!"

She heard Crunch barking somewhere in the distance. The interior lights of the van suddenly came on and she saw Jack scrambling inside. He slammed the door just

as she approached. She tried the door but it was locked.
"Jack, open the door."
"No! Go away!"
"Come on, Jack. Why are you doing this?"
"Because you don't believe me. Nobody believes me."
"Believe what?"
"Go away!"
She looked around at the darkness. Again, she could hear Crunch barking. She peered toward the lane that led to the main house but the heavy canopy of trees blocked out the moon, and all she could see were shadows against darker shadows. She peered back inside the van and clinched her teeth.
"If you won't let me in so that I can keep from being knifed in the back by the boogeyman, would you at least hand me that bottle of scotch so that I can be murdered in peace?"
The window rolled down just enough to push the bottle through. She grabbed it by the neck. The window went back up.
"Thanks," she said.
"You're welcome."
She took a long slug. The stridulation of a million crickets filled the air. The sky twinkled mockingly. A mosquito bit her. The window came down a crack and a screwdriver was poked through.
"What's this for?" she asked.
"In case the boogeyman . . ."
"No thanks. I'd rather have a cigarette."
The screwdriver retreated. The window went back up.
"You're not going to give me a cigarette?"
"Smoking isn't good for you."
"Please?"
"OK. Where are they?"
"In my purse. There's a lighter in there too."
"Can I light it for you?"

"You're the boss! Just don't burn yourself."

The window came back down a few inches. The cigarette came through the slot, ember first, and just as she was about to take it two large hands grabbed her from behind.

Thirteen

Three involuntary reflexes occurred simultaneously: her right forefinger and thumb pinched off the red-hot coal of the proffered cigarette; she screamed with a violence that nearly tore out her tonsils; and her left hand, still clutching the bottle by the neck, ramrodded back into the soft groin of her assailant.

She spun around.

Al dropped to his knees, clutching himself. He was desperately trying to catch his breath, his face horribly contorted.

The van door flew open, slamming into her back and throwing her forward to the ground. She landed on top of Al, her elbow catching him in the eye. He cried out in pain.

Crunch scrambled on top of them and licked her face. She backhanded him, sending him up and out into the darkness like a pop fly.

She rolled over onto the ground.

"What happened?" Jack implored, kneeling down between them.

Nobody answered.

Al groaned in a rocking fetal position, cupping his

scrotum with one hand, his eye with the other. Rhea stared idiotically at *her* hand, which was fanning itself of its own volition.

She wanted the words to come spitting out of her face: "A slight misunderstanding . . ." Her voice sounded like a stepped-on bagpipe.

It was only then that she realized that Al hadn't seized her by the neck. He had placed his hands there for moral support.

She gazed up to where the moon would soon be peeking over the treetops. The crickets or cicadas or whatever they were vibrated at a suffocating decibel. A thousand bits of gravel goaded her bruised back, but she was too hurt and tired and full of scotch to want to move, let alone to get up. She closed her eyes.

Her thumb and forefinger were really beginning to throb. A laugh jumped out of her throat.

"What's so . . . fucking . . . funny?" Al panted in a pinched voice.

She nudged his buttock with the bottle of scotch. His hand reached backward and yanked it from her. She heard a slurping sound followed by convulsive coughing. She leaned over on her side and gently lay her hand on his temple.

"Are you OK?" she asked.

"I'm gonna throw up."

"You shouldn't sneak up on people."

Al moaned.

"I'm sorry. Really I am."

"Shut up and let me die in peace."

"You're not going to die!" Jack interjected.

Al grabbed hold of Jack's shoulder and pulled himself up in a sitting position. "I'll be all right in a minute." He managed a facsimile of a smile.

"OK, Dad," Jack said. But he was looking in the direction of the house, obviously thinking of the wrecked studio.

"And *never* walk up behind horses or women," Rhea tried to joke, but no one laughed. Rhea leaned over and kissed Al—a strategic difficulty since he was once again in his double-cup position.

"Vasectomizer," he muttered through his teeth.

She withdrew her lips, reclaimed the Dewar's, leaned back and took a swig. Was there a difference between eroticism and horror? A powerful urge to make love then and there . . . It was all so crazy. The last few days had propelled her into a suspended disbelief of just about everything. Scar against scar, and they were getting more numerous by the minute.

In the distance they heard tires grinding over gravel. A car was approaching. Rhea looked up. "Who's that?"

"Probably the police," Al took a deep breath. "I called them from the main house."

"Was it broken into?"

"No, damn it. I mean, I almost wish it had been. It was just my studio . . ."

"Who hates you enough to do all this?"

She had wanted to say, "Does your ex-wife hate you enough . . ." but she couldn't with the boy there. And then she realized, not without pleasure, that her way of thinking about the case had changed. There *was* no other way of thinking about it. The crimes had been directed toward Al. Not Emil, not herself, but Al. This would surely put him in the clear with Tennyson. Then she thought of the police coming up the road. What would they think when they found them all maimed and sprawled on the ground? She scrambled to her feet.

"Can you get up?" she asked him

"No."

"Let me help you."

"Forget it. It doesn't matter anyway."

She wasn't so sure. It was stupid to complicate the situation any more than necessary. But before she could object, the police car wheeled into the drive, blinding them with its lights. She shielded her eyes with her forearm.

The lights went off. The door opened, and the broad-shouldered, silhouetted form of a cop approached.

Emerging from the shadows, he stopped. She could see that he was good looking and probably Italian. Christ, she thought, just what I need in my life, another good-looking cop.

He was appraising the situation, looking from Al to Rhea and back to Al again. Was he smiling or grimacing or scowling? She couldn't quite tell. She felt ridiculous. It was all she could do to keep her arms down to her sides, although she had an overwhelming desire to fan her blisters and rub the crease in her back. He walked toward her, passed by her and, leaning down, helped Al get to his feet.

"What happened to you?" he asked.

"Rhea whacked Dad in the nuts and then she gave him a black eye," Jack explained.

"Did she," said the cop, throwing a leer in Rhea's direction. Then turning back to Al, he asked, "Do you want to press charges?"

Al took a deep breath: "If you would have asked me that ten minutes ago . . ."

Both the cop and Al laughed.

Then she understood. It *didn't* matter: they were obviously friends. His name was Steve Sachetti. Several years earlier, Al had helped add a porch onto Steve's father's house. They exhibited the easy, impersonal intimacy of drinking buddies—a form of male camaraderie that always put Rhea in a bad, if not vaguely jealous, mood. But she was also relieved. There would be no incriminating, tough city boy third degree."

Which reminded her of her burn . . .

Steve tousled Jack's hair and they all headed toward the house, Rhea trailing, thwarted by the sinking apprehension of yet another investigation.

When they entered the studio, Steve briefly patted Al on the shoulder. Al told him the whole story: what had happened in New York and how there was an obvious connection between the two crimes. Steve nodded, becoming more solemn with each new detail. Finally he asked who was in charge of the case in New York.

Reluctantly, Al gave him Tennyson's name.

A series of phone calls ensued. During this time, Rhea kept her hand under cold running water, even though she knew it to be a little late for preventative measures. Jack helped her with the bandages.

Al had a dish towel full of ice mashed against his eye.

"Let's see," she said.

He dropped the ice pack. She winced. A first-class shiner. The white of his eye was blood red. Steve got off the phone and said that John Tennyson was on his way. Al and Rhea exchanged glances but didn't say anything. What was to say? From the beginning, Tennyson's omnipresence had been an essential part of their relationship.

While waiting for Tennyson's arrival, Rhea took Jack upstairs and prepared him for bed.

It wasn't an easy procedure. Other local cops had arrived, and Jack resented not being a part of the investigative drama. He was also hopelessly exhausted and correspondingly cranky. She drew him a bath, which helped to relax him. But every time the phone rang, which was frequently, he managed to rouse himself into renewed protest.

"Get your pajamas on."

She disconnected the upstairs phone. She also discovered an attic fan, which she turned on and which helped to vibrate away the noise from downstairs. She got him in bed, located an oversize book of fairy tales, closed the door, lay down beside him and read to him.

Halfway through the second story she realized that his eyes were shut and his breathing had taken on a kind of self-enveloping pattern. She kept on reading anyway. Aloud.

Not once, during all the stressful trials of the last few days, had Jack asked for his mother. Did he keep his need buried or did he just not know what he was missing? She kept reading.

Someone's been sleeping in my bed. Had the bitch been here during the weekend?

Rhea's mother had died in childbirth. Rhea had never known what *she* was missing. Was she now playing make-believe? Did she want to be the mother she had never known? She turned the page with her stupid bandaged fingers. In Greek mythology, Rhea was the phantom mother of Zeus, king of the gods. She gave birth and then she just sort of faded from the epic.

She kept reading.

Suddenly there was an entire universe of spectral mothers pushing and shoving their way into the room for the privilege of listening to Rhea read. Story after story. Page after clumsily turned page. Al's mother was there. Who had she been? When had she died?

Why was the grandfather, HoHo, as Jack called him, the only ghost in his secret world? *I hate him I hate him I hate him.* Had Jack been talking about HoHo? Was that who he thought had shattered the boxes?

Anne's mother walked in, and so did Catherine Miller's, though she had never met the woman before. She read the story of Hansel and Gretel to the crowded room of she-ghosts. When Gretel stoked the oven, Rhea remembered her long-gone Emil.

"Once upon a time," she read, "even Véra Orloff Vertbois had a mother."

And now Véra's mother was here, too.

And the Véra that would never be a mother, who had probably never wanted to be a mother, was here.

They were all here, listening to Rhea's moonlit recitation.

She read and she read and she read until the book went slack in her hands and she, too, fell fast asleep.

Fourteen

She woke up with a start. She could have sworn that someone had come into the room.

"Hello?" she whispered. She sat up. She must have been dreaming. The boy was next to her, sound asleep.

The one small window in Jack's bedroom faced the west. The sky was still dark, though there were signs . . . she consulted her watch. Six o'clock. She brought up her other hand to rub her eyes and was greeted with gauze and tape. The night before began to return to her.

She got out of bed, walked across the hall to the bathroom, squeezed some toothpaste on the edge of the sink with her one good hand, put down the tube, daubed her left forefinger in the paste and smeared it across her teeth.

Something about ghosts . . .

She rinsed, splashed cold water on her face and looked in the mirror. She looked like hell and felt worse. Her head throbbed, her right hand throbbed, her back throbbed. She found aspirin in the medicine cabinet, took six, and sat down to pee. How many days has this been going on? Friday, Saturday, Sunday, Monday, this was Tuesday. Tonight, the new opening. She groaned.

Round five coming up.

She walked out into the open loft. Again, she was struck by how handsome it was. Daybreak pushed in through the eastern windows and softened the bare, plank floor, and settled down upon it like a gold-embossed carpet. At the far end of the room, she could see that Al's bed had not been slept in. A feeling of impatience swept over her. Had Al been up all night?

She heard car doors slamming. She peered out one of the windows overlooking the drive. Cops in groups, some of them storing equipment in trunks, some pulling on cigarettes, were chatting, probably waiting to be released by a higher authority.

Tennyson.

She spun around and felt dizzy. She took one last regretful look at the loft, took a deep breath and descended the staircase, down into the harshly lighted kitchen.

It was the gallery investigation all over again, except this time she had come in on the tail end. Forensic people, none of whom Rhea recognized from the gallery, were just leaving. Shears, the ever-earnest vulture from the DA's office, was conferring with Tennyson.

"Good morning," he said, turning his back on Shears's words in mid-sentence.

"Morning, John. Any coffee?"

"Instant, if there's any left."

"Morning, Shears. You're looking well, as always. But don't you have your spurs all tangled up? Last time I looked, we were in Connecticut."

"Fortunately," Shears retorted, "the local police aren't as territorial as you. It's common practice to notify other departments about a crime if there seems to be a connection with one they're already working on, even in another state. Particularly if there's a murder involved. It's a matter of courtesy and fraternal wisdom."

"'Courtesy and fraternal wisdom,'" Rhea repeated with a dull smile. "Then this is a whole new world for you, isn't it? How much you have to learn!"

Rhea proceeded to a large but mostly excavated jar of instant coffee. She held it up to the light and examined the granules still clinging to the inside corners of the glass. The kettle was still warm. She filled the jar with hot water, swished the darkening contents until it turned into ink. She sampled straight from the jar. The taste was bilious but she was satisfied: out of the corner of her eye she saw that Shears was appalled.

Tennyson came over. "How do you feel?"

"Like someone pushed me off a mountain. Nothing unusual. Got a cigarette? Thanks. I'm afraid you'll have to light it for me. I burned my fingers."

He took her injured hand in his. "Who wrapped this?"

"I did. What's wrong with it?"

"Dummy. Don't you know that you wrap a burn *loosely?* Here. Stand still. Let me do this right."

She shrugged as he unwound the bandages, but the relief was immediate and god-sent. The throbbing suddenly ceased. She felt herself become passive to his expertise. He reached over and grabbed the scissors and fresh gauze left from the night before, and began applying new bandages.

"You have very feminine hands," he murmured. Repetitions within repetitions: she was struck by his attractive, clean-scented, creepy . . . that hale version of Emil's cynical, desiccated face.

"And you have extraordinarily bad timing, John. Are you going to wrap it or fuck it?"

"Christ, can't you take a simple compliment?"

"No. At least, not before coffee. What have you found out?"

He finished the bandages before answering, "A few things. The unidentified fingerprints from the gallery?"

"Yes?"

"They're crawling all over this place. Whoever wrecked your gallery wrecked Al's studio."

"Hmm. Does that make it any easier to figure out who did it?"

"In a way. Whoever did it knew where Al lived. Lots of country roads . . . not easy to find if you're coming out from the city. I got lost twice. The question is, what's the motive?"

"At least it gets Al off the hook . . . or do you still believe that— "

"I believe more than ever that Al knows something that I don't know and that probably you don't know. And I also believe that if you did know, you probably wouldn't tell me."

"Why?"

"Well, things have warmed up between you, haven't they?"

She averted her eyes—a sign of weakness she instantly regretted. She still wasn't sufficiently awake or mentally prepared for this interview. She hated the disadvantage. She despised herself for having allowed Tennyson to improve her bandage. And above all, she was maddened by the fact that she didn't know if she and Al had "warmed up" or not. The truth was that she would have done anything to stop thinking about Al altogether.

"Anyway," Tennyson continued, "he's sticking to his story, that he doesn't know anyone who would want to do this to him."

"Have you located his ex-wife yet?"

"No, but we will. I hope she's more forthcoming than you."

"I'm not holding back on anything. Goddamn it, I don't know anything."

"Yeh. You don't know anything. Al doesn't know anything. Nobody knows anything. It's downright miraculous how ignorant everyone is in this case. Your artist is lying about something, Rhea. I'd stake my job on it. What and why, I still don't know."

She turned on the tap and doused her cigarette. "Where is he, anyway?"

Tennyson tilted his head toward the studio door.

Clutching her jar, she snaked her way around the various cops and equipment and walked into the workshop.

His left eye was completely swollen shut. He was seated at a work table with one of the ruined boxes in his lap. Embracing the box with one arm and using a metal scraper with the other, he was removing the broken contents in much the same way as someone would disembowel a pumpkin. She bent over to kiss him. His long hair reeked of cigarettes.

"Some night."

"Yeah," he said, barely looking up.

"Sorry about the eye. What are you doing?"

"Making a box."

"Now?"

"Do you remember your conversation with Tennyson last night?"

"Last night?"

"At the gallery before we came out here."

"God, was that last night?"

"Do you remember what you told him?"

"No."

"You said . . ." Al smiled. "Never mind what you said. You'll remember when you see this finished. It gave me an idea for the penultimate box. It won't take me long to do. I'll have it ready for tonight. It'll come back to you then."

"You want to include it in the show?"

He nodded.

"Then tell me now."

"Nope. You'll have to wait until I bring it on tonight.

Which reminds me: Tennyson has offered to drive you back into the city."

"So what? I don't want to go in with Tennyson. I want to go in with you."

Al shook his head. "I've got things to do here. Jack's got to go to school and I'm not going anywhere without him. Not now," he added, looking around the room, "that this has happened. Jack and I will drive in later."

"You don't want me to stay?"

"What for? Besides, you've got things to do."

"Like what? The installation's finished. Simon and Felix and Anne can take care of all the last minute . . ."

She stopped herself. Al raised his one functional eyebrow with beleaguered prescience. "Ach!" she said. "I forgot about the new keys. They can't get into the gallery without me. Well, surely there's a train I can catch."

"What about Crunch?"

"You bring him in."

"It would be easier to hitch a ride with Tennyson."

"I'd rather hitch a ride with the devil. I don't want to be alone with him for two hours—"

"An hour and a half."

"Whatever. I'm too tired to be with him. I don't trust him."

"If he gets out of hand, slam him in the balls with a bottle of scotch."

She paid little or no attention to the surrounding countryside as she drove back with Tennyson. She didn't want to return to New York and she didn't have the heart to reexamine what, only last night, had been the mesmerizing sideshow to a dreamy escape. Now, they were driving directly into a particularly uncharming sun. Without asking, she helped herself to John's sunglasses on the dashboard and sank into a kind of self-induced coma.

"Where do you want off?"

"Hunh?"

She opened her eyes. They were bumping along the FDR Drive just north of the Queensborough Bridge. Her watch said 9:15. "God, that was fast."

She turned toward Tennyson feeling much refreshed.

"I feel like a new person."

"Great."

He grumbled something at the taxi in front of him and swerved into the left lane with a jerk. A night without sleep had taken its toll, and she could see that it was his turn to be truculent.

"Sorry I wasn't better company."

"Right. Where do you want to be left off."

"At the gallery."

They exited the FDR at Houston.

He didn't turn off the engine when they pulled up at Prince Street. She reached for the door handle and then stopped herself.

"Would you mind going in with me?" she asked.

"Why?"

"All this breaking and entering is becoming a habit. What if, while everyone was in Connecticut, they decided to . . ."

Tennyson pointed across the street to Emil's loft.

"Makes a good place for a stakeout."

"I see."

"Don't thank me or anything."

"I'm sorry. I'm a bitch. Thank you."

"I'll see you tonight."

She leaned over and pecked him on the cheek. He grabbed her and kissed her on the lips. She fumbled with her purse and got out of the car. The car sped off and turned right on West Broadway.

She walked into the gallery. She went to Anne's Roladex and searched for Al's number and then remembered that he didn't have a telephone. Then she remembered that Steve Sachetti, the cop, had used a phone in

Al's kitchen and that she herself had disconnected the upstairs extension. Why had Al lied to the gallery about having a phone?

She called information, got his number and dialed it. "Hello?"

"I thought you didn't have a phone."

"I like my privacy."

"Then you should have it unlisted."

"Is that why you're calling me? I'm working."

"Sorry, I was just wondering . . . you said penultimate box."

"Penultimate box?"

"Yeah, you said you were building the penultimate box."

"That's right."

"So what's the ultimate box?"

"A coffin, of course."

She closed her eyes. "Whose coffin?"

"Anybody's coffin is the ultimate box for that particular person, wouldn't you say?"

"I guess so. So why piddle around with the penultimate box when you could build the ultimate box?"

Al laughed. "I don't know."

"See you tonight," she said and hung up.

A few minutes later the phone rang. It was Al. "Why not take the penultimate and the ultimate and combine the two?" he asked.

"Sounds good if you can do it," Rhea answered.

"I think I could bang it together. It's all idea, of course, no technique."

"If you say so. You still haven't told me what the penultimate box is so I have no way of visualizing it."

"See you around six."

"Good-bye, Al." She hung up.

Tennyson's scent was still on her lips.

Fifteen

All of her staff arrived promptly at 10:00. She had ready for them three lists of tasks to be completed by 5:00.

"Read your lists carefully," she said. "If you have any questions, ask now. I'm leaving and won't be back until around five."

Felix, his eyes still glued to the list, smiled and raised his hand. "You want me to call up Catherine and invite her?"

"Well, Felix, you're the logical candidate. She spit in Simon's face. I fired her. And Anne's inheritance has given her a nasty case of zelophobia."

Zelophobia: fear of jealousy. Though it wasn't in the dictionary, no one needed the definition. It had been one of Emil's favorite words. They'd all heard him use it a hundred times. Hearing herself use it for the first time was creepy. It was as if Emil were rustling around inside her, using her as a mouthpiece.

"She won't come," Felix said.

"How much do you want to bet?"

"Five dollars."

"You're on. Any other takers?"

"Five dollars says she won't," Anne said, giggling.

"How about you, Simon?"

Simon held up his palm to indicate that the wagering was distasteful.

"OK. Are there any other questions?"

"Not a question, exactly . . ." Again, Felix raised his hand. "I ran into Jamie Kheel last night."

Rhea's mouth dropped open. "Where! The police have been . . . how do you know her? She left Al long before you started working here."

"I don't know her. Or I didn't."

Felix had been at Raoul's, standing at the bar chatting up his girlfriend of the moment, when several staff members from a neighboring gallery came in. One of them knew him and approached him.

"The word's out on the street," Felix continued. "Everyone knows that something is cooking at the Orloff and they want to know. Anyway, he was trying to bleed me for information, I wasn't giving it to him and this lady comes up beside him, puts her arm around him and he says, 'Felix, I'd like you to meet Jamie Kheel,' just like that."

"What did she look like?"

"I thought you knew her."

"I mean, how did she look?"

Felix lowered his eyelids half a notch. "A very mean piece of equipment."

"Is that meant to be a tribute?"

Felix nodded in the affirmative.

"Charming phrase, Felix. So what did you say to her?"

Felix took a deep breath. "I invited her."

"She's coming tonight?"

"I guess. She *said* she wouldn't miss it for the world. I figured you'd want her here."

"You did splendidly. You've all done splendidly."

She went into her office for a moment. She returned

with three checks for $500 each, and distributed them. It was an embarrassing moment. Beneficence wasn't exactly her forte. "It's time to gladden hearts. We're all about at the end of our tethers. You've toughed it out with me and . . ."

She realized that she was overexplaining. She tacked to a different subject: "I'll be home for most of the day if anything important comes up. But please, be sure it's important before calling. Any more questions? Good. I'll see you at five."

She walked very quickly to her apartment. *A mean piece of equipment.* Jamie must have got off the drugs. Either that or she had discovered new, improved ones. God, would Tennyson be surprised. The thought rejuvenated her. It reminded her that, whatever happened tonight to exacerbate her mental instability, the party would not be without its little moments.

Then she took a look at herself in the bathroom mirror. Bad news: macho girl as grieving widow.

She put on jogging clothes and left the apartment. She chose a circuit that would be a three-mile run, but halfway through she limped to a stop. She was sweating profusely, too much for a mile and a half. She didn't have it in her. She started walking back home. At Thompson and Bleecker she noticed a large yellow and black awning that advertised toys. She went into the store.

"What's the top-selling toys for six-year-old boys?" she inquired, still short of breath.

The woman brought out several items—some grotesque, all violent. Rhea said she would take all of them. Then she realized that she didn't have any money. She called the gallery and instructed Simon to come pick them up.

She tried to run again but ended up walking the rest of the way to her apartment.

She rifled through the refrigerator, humming. She drank copious amounts of orange juice, ate the leftover tossed salad and tamped it all down with a large slab of ham. Her worst enemy right now, she reasoned, was her body. In the last few days she had abused it, neglected it, fucked it, and now, just when she needed it most, her energy was gone.

Wouldn't do. Wouldn't do.

She put a large pot of water on the stove. She gnawed at a raw carrot, then stood on her head until the water came to a boil. She dumped in the pasta and made a simple butter-garlic sauce. She gorged herself until she thought she would explode. Then she drank two large glasses of water.

She unwrapped her bandages. She took off her clothes. She took a hot, then cold, then hot, then cold shower. She brushed her teeth. She peed and condemned its bright yellow color. She drank two more glasses of water.

She padded into the bedroom, pulled down all the blinds, turned on the fan of the air conditioner for the lulling effect of the white noise, and, still naked, climbed into bed.

She prayed that the phone wouldn't ring and passed out.

―――

She woke up a little before three, thinking: I wonder if I have anything to wear? But she passed the closet without entering. She turned on the sauna and then returned to her closet. She rifled through hangers for a moment and decided to forget it. She'd figure it out at the last minute just like she always did.

She walked into the living room. One of the giant windows had been left open. Simon's painting had been propped up against the adjacent sill and had been blown down. She bent down and picked it up. As she was setting it back up on the sill, her face two inches from the canvas, she froze.

She stepped back.

It couldn't be.

She took the canvas, turned it upside down and stepped back again. Her eyes clouded over.

It was a coincidence, that was all.

She checked the temperature in the sauna. It still wasn't as warm as she liked it, but she sat down anyway. She looked at her blisters. She got up and went back to the living room. She looked at Simon's upside-down picture, which wasn't upside-down at all.

Don't look at that one. I've only been working on that for a couple of weeks.

It was just a bad joke her imagination was playing on her. An unfortunate coincidence. But the image remained. She couldn't absolve what was planted before her eyes. She had thought of it as a deep valley with a television antenna running up one side of the incline. Upside-down it could be—was it?—a pyramidal stack of boxes with a broom leaning against it.

Maybe the painting was right side up. Maybe it was Rhea who was upside-down.

She strode into the gallery at 5:00 on the dot. The place was impeccable. The table where Simon would fingerprint had been set up at the entrance.

She walked into JAN, asked if there were any problems and, getting a negative response, told them to be back by 6:30. Simon and Felix would have time to go home and change. Anne's place in Queens was too far away. She gave Anne the keys to her loft so that she could clean up there. It was the usual format for Anne on opening nights. Before she left, however, Rhea asked her a question: "Does Simon have a car?"

"No. He doesn't even have a driver's license. He grew up in the city and he never—"

"Yeah, that's what I thought."

"Why?"

"Oh nothing. I thought it might be useful, that's all. I put out clean towels for you."

Rhea walked her to the door and locked it after Anne had left.

She went into the gallery bathroom and consulted the mirror. She was shocked at her reflection. There was something so weak or unfinished about her look. The black suede dress was fine: short and simple, with a high neck in front and a moderate plunge in the back. Makeup was OK too: minimal except for the deep orange lipstick, which matched the message on the wall. It was the hair that wasn't doing much of anything. She found a comb in a drawer to the side of the sink, watered down her hair, and combed it back into a modified James Dean. She looked down at the comb. A man's comb. Emil's comb. She dropped it into the wastebasket and exited the bathroom.

She walked around the double gallery several times. Her black high-heeled sling-backs clicked against the floor. She stopped and raised her hands.

"What the fuck have you gotten me into?" The words came out of her mouth like ashes. Even if he were still alive, the Supernatural King of Assholes wouldn't have answered.

Sixteen

Someone knocked on the door. It was 5:30.

She opened it, Crunch zipped between her legs and charged into the gallery. Jack came running in after Crunch. Al brought up the rear, wearing large opaque sunglasses.

"Let me see it," she said.

Carefully, he slipped the glasses down an inch. His eye was still swollen shut and the surrounding tissue was kaleidoscopic.

"Mm." She gritted her teeth. "Pretty ugly. How do you plan to explain that to the press?"

"I was hoping the sunglasses—"

"No way. You'd have to have wraparounds."

"Well, you could circulate a story about me blinding myself in despair. How's your hand?"

"Thing of the past," she said, waving off her injury.

But he caught her hand in mid-air and examined her unbandaged blisters, bringing her closer to him "You look great. All I kept thinking about last night was . . ."

He backed her up against the table and kissed her with an avidity that made her fidget. Like she was going to

141

pee. She had all of these half-baked ideas incubating inside of her and it was as if one more kiss might start the hatching process prematurely. Ridiculous. Here she was, pushing forty, feeling seventy, on the brink of a major nervous breakdown, in her own place of business, tongue-wrestling like a horny school girl with a one-eyed artist. In spite of herself she kissed him back as hard as she could, grateful for the surprise abandon and, she couldn't deny it, grateful for the chance to erase Tennyson's lips.

"There's not time," she mumbled.

"I know. I know."

"You're spending the night?"

He nodded.

Jack emerged from JAN holding the plastic bag of toys she had purchased that morning. "Whose are these?" he called.

"Whose do you think?" she called back. "But you've got to promise me that you'll keep them in my office."

She dislodged herself, regretfully but forcefully, from his embrace.

"Did you finish your box?"

"It's in the van," he said, pushing his hair back away from his forehead. "I don't want you to see it, though . . . not before I've set it up."

"By the way," she said, squeezing his butt, "you were rude to me this morning."

"I can't defend myself. I was dead on my feet. I still am."

"You didn't take a nap or anything?"

"There wasn't time."

They both looked at their watches. They looked at each other. "Let me get to my work." Rhea sighed and relented. It was the kind of request she, of all people, couldn't refuse. Al went back out to the double-parked van. Rhea retreated to her office, where Jack was expertly separating the plastic packaging of a space warrior.

"Did you go to school?" she asked.

"I've got a lot of homework."
"At your age? That's stupid."
"You're telling me."
"Did you see HoHo?"

Jack pretended not to hear. There was an imperceptible improvement in her posture.

"Did you see HoHo?" she repeated.
"Dad told me not to talk about that."
"Why?"
"Because."
"Because why?"
"Just because."
"Just because why?"
"He says we don't talk about family stuff."

The taste of Al soured in her mouth. She'd given him her gallery, her trust, her body—what the fuck constituted her right to know? And what was so precious, so top secret about Al's family? The more she thought about it, the more it pissed her off. Christ, artists! They were driving her out of her mind. She'd gotten so far away from herself. How could she have allowed a little sex to crowbar its way into common sense? It was her own blubbering fault for not pressing the point.

Of course, she *wasn't* family. She'd gone to bed with him, big deal. This was schoolgirl bullshit. Al didn't owe her anything. She made some quick mental calculations about her menstrual cycle: that wasn't it.

Then she *really* got pissed off. Why should she blame this scatterbrained attack of jealousy on her bodily functions? She *was* out of her mind. She shot up out of her chair. Jack and Crunch looked up expectantly. She sat back down. She smoked a stupid cigarette. She crossed her legs and jiggled her foot.

Chill out, Rhea. Think . . .

This was the first time she had developed an intimate relationship with a gallery artist. (Mingling and schmoozing and fucking had always been Emil's department.) It didn't appear that she was filling her partner's shoes very well. Emil had always managed to keep an arm's distance from any relationship, and with a sense of humor to keep everyone feeling cozy. For the first time in her life, she wondered if she was incapable of straddling . . .

Double bullshit. What she really needed was a drink.

Al called for her from the other room. Be cool. She found him in the smaller gallery.

Standing upright against the wall, next to the roped-off stairwell, was a dark gray wooden coffin. The lid, unconnected to the main construction, was leaning against one side. Just like a broom was leaning against boxes, she thought. Just like she had been leaning against a conspiratorial pyramid of unanswered questions.

On the inside of the coffin, in orange paint, was the message:

Fire into gold?
Turn up the heat, chicken-shit.

"Who did you write this to?"

Al darted a look at her, his sunglasses flashing momentarily from the reflected track lighting.

"Who did you write this to?" she repeated.

"To the chicken-shit that you'd like to flush out into the open. Your conversation with Tennyson, remember? What do you mean, 'Who did I write this to?'"

"You couldn't wait to get rid of me this morning, could you?"

The message was inflammatory all right, but not the way in which Al had intended. Something had suddenly snapped in Rhea. He couldn't make it out, but he was hurt.

"Don't come at me like that. What's wrong with you, anyway?"

She didn't answer.

"Look, do you like the box or not? If you don't like it I'll take it back to the van."

"I'm sick to death of all these unanswered questions."

"You don't think I am?" Al said, laughing bitterly.

"That's not what I'm talking about. You've intentionally kept me in the dark. Why don't you trust me?"

"Why don't I trust you? I don't even know what you're talking about."

"Tennyson maintains—"

"Tennyson! What is this?"

"Tennyson maintains that the message means something to you, that it's a very personal message."

"So what?"

"I'm asking and I have the right to ask. Do you or don't you know who wrote it?"

"Oh come on, Rhea—"

"No, you come on."

"If I knew who wrote it I'd have the son of a bitch inside this box. And don't raise your voice at me. Now why don't you just tell me what all of this sudden paranoia is about."

"And why don't you tell me how you got those burns?" she blurted, her eyes clouding over.

"Burns . . ."

"And why is Jack terrorized by HoHo, your father? You know, the more I think about it . . . I don't know a thing about you. I know you're not big on self-pity. I know that you're the first man in a long, long time who's made me behave like a goddamn fool . . . sometimes I think the silence between us is enough and other times I feel like you're not really there, that you never will he . . . and just listen to me! I sound like a nagging wife, like we've known each other for—"

"Rhea—"

"Don't touch me. Look at this fucking place! You've got me dancing with the devil and I don't even know what you want out of it."

Al backed up to the bathroom door by the stairwell and slid down into a sitting position. He took off his glasses. "What do you want from me? My life story?"

"At least."

He suddenly looked depleted and small. She shook with surprise and disgust at her outburst, which must have appeared to Al as totally unmotivated and boorish. She longed to put something soothing on his battered eye. She was ashamed of her own display of self-pity. But above all, she was angry at his silence. "I want to know how you got those scars. They got me in bed with you and . . ."

"And what?"

And she wanted to get out of bed? Was that what she was going to say? She bit her lip and stared down at him.

"Your timing is great, Rhea. OK, you want to know about scars. You've got yourself all cranked up for a melodrama. Then come over here and sit down and I'll tell you a nice big melodrama. Once upon a time—"

"Al, I—"

"Sit down and shut up. You want to know about scars and I'm going to tell you about scars."

He took the sunglasses and flung them through the air like a frisbee. They smashed against the far wall. "I grew up alone with my father on a two-thousand-acre cattle ranch in the middle of nowhere in the ass-end of the Ozark mountains. Until the state forced my father to send me to school, he and the two hired hands were the only people I knew. You don't know what isolation is.

"I guess I was as close as any kid can be to his father. But there were times when I was so jealous . . . he was a sculptor, he had a workshop and, late at night, in bed, I'd hear him down there becoming whatever it was he was creating and I knew that I had no place, no existence for him there. I was even forbidden to play in there. It was the place I most wanted to be, of course. It was like a forest of large wooden sculptures. He never tried to sell them. As far as I know, no one ever came to look at them. It was his inner life, that's all. Wooden women made out of walnut trees that grew by the side of the creek that ran through the valley of our ranch.

"One day I sneaked in. I was six. I was paying with some matches, another thing I was forbidden to do. I caught the place on fire. I didn't try to run for help. That never occurred to me. All I knew was that if I allowed his workshop to burn down I would loose a father. So I tried to put it out and it got bigger and I tried to put it out and the more I tried, the bigger it got.

"One of the hired hands was on a tractor in the pasture below the house. He saw the smoke and pulled me out of the rubble . . . that's where the scars came from.

"I was right. I did lose my father, just like he lost twenty years of midnight secret work. He always pretended to have forgiven. And there were times when I thought he had. But there were other times . . . he never sculpted again. He took up drawing and watercolor. But he never went back to wood.

"So you see, the automatic conclusion to be made is that my father did this. The motive: revenge."

Rhea moved closer to him.

"There's only one problem," he said with a laugh. "My father died nearly ten years ago."

"But what about Jack?" she asked. "He thinks he's still alive."

"No he doesn't. He thinks he's a ghost."

"Why does he call him HoHo?"

"My father's real name was Horace. HoHo's bad but Horace is worse. It was a nickname he'd always had. The hired hands called him that and so did I."

"But why does he think there's a ghost?"

Al sighed, then laughed. "That's the second half of my soap opera. When I was born, HoHo gave me a heifer calf for my birthday. It became a tradition. Each birthday I got another calf and by the time I was twenty-one I had a pretty good-sized herd of cattle. These heifers grew and had calves of their own. Anyway, when I came of age, I sold the herd, took the money and left. Moved to Europe and wandered around there for a few years, which I think you already know about.

"I got word that my father had been killed.

"There was a large valley that followed the course of the river through our ranch. Once every few years, the river would flood and turn the whole valley into a destructive . . . oh I don't know, it looked like the Mississippi. It was wild. It took down huge trees, washed away cattle that couldn't get to higher ground, washed them as far away as the Oklahoma state line, which was five miles from our place.

"It had been raining hard all day. After dark, it got serious. HoHo woke up Gar, one of the guys who lived on the place, and said he needed some help . . . you know, to open some gates so the cattle could go up into the hills. They couldn't go very far in the truck. The water was already way over the banks. The rain was torrential. Gar and Dad got into a fight. Gar said it was already too late. Dad didn't listen. He never listened to anybody. He took off wading into the dark by himself with a flashlight. That was the last they saw of him.

"Your father drowned?"

Al laughed again. "I guess."

"You don't know?"

"Here comes the juicy part. They never found the body. And that's the source of Jack's ghost."

"But if they never found the body . . ."

"He *died* out there. Period. That ranch was all he had. If he didn't die, then he just left. And HoHo never would have left that ranch. It was an extension of his body, his soul, if you want to think of it that way. He's dead. He hasn't been wandering secretly around the world for the last ten years waiting for revenge. It's too preposterous. It's the kind of thing a kid Jack's age can believe in, but I can't.

"When Tennyson handed me the note and I read the

word *fire*, I nearly shit in my pants. Of course I would react. I *did* react, and I knew Tennyson had found my reaction suspicious. The grim coincidence . . . a very black joke, I was determined to keep to myself. I figured if I told the police, then they would go off on a wild-goose chase looking for the long-lost father, when what they should be doing was going after *him*." He pointed to the coffin. "The chicken-shit who's been wiping me out."

"So you don't know who it is."

"Nope."

"And you refuse to believe that it's possible that your father . . ."

"Look. The only thing I can tell you is that I know who my father was. He was a man of sorrow, of loneliness, of profound loneliness, maybe crazy, but he wasn't vengeful. He's not walking around still alive. And he's not walking around as a specter. He's gone. And to let the cops in on this would just turn the whole thing into more of a circus than it already is. Besides, even if it were my old man—and I know it's not—do you think I would rat on him? After all, he would be doing to me what I had done to him. It would be between the two of us, wouldn't it?"

"I just don't understand why you didn't tell me this before."

"I almost did, several times."

"What stopped you?"

"Why! The last few days have been a free-for-all. Have you had time to think one fucking thought through since this all started? I haven't even been to bed since . . . what day is this? I haven't been to bed since Sunday night. I don't even know if I have the stamina to make it through the next few hours. In fact," he got to his feet, "I feel like getting Jack and just going home."

"Don't say that." Rhea stood up, too.

"I've suddenly lost my appetite for all of this. It's all bullshit anyway."

"It's not bullshit."

"Well, it's a commentary on bullshit, which amounts to the same thing. It's like . . ."

"Simulationism?"

"How did you know I was thinking that?"

"I've already had this conversation."

"It makes me want to puke."

"How about having a drink instead?"

"OK."

They looked at each other and laughed. "This *is* crazy, Rhea. And so are you. Maybe that's why I . . . I'm tired of all this. My art, it's a fight every inch of the way."

"So, what isn't? Don't you start sulking on me now. Both of us have gone too far already. No matter what happens tonight, you're going to go home tomorrow and start working on a new series. Build up inventory for a new show, and don't think about anything else."

"New show," he said, laughing derisively. "That could be two years down the road. Between the carpentry and raising Jack—"

"Forget about the carpentry."

"And how do you propose I eat in the meantime? Sell my story to a magazine, like Catherine? Advertise for movie options? Who knows how long it will be before the insurance company pays up?"

"The insurance company. I'd forgotten about that."

"Have you even called them?"

"I'm ashamed to admit it . . . but no. It just slipped my mind. Listen, the gallery can take care of your expenses."

She was as embarrassed by her sudden largess as she was of having forgotten to call the insurance company. She adopted a tougher tone. "You're an investment, bub. And like most investments, it boils down to a matter of timing. You've got to keep pumping in money before . . . this installation has already attracted a lot of attention. But the public has a short memory. You've got to come back with another show and quick, before the public forgets. The April slot is still open. That's six months away."

"April!" Al shook his head incredulously.

"Let me concentrate on the bills. You concentrate on your work. Don't even say yes or no. You're all talked out. So am I."

"What are you going to tell Bill Whitehead? He thinks that slot is his."

"There was never any question of that. You've seen his slides. I couldn't sell his stuff if I had a sidewalk sale. Buy one, get one free—no way. I'll just have to break it to him gently somehow."

"Well, don't tell him I'm taking his place."

"Why not? He's bound to find out."

"Not for the time being. I couldn't handle him being mad at me—not on top of everthing else."

"Don't worry about it. You just concentrate on your work. Now—you stay right here. Don't move."

She started to open the bathroom door, but he caught her.

"Wait," he said.

"What is it?"

"You've got crap all over the back of your dress . . . I guess from the floor."

He half caressed, half brushed off her ass.

She opened the bathroom door and stooped down at the mini-refrigerator. She pulled out a bottle of her private stash of champagne and held it in her left hand. With her right hand (ouch! the blisters!) she managed to thread, then curl her little finger through the loops of two coffee mugs. She brought them outside with a wink. But then, to her surprise, he grabbed her and kissed her—mugs and champagne bottle in all the wrong places. Again she had the sensation that their fondling was amateurish, even corny, as if the coffin were their chaperon, as if they could only go so far before they were separated by a higher authority.

Al started to pour champagne into the coffee mugs and then checked himself. He grimaced at the mugs. "Why bother?" he said and took a swig straight from the bottle. Foam ran down the sides of his mouth and he grinned. He passed the bottle to Rhea.

Someone knocked on the front door. She looked at her watch. 6:20. Simon was waiting to be let in.

Seventeen

Felix and Anne returned to the gallery at the same time Felix had a handful of cassettes. (Shostakovich's string quartets, one of Emil's many gloomy enthusiasms).

"Let's hear what it sounds like."

A sound system had been set up, and four large speakers had been placed strategically in the far corners of the galleries. The music came on with a dramatic, self-serious groan.

Anne and Rhea laughed.

"What's the joke?" Al asked.

"Oh . . ." Rhea tried to wave off the question while pouring champagne for the staff.

"Tell me."

"'Orthogonal toil,'" Anne offered.

"What's that mean?" Al turned to her.

"Orthogonal: composed of right angles." Anne rolled her eyes. "The only reason I know is because I had to type it up for him. It was in an article Emil wrote, several years ago, on Picasso's Blue Period."

"He was talking about Picasso's *The Ironing Lady*," Rhea inserted.

"Right," Anne continued. "I'd forgotten. Anyway, he said that the configuration of the working woman was 'evocative of the orthogonal toil of Shostakovichian string quartets.'"

The joke, if that was what it was, would have been better off left unexplained. Everyone stared at the floor. The ensuing silence was, perhaps, the closest Emil's staff would ever come to giving their dead boss a eulogy.

And, Rhea mused, 'orthogonal toil' was an apt description of her belabored attempt to get a grip on the case. Had she learned anything since she stumbled upon his corpse? She was so tired. She worried that her powers of perception were worn out, or at least temporarily desensitized by the barrage of events.

Al asked Simon to help him direct a pinlight down into the coffin. Rhea watched Simon as he read the message inside the box. He didn't laugh. But then, he seldom did.

And that suddenly bothered her. Humor (albeit of the lachrymose variety) had been an essential ingredient in the destruction of Al's work—or at least it seemed that way to her. Was Simon capable of such wit? She remembered Saturday morning, when she had gathered the staff in her office and told them that Emil was dead. Simon had giggled before he realized she was serious. Pretty good acting, if that was what it was. As the light went up on the coffin, Simon's credibility as The One and Only Chickenshit somewhat dimmed.

The group consensus was that the coffin "worked." Felix proposed a toast to Al. Rhea watched to see if Simon drank to the toast. He did.

Nothing but sluggish fragments of contradictory ideas and evidence in her head. Fancy footwork from an overdanced mind. This was no time to be considering anything but business. Business was the single element in her life in which she felt on solid ground. She checked her watch as if to slap herself awake.

"OK," she said, clapping her hands together and

barely missing one of her blisters, "let's get this thing going. Got your stamping pad, Simon? Guard it and the guest book with your life. Think of yourself as a bouncer: no fingerprints—no entrance, and no exceptions. And don't give them their In Memoriam cards until after they've used the Handi-Wipes."

"Right."

"What else? Felix, keep your eyes peeled for Joan McCabe."

"Who's that?"

"The reporter from *Manhattanite* . . . supposedly doing Catherine's big exposé. Spend some time with her. If you can, make yourself indispensable to her—"

"Is she good-looking?"

Rhea and Anne groaned in unison. "Listen to you. I'm not asking you to boff her in the coat closet, I'm asking you to get the slant on her story."

"OK," Felix said, smiling, "But what if Catherine comes with her?"

"In that case, make yourself indespensable to both of them."

She suddenly froze as if she were at the brink of some major revelation. "Anne . . ."

"What?" Anne asked nervously.

"We should be drinking champagne."

"We are."

"No, I mean the guests. We should be giving them champagne. Do you think there's time to order some?"

"I doubt it," Anne fidgeted. "I don't know."

"Sure there is. There's got to be. Call all the neighborhood liquor stores and get everything that's cold and Moët-Chandon or better. I don't care about the cost."

"Now?"

"Tell them . . . tell them there's a big tip if we can get it here in twenty minutes. Oh, and we'll need more ice. Felix, don't we have something downstairs to hold more ice?"

"I'll find something."

"God, how could I have been so stupid," she said to nobody in particular. "This is a champagne crowd coming to a champagne event and I'm offering . . ."

She stepped into her office to check on Jack. He was playing contentedly with Crunch underneath her desk. She took another look around the gallery. Anne got off the phone and said the champagne was on its way.

"Great. Now why don't you put on some lipstick."

"I have on lipstick."

"Oh. Then why don't you put on some visible lipstick. Here, try mine. And don't be skimpy."

She thought of a dozen last-minute details. She had everybody scrambling.

An assortment of twenty-seven (more or less) chilled bottles of good-to-excellent champagne managed to arrive before the guests. Felix and Al iced it down at the side of the makeshift bar in JAN. Rhea breathed a little easier.

She took one last look around. It was 6:55.

Simon opened the front door and seated himself behind the desk. He straightened the stack of announcements with ostentatious fussiness. Felix dimmed the lights to the proper intensity. The place became downright spooky. The violins simpered. The cello moaned.

"Someone turn up that hideous music."

"Did you say up?"

"Up."

She hated social functions, she hated Emil for not being here to take up the slack, and she hated herself for being, all of these years, socially recalcitrant. It was such an integral part of her business. She'd relied on Emil too much. She'd been lazy. She could have learned so much from him about the social intricacies . . . and now it was too late.

Al approached. "What's the matter?"

"Nothing's the matter."

"Then why are you biting your lip?"

"I'm not."

"Yes you are. You're not nervous, are you?"

"Of course not."

"You *are* nervous."

"I'm not. Well, maybe a little. Dealing with a crush of people has never been my forte."

"You'll do fine. Just keep smiling. That's what glamorous hostesses do in the movies."

Rhea donned (what she hoped to be) a *non*-misanthropic smile and tried it out on Al. "Like this?"

Al stepped back and observed, "Looks like there's a guillotine lodged in your throat. Forget the smile idea."

"Some expert. You're at least as antisocial as I."

"Rhea." Anne approached, complaining, "I look whorish in all this lipstick."

"The table wobbles," Simon whined.

Crunch trotted over to the boxes and peed on the leaning broom.

"Let the cartoon begin!" Felix sang in the distance.

"Fuck all of you!" Rhea sang back as the first guests stepped through the doorway.

Ironically, the first to arrive were the last to have left Emil's last Friday night: Arlene Brice (the horny art consultant), James Drummond (the uptown gallery owner), and Drummond's lover. Had they come as a group—newly bonded by Emil's deathbed insults? Rhea watched apprehensively as they confronted Simon's table. Their willingness to be fingerprinted, after an initial puzzlement and an exchange of surreptitious smiles, was an encouraging sign.

An older man was next in line. He had purchased one of the boxes that now lay in the heap. Rhea would have to tear up the check he had given her Friday night. He saw the fingerprinting process and balked. Was it the money he had coming to him that made him hesitate, that kept him from turning around and leaving in a huff? You could see his irresolution. Arlene gave him flirty, good-natured encouragement, which seemed to make up his mind for him. He submitted to the fingerprinting.

Two artists were next. They were no problem.

Next came a scruffy-looking and savvy society photographer. No problem there, either.

Then came her lawyer, Becker. He was having none of it. He spied Rhea and, gesturing to the display on Simon's desk, appealed to her with his eyes. She shook her head and pointed to the others who had already undergone the fingerprinting. He heaved sigh in her direction, but he relented. The photographer took his picture.

On they came: buyers, publishers, museum representatives, consultants, the press, hungry-looking artists, murderers . . . ?

Matt the printer submitted. Sergeant Lipski, in full uniform, submitted. The Karl Tompkinses (Al's uptown alibi) submitted.

With each new conversion at the desk—and the gallery was rapidly filling, she'd never seen such punctuality—an unanticipated group bonding gained strength. It was like a challenge of allegiance: "Are you coming over to our side or not?" It was the initiated staring down the uninitiated. Trenchant reverse snobbism centered around a stamping pad.

She'd never seen anything quite like it. Rhea eased into a half-amused, half-bitter understanding of the perversity feeding on itself. For the first thirty minutes, the fingerprinting *was* the show. A well-known art critic who had pointedly and repeatedly refused to review any of Emil's shows entered the door. He all but licked his lips as Simon pressed his fingers onto the blank page.

Inez, Emil's housekeeper, arrived accompanied by a retinue of assorted, uninvited relatives. She was still in what Véra had dubbed her swarm of flies getup. Her entrance rocked the gallery for a good two minutes. She was putting up a fight.

"I'm no criminal!" she bellowed at Simon. Shostakovich's complaining was no match for hers. Rhea quickly moved up.

"Of course *you* don't have to be fingerprinted," Rhea demurred. "What's wrong with you, Simon! Inez is family."

"But you told me—"

"And I'm sure Inez's family is our family, right, Inez?"

"Well, I . . ." Inez sniffed.

"Come on through. You must introduce me to everyone. This must be your son . . ."

Grudgingly accepting the special attention due her (she was very big on her dignity), Inez hurled one last glare at Simon, rearranged her mourning regalia, and (grown children in tow) cut water to the bar.

"Rhea," Simon complained, "you told me that everyone—"

"Relax, I just saved you a trip to hospital."

Time for a drink.

She walked into JAN. It was immediately clear that there wouldn't be nearly enough champagne. She could easily (and no doubt would) drink two bottles on her own. Inez and company would be good for eight. She took Anne to the side and told her to phone for more . . . all points bulletin . . . as much as Anne could lay her hands on. She poured herself a drink.

An overweight German (a heavyweight buyer), grabbed her by the arm and pulled her into his group of friends. She loathed the feeling of being folded in like so much batter. But it was German batter and it was soothing to momentarily revert to her native tongue. She'd almost forgotten . . . a little girl with black braids reaching out and touching her handsome father's blond hair . . .

A camera flashed. Her head began to buzz with the reality of what Al had concocted. Where *was* Al? She poured herself another drink and began to circulate. It was working. It was happening.

Old Names, Big Bank Accounts, Art Nabobs, Wry Reporters, Pretty Faces—one by one, they queued their way past the "booking," took in the scene (Al's scene) and adopted it as their own. They worked with each other like a gang of conspirators: dusting off one another's egos. weaving in and out, coupling for a camera-clicked moment, threading through the galleries like some great anthropomorphic loom thumping out a tapestry that unwittingly incorporated into the final design the phantom sneer of Emil Vladimir Orloff.

Al's boxes were all but hidden from view. For all practical purposes, the people had created an installation of their own.

A contributing editor for an art magazine stopped her with congratulations followed by the question: "Did Art kill Emil Orloff?"

"Hmm. Interesting concept," Rhea responded. "Which Art did you have in mind?"

"What do you mean?"

"The Art of Business? The aesthetics of Art? Or better yet, what about the real nuts and bolts of Art: the chemical dangers that tag along with Art."

"Rhea, I'm afraid I don't follow—"

"Poisoning from inhaling art supplies," Rhea interrupted. "Ninety percent of them *are* harmful, you know. They say Goya's insanity was the result of lead poisoning. Van Gogh's, too, for that matter. Breathing cadmium is no cakewalk, either. Morris Louis died from the fumes of acrylic paint. And who has the time or money for ventilation? Not to mention cigarettes—we nearly all smoke like fiends. Brain cancer, lung cancer, leukemia, drug addiction . . . take your pick. Art's a toxic business . . . and a hostile witness to its creators."

She couldn't believe herself. Had she really just said all that juvenile shit? Rhea's interviewer was at a loss for words. Finally he said. "Let me ask you a different question."

"Shoot."

"How would you describe this installation?"

"Accurately."

Why was she being so impossible? The reporter presevered. "Well then, let's talk about the quality of Al Kheel's work."

"Irrelevant, since it's now non-existent except for those fortunate buyers who already own his earlier work. I've no doubt that it's just gone up in price."

"Ah! So *money's* the issue."

"Listen, do you see any price lists floating around?"

"Well—"

"Does it look like I'm going to make any money here? Would you like to buy one of these piles of refuse? I'm sure we can work a bargain basement deal."

At the entrance, two delivery boys came in with boxes of champagne on their shoulders.

"You want to talk about art? There's art: men with champagne on their backs. Something you can really wrap your tongue around. Performance art of the highest caliber. Would you excuse me?" She followed the delivery boys, who were disappearing into JAN. All sorts of people waylaid her during her return to the bar, gravid with compliments and congratulatory adjectives like *inspired*, *outrageous*, and *disturbing*.

And all the while she kept thinking, why am I putting myself through all of this? It *isn't* the money. Right now I could be sitting on the veranda of the Gritti Palace watching a garish sunset. Or in Antibes. Or any place on earth.

"Hello, Madeleine. I was hoping you were in town . . ." She caught herself bestowing hypocritical smiles like a parade queen. The champagne, mixed with the apparent success of the party, played games with her frazzled mind. It was wild, what was coming, effortlessly, from her mouth. It wasn't her style at all. Usually in this kind of crowd—a crowd she could accurately claim as her birthright—she clammed up. But tonight . . ."Claude, Robert, how are you two? I haven't seen you since the afternoon Emil got thrown out of 21 . . . yes, well the old bitch deserved to have a peach thrown at her."

It was as if she had just emerged from a pool after completing an excellent dive. That was Emil's little social trick, wasn't it? Springing off tongues like so many diving boards, adding that little twist at the end, achieving as much altitude as possible before going on to the next feat of feigned levity. Emil's department, not hers. And yet . . . it was almost as if he were inside her, prompting her with cue cards. Odd as hell and, she couldn't deny it, intoxicating.

A hand grabbed her by the elbow.

"Remember me?" It was Jamie Kheel, Al's ex-wife. Rhea immediately saw what Felix had meant: she *was* a mean piece of equipment. She wore a skin-tight candy-apple-red mini-skirt, and her motor was still humming after all of those thousands of miles. As ravishing as she was contemptible.

"Of course I remember you," Rhea said. "Though I don't remember the blond hair. Maybe that's why the cops can't find you. Out of date root description. They are looking for you, you know."

"Well, I haven't been hiding. The cops can find me anytime they want." She dropped the name of an East Village artist who had, in the last year, emerged as a star.

Bullshit on top of bullshit.

"Wow," Rhea exclaimed, "a man with a high recognition factor. You *are* hobnobbing. The last I heard, you were with a drummer. The Van Gogh-Goghs, wasn't it?"

"That was ages ago." Jamie was triumphant. "Ancient history."

"Sort of like your son."

Jamie dropped the smile. "What's my son got to do with it?"

"Not much, I would imagine. He's here, you know. Back there in my office. Want me to go get him for you?"

Jamie swallowed. "Jackie's here?"

"That's right."

"Oh. I hadn't thought . . . I don't think . . . let's not tell him, shall we? It would only upset him. Anyway, I can't stay long."

Rhea smiled and said very slowly, "You got that right."

"What gives you the right to . . . you're so superior with your second-rate artist, aren't you?"

Rhea laughed. "Who are you calling second-rate?"

"Al."

"The only second-rate thing in this gallery is your tawdry belief in reflected glory. Aren't you a little old to be a groupie?"

"Go to hell," Jamie said, seething, and stormed off.

The gods must have been with her! Just at that moment, Rhea spied Shears standing next to the entrance of JAN, holding a clear plastic cup of red wine with both hands and looking around the room self-consciously.

"Shears," Rhea said, "am I glad to see you. Wouldn't you rather have champagne?"

"No. Thank you."

"Suit yourself. What would you say if I told you I had a great tip for you?"

"I probably wouldn't believe you," Shears answered honestly.

"If you look around my right shoulder—don't be too obvious—you'll see a hot little sports car all in red. See the one? Masses of fake gold hair? Know who that is? That is Al Kheel's ex-wife . . . I thought you'd be interested. What do you want to bet that she's dying to talk to the authorities?"

Shears looked up at Rhea distrustfully. "Does Tennyson know she's here?"

"As far as I know," Rhea answered, "he hasn't got here yet. At least, I haven't seen him. You're the first to know."

Shears still wasn't taking the bait.

"Look, if you don't believe me . . . how about if I take you over there and introduce her to you?"

"Let's go."

"Want a pad and pencil?"

"I'm not here officially."

"Yes." Rhea tried to ignore the large pink bow in her hair. "I can see that. Still, when opportunity knocks . . . and I can guarantee you that she won't be here for long. Ah, here we are. Jamie Kheel, I'd like you to meet Ms. Shears, from the DA's office."

Jamie looked from one woman to the other. Rhea backed away smiling, and all but waltzed into JAN.

Humming, she filled her glass. She looked up at Anne. "Having a good time?"

Anne creased her eyebrows. "It looks like you are."

Rhea eyed her glass: "I wish I could believe that. You may be right, though. Have you seen Al? I need to talk to him."

"You might try the coffin. That's where he's been parked so far."

"Yes, it's dimmest there. I think he's self-conscious about the black eye."

Rhea suddenly blurted out a laugh that made her sound like a giddy coed. Anne stared in amazement. Someone tapped Rhea on the back. It was Felix, with a tweed-tailored woman by his side.

"Rhea, I'd like you to meet Joan McCabe."

"Nice to meet you, Joan," Rhea shook her hand, still laughing. "Forgive me, but Anne was telling me the most amusing story, weren't you, Anne?"

Anne vigorously shook her head.

"Don't pay any attention to her. How's your brother,

Taylor? I haven't seen him for ages. Did you bring Catherine with you?"

Joan McCabe, unsmiling, cleared her voice: "Surely you didn't expect her to come?"

"Well, I'll be disappointed if she doesn't. The staff and I have a side bet going. If she doesn't come, I'm out ten dollars."

A group came in, laughing. Rhea, Joan, Anne, and Felix jostled sideways to make room for them at the bar.

Joan observed. "I think it would break her heart if she saw all of this."

"Oh, I forgot," Rhea lighted a cigarette with Felix's help. "She's still in mourning, isn't she? And you're going to spill the gossipy beans in the splendid magazine you work for. How *is* the 'Rhea, the Murderess' article coming? Or am I not allowed to ask?"

"There's several questions I would like to ask *you*," Joan returned.

"Fine . . . but first let me ask you one. Since you believe that Catherine was so close to Emil—never mind that she wasn't mentioned in his will, no doubt an oversight on his part—she would be intimately aware of his daily comings and goings, right?"

"Yes."

"So why don't you ask her where he was getting his drugs?"

Joan McCabe's mouth twisted at one end. "She doesn't know anything about that."

"So where's your inside story?"

"What?"

"McCabe, you're fishing, and you know it. If Catherine doesn't know where the drugs came from—and to tell you the truth, I don't really think she does—then she knows very little indeed. Don't you see?"

And for the first time, it suddenly became clear to Rhea as she continued: "There's a mystery about fingerprints and there's a mystery about Emil's drug connections.

He had drugs that night. Plenty of them. Too much of them. And I'd put my last dollar on the probability that there's a connection there. You find the drug dealer and you've got a man . . . or woman with some answers."

"That still doesn't eliminate you," McCabe returned.

"That's true." Out of the corner of her eye, Rhea noticed that Sergeant Lipski had come up and was listening intently. She quickly introduced him and pulled him into the conversation. "What's your opinion, Lipski?"

"I don't have an opinion," he said with a smile.

"That's boring. Which reminds me . . . you know Shears, right? Well, right now she's got Al's ex cornered. That's right. Right out there. Why don't you go see how things are going?"

Then she turned to Joan McCabe. "Now, you said you wanted to ask me some questions?"

"Word has it that you and Al Kheel are lovers."

Rhea paused. "That's not a question."

"Then I'll make it a question: are you lovers?"

"Certainly not."

"You deny that you and Al—"

"Absolutely. What else?"

It was evident that Joan McCabe wasn't quite geared for the rapidity of Rhea's answers. It took her a moment to gather her thoughts: "The question of insurance on Mr. Kheel's work—"

"The gallery is totally insured, provided I'm found innocent of any wrongdoing. The carnage at Al's studio is a different story. Oh! You didn't know about that, did you? I'll give you a little scoop: last night, in Connecticut, it was discovered . . ."

She was just about to fill her in on the details when a sudden atmospheric change made her prick up her ears. Without excusing herself, she darted back into the main room.

First came a kind of group gasp, an abrupt ending to the cacophony usually associated with a tightly packed crowd; a unified hesitation that spread down the channels like overturned dominoes and that left nothing standing but the grueling string quartet and John Tennyson's approach. She immediately understood.

He was in a dark navy suit of a better cut than anything she'd seen him in before. In the theatrical lighting he was a dead ringer for Emil Orloff. As he walked toward her, she could almost believe . . .

He came up and shook her hand.

"Well, John, you've made the entrance of the night. I feel like I ought to be paying you something."

"Maybe you are," Tennyson said, smiling.

An older, white-haired woman came up from behind him and smiled. She offered her hand, which was broad and rough to the touch.

"Rhea," Tennyson said, "I'd like you to meet Gabby, my ex-wife."

"Hi. Nice to meet you. You're a sculptor, right?"

Gabby shrugged good-naturedly. She had nice, trustworthy smile lines that crinkled around her eyes. She had thickened with age, but Rhea could tell that she had once been pretty.

"Some people have called me that," Gabby said. Her voice was as solid and as pliable as a piece of clay. Rhea immediately liked her even though she was vaguely saddened by her existence. It was sort of the same feeling she had when she was around Jack . . .

"How in the world," Rhea joked, "could you have lived with this man all those years?"

"Wasn't easy."

By now, the photographers had caught up with Tennyson and as they began to snap, Gabby instinctively moved to the side. Her modesty made Rhea feel silly by comparison. Rhea was just about to pull Gabby into the picture frame when, suddenly, the gallery went black.

People panicked. There were screams in the darkness.

"Where's the light panel?" she could hear Tennyson yelling.

"To the right of the front door!" she yelled back.

Someone nearly pushed her over. How long were the lights off? Ten seconds? A minute? In the darkness, time went beserk.

Just as suddenly, the lights came back on.

The stirring and the noise subsided. Nobody knew what to do. She stood on her tiptoes for a better view of the front entrance. Al climbed up on the ledge underneath the light controls. His bruised and swollen face beamed like a little boy's. He waved his arms.

"Sorry!" he yelled. "But I've always wanted to do that!"

Booing and groaning ensued, then general laughter.

"That son of a bitch," Rhea hissed. Her heart was still beating fast. Then she thought of Jack in her office. Her hand went up to her mouth.

"Rhea?" Tennyson asked.

"I'll be right back."

She ran into her office. Jack and Crunch were quietly sharing a glass of champagne. Of course! The lights had remained on in here and in JAN. She rushed over to Anne and told her to keep an eye on her office. No one was to go in there and bother the boy.

She hurried back to John and Gabby.

"What was that all about?" Tennyson asked.

"Nothing. Just checking on something."

Shears came up to the group, nearly in tears. The front of her pink blouse was covered in spilled red wine.

"Shears, your blouse!"

"I know," Shears said, seething. "Jamie did it on purpose, I'd swear to it. The second the lights went out . . . and what's worse, she got away."

"Jamie Kheel's here?" Tennyson exclaimed.

"She was."

He quickly pushed his way toward the front door. The three women looked at one other in embarrassment.

"I'm going to wring Al's neck," Rhea said.

Shears wasn't mollified. "It's ruined."

"Don't say that. Look," Rhea said, taking Shears by the arm. "You just come with me. Gabby, we'll see you later."

"Where are you taking me?"

"Never mind," Rhea said, expertly making a path to the bathroom, pulling a reluctant Shears behind her.

Once inside, Rhea locked the door. "Ah," Rhea exhaled. "Sweet silence. Now then, take off your blouse. Do as I say. You don't want the stain to set, do you? What is it, silk?"

"No, it's synthetic," Shears said, holding onto one of her buttons in hesitation.

"Well, that's better. Come on, don't be shy. I won't look."

Rhea opened up the minirefrigerator, extracted a bottle of Perrier, took the proffered blouse and daubed the stain until it disappeared. Then she opened a cabinet under the sink, pulled out a hair dryer, plugged it into an outlet, and dried the blouse. Shears stood silently, motionlessly in her bra, embarrassed and impressed at the same time.

"Here," Rhea said, handing back the dried garment.

"You fixed it."

"Well, it's a little wrinkled but at least you won't look like a murder victim. You see, I'm not entirely wicked. When I get my hands on Al . . . that was a stupid stunt. Someone could have been hurt. For all I know, someone may have been hurt."

"Why did you do this?"

"Do what?"

"Fix my blouse."

"Why is everybody so incredulous when I try to save things? Why can't you just thank me?"

Shears thanked her but she remained unconvinced.

"OK, maybe I just wanted to get away from the people for a while . . . and that ghastly music. Or maybe I realize I need all the help I can get, including from you. Or maybe I'm just a really wonderful person."

"I never thought of that," Shears said with a laugh.

"The woman can laugh!" Rhea laughed too.

Rhea pulled a bottle of champagne out of the mini-refrigerator. "Could you open this for me? My blisters."

The cork popped. Rhea found some Styrofoam cups. They drank in silence for a moment.

"Careful, Shears. Drinking with a suspect. You're compromising your objectivity. I might even demand that you be removed from the case."

Shears arched an eyebrow.

"What's your first name, anyway?"

"You'll just laugh."

"No I won't."

"Yes you will."

"I promise, I won't. Cross my heart."

Shears took a deep breath and exhaled. "Gazelle."

There was a moment of silence, then Rhea screamed with laughter.

"I told you you'd laugh," Shears said, eyes clouding over.

"Sorry. Is it really Gazelle?"

"Thanks for fixing my blouse," Shears said, sighing and putting her hand on the doorknob.

"Wait!" Rhea exclaimed.

"What?"

The idea of once again facing the crowd . . . a sinking feeling overcame Rhea. She had endured the roller coaster as long as she could. She felt she could jump off at any moment. She was stalling, and she grasped at the first question that came to her.

"Do you have any idea who's been doing this?"

"Apart from you? No, not yet."

Someone was knocking on the door.

"What about Jamie?"

"Possibly. Look, Rhea, it's really claustrophobic in here."

"You're right," Rhea refilled her cup.

"You shouldn't drink so much."

"Yeah, well, there's a lot of things I shouldn't be doing."

Shears opened the door, and the noise rushed in. Several people were waiting to use the toilet. Drummond's lover was at the head of the line. "You girls have been taking your sweet time," he said, leering. "What have you been up to, anyway?"

"Not much," Rhea answered. "She'd only take off her blouse, right, Gazelle?"

Shears nearly dropped dead from mortification.

"It's just a joke."

With the aid of her bottle of champagne, Rhea forced her way back into the crowd. The rooms were thunderous, hot, and smoky. Rhea had the slurry-brained notion that she wasn't even there.

Eighteen

Rhea looked down at the dead arm stretched across her breasts. She was fascinated by every detail in the musculature—sinews hardened by years of driving nails, sawing boards . . .

She checked the clock on her bedside table: 6:25. Much too early to get up. She gently lifted the arm and got out of bed.

She put on a robe and tiptoed out to the living room, where, propped up against the television, Simon's painting awaited her. She sat down and stared. All doubts had been wiped away when, last night, Al had been shown the upside-down version.

Of course they had both been in an excitable mood. They had just returned from what was surely one of the major publicity coups of the season. Would Al still see the painting as incriminating evidence in the sobering morning light?

She did. She padded into the kitchen and loaded the coffee maker with double ammunition. Where had she put Tennyson's card? She rifled through a stack of unopened mail, located it, and dialed his number.

"Yes," he snapped, "who is it?"

"It's me. Did I wake you?"

There was a muffled sound as if John were repositioning or trading hands with the receiver.

"Rhea," he finally said, "It's not even seven yet. I must be foremost on your mind."

"You told me to call this number if anything—"

"What's happened."

"I'm OK but I need you to come over right away."

"Why? What's up?"

"Sorry, John, I really can't explain it. It's something you have to see for yourself. Here, in my apartment. I was going to tell you last night but everything was so crazy . . . and I couldn't rule out the possibility that *I* was crazy . . . still can't, for that matter. Up one minute, down the next . . . anyway, I wanted to see Al's reaction before I showed it to you. John, are you there?

"Yeah. Give me thirty minutes."

After she hung up, she wrung her hands. What if it *was* just coincidence? He'd think her a fool. She couldn't just sit around worrying while she waited.

Quietly she slipped into some jeans and a T-shirt and ran down to the corner of Prince and West Broadway, where there was a newsstand. She hadn't spotted anyone tailing her, and the streets were virtually empty. She bought the morning papers and returned home. The coffee was brewed. She poured herself a mug, stiff as mud, and opened the *Times* to the sports page.

Damn! She'd missed a great Mets game. While she was waltzing around coffins, Keith Hernandez, getting the 2000th hit of his career, had led the Mets to a 12 to 4 victory over the Chicago Cubs, putting the Mets only one and a half games behind the first-place Cardinals.

So close, so far away. The Mets had survived, at least for the time being . . . and so had she . . . maybe that was why she loved the Mets. Their victories had always seemed transferable. It was encouraging, invigorating, and it put her minor-league hangover on the back burner. She slid her coffee mug across the kitchen counter, over to the computer, and booted it up. She retrieved last night's guest list and scrolled down the names. Nothing. Then she had an idea: she tapped in a command to alphabetize the list. Maybe if she looked at the names from a clarified angle . . . still nothing.

There was a name that wasn't here, a name that belonged to the fingerprints, a face that she sensed was missing, a name-face as blatantly obvious as it was elusive. Damn! why couldn't she get a hold on it? She stared at the screen as if to bully it into answering her. Son of a glitch.

It was like the word *separate*. For some reason Rhea had never been able to commit to memory the proper spelling. She wasn't a bad speller and it wasn't a difficult word, but she inevitably spelled it *seperate*. And the longer she stared at the two—seperate, separate—the more entrenched she became in the misspelling. It was as if the two were in collusion.

That gave her another thought. She scrolled back up through the guest list while trying to think of people who could be grouped together as a team. Still nothing very convincing. There was a knock on the door. Tennyson looked showered but haggard, "This better be good," he grumbled.

"Don't say that. You want some coffee first?"

"No, I want to know why I'm here."

"Follow me."

She led him into the living room and pointed toward the canvas. "Remind you of anything?"

Tennyson frowned. It wasn't clear if he saw the boxes and the leaning broom or not. "Did Al paint this?" he asked finally.

"No, Simon Golden."

Tennyson scratched the palm of his hand for a moment. Then he said, "I'll take some coffee now."

They sat at the kitchen counter and Rhea told him the story of how she had acquired the painting and how, by accident, it had fallen over.

When she was finished, he rubbed his eyes and sighed. "You'd make a great midwife."

"Why do you say that?"

"You keep pushing till something comes out."

"You mean Simon's painting? You think it's incriminating?"

He shook his head. "It's what I know that counts, Rhea. That painting could be anything you wanted it to be." He changed the subject. "Yesterday afternoon I got a call from Steve Sachetti, the cop out at Redding. He's narrowed the time of break-in between late Saturday afternoon to Monday night when you arrived."

"How did he do that?"

"The garbage man picked up the garbage on Saturday around four-thirty. The two cans were right next to the front door. He is willing to swear that the door was closed, but Jack says that when he went in the door was wide open. I may as well tell you that I've had a tail on all of your employees since Saturday. Simon has been nowhere north of Fourteenth Street since then. He's clean. And as far as the Connecticut break-in goes, all of your employees are clean.

"As for that painting . . . as evidence, it's laughable."

"So what can we do?"

"Watch and wait." His face clouded over. "Something I'm not sure you're capable of."

The telephone rang. It was for Tennyson. When he hung up, he was smiling. "The fingerprint report just came in on your guest book."

"And?"

"The ones we're looking for aren't in there."

"Yeah, well," Rhea said with a sigh, "it was a screwy idea anyway . . . I mean, apart from the fact that it pandered to the general sensationalism of the night. It's possible that we'll never find out, isn't it?"

"Remember, it's only been six days."

"Seems like an eternity."

"Cheer up. There's something else." John's smile widened. "We've located Jamie Kheel. She's not at all happy. Seems she's not an early riser like you. They're bringing her in for questioning right now."

"Love to sit in on that one."

"I'm not sure that would be beneficial."

"It would do *me* a world of good."

She poured him another cup of coffee. "I liked your wife."

"She liked you too. My ex-wife." he corrected her.

"Nah. You'll always think of her as your wife, even if you were to remarry. Gabby's too good of a woman . . ."

"She is a good woman," he admitted. "And she can still make me laugh."

"Well, if you can find someone to make you laugh . . . that's practically the whole ball game."

"You're in a generous mood this morning. I was sort of expecting a repeat of yesterday's hangover."

"I avoided the spirits last night. Stuck to champagne. I may still be a little drunk."

"You're not let down from all the excitement?"

"I don't know what I feel. It's weird. In spite of all the confusion, I do feel strange relaxation or self-satisfaction or something."

"Good night with Al?"

Rhea looked at her fingernails; a gesture that when she saw other women do it, made her want to throw up.

"Rhea Buerklin at a loss for words. That's a new one."

"Shut up. Al and I are like two beaten-up puppy dogs. All of this crap has flung us together, that's all. We're good for each other. We know how to lick each other's wounds—"

"I don't want to hear this—"

"Then don't ask."

Tennyson sipped his coffee reflectively.

"Then how come you told Joan McCabe last night that nothing was going on between you and Al?"

"I didn't say that. How did you hear about that? I didn't say there was nothing going on between us. I told her we weren't lovers. There's a difference."

"If you say so," he answered dryly.

"OK, maybe there isn't any difference. So what? Does she or doesn't she. Is Rhea or isn't Rhea. Who cares?"

"I do."

She cast him a sidelong glance and continued, "Anyway, that wasn't what I meant when I said self-satisfied. For one thing, I survived the opening. For another thing, the Mets won while the dumb-fuck Yankees, *your* team, are back in third place. And for another thing—"

The telephone rang again. This time Tennyson answered. His brow creased. After a few seconds he said, "Who is this?" Then he looked at the receiver and hung up.

"Who was it?" she asked.

"Didn't you tell me that you just had your phone number changed?"

"That's right. About two weeks ago."

"Well, you'd better get it changed again. The guy thought I was Al. 'Morning, Al,' he said, 'Did you know that there is an exchange for all things, just as there are goods into fire and fire into gold?' Then he hung up on me. I didn't recognize the voice. Very low-pitched and hoarse-sounding as if, whoever he was, he was trying to disguise his voice or sound like a ghost or something."

"Ghost," she repeated.

"A bad imitation of a ghost."

"It could have been a crank call," Rhea said hopefully.

"It could have been."

"John, I'm getting scared."

He walked over to her and held her by the shoulders.

"I'm not going to let anything happen to you. You've got to trust me."

"I do trust you."

"Yes, but I mean entirely. You've got to do as I say from now on. That means quit trying to take control."

"What do you want me to do?"

"I want you to wait and watch. But mostly I want you to wait. Promise me you'll do that. No clever innuendoes thrown in Simon's direction . . . that sort of thing. And on second thought, I don't want you to change your number."

"It's tapped, isn't it."

John nodded without apology. "It could be of great help to us now. If the hoarse voice calls again, try to stall him."

"Great."

John suddenly looked up. Rhea turned around to follow his gaze. Al was standing in the doorway. "How long have you been there?" John asked.

"Long enough to hear about the phone call."

"Do you know anybody with a low, hoarse voice?"

Al shook his head. They watched him walk over to a pack of cigarettes and light one up. They could see the irritation building in his movements. "You know what's really beginning to piss me off?" he finally said. "All these extra dramatic gestures. There's too many of them. Someone sees this whole thing as fun."

"It may be the very thing that catches him up," John responded.

"Too many details," Al continued as if he hadn't heard. "The whole thing is overworked, like . . . like . . . Simon's painting. Rhea, didn't you say that you picked this one because it *wasn't* completed? That the finished ones looked overfinished?"

Rhea bit the inside of her cheek.

"Yes, I said that."

"Why was he calling you?" John asked Al.

"What?"

"He didn't ask for Rhea. He was calling for you. Or at least he knew you were here and didn't care if he talked to you."

Al didn't answer.

"Al," Rhea said, almost pleading. "I know I promised that I wouldn't say anything. John said he sounded like a ghost."

Al exploded. "That's fucking ridiculous and you know it."

"I know it's ridiculous, you know it's ridiculous, but John doesn't know it's ridiculous and whoever called may not think it's ridiculous."

The phone rang. Tennyson seized the phone.

"No," he said, "Don't start without me. Well, Jamie Kheel can just wait until I get there." He hung up.

John walked back over to his stool. "Jamie lived out there with you, right?" he asked.

Al poured himself some coffee.

"In the beginning, yes."

"Anyone else from the city know how to get to your place?" Al shook his head and sat down. Rhea took the phone off the hook. "Come on, Al," she said. "Tell him about HoHo."

Under duress, he told Tennyson the story of his father.

Nineteen

It was 8:30 by the time Al finished his story. Tennyson made ready to leave for the police station, where Jamie Kheel was waiting for him.

"Bet you don't find out anything," Al said, stopping Tennyson at the door.

"Why?"

"Because Jamie's got what she wants. She's right in the middle of the local dog and pony show. She's shacking up with a star of the moment. She's got someone to take care of her kid so she doesn't have to feel guilty about leaving him. What's her motive? The last thing she wants to see is me mixed up with the police."

"Did you talk to her last night?" John asked.

"For a moment. She wanted to know if I was the one who had killed Emil. I said no and she was visibly relieved."

"Why didn't you say something before?" Rhea asked with a peeved expression.

"What time slot did you have in mind? Christ, ever since I saw Simon's portrait of my work . . . which reminds me: I've been doing some mental calculations about the time that's gone into his canvas. Let me show you."

They all retreated to the living room and gathered around the painting.

"The grid Simon's set up here has well over five thousand quarter-inch squares. I'd say about half of those have been painted in. Now . . ."

Al pulled a pencil from his pocket. "This'll do," he said, holding it up like a paintbrush. "If you put the paintbrush up to one of the squares and pantomime filling it in like this . . . boom, boom, boom, boom . . . and remember, all of these squares are carefully delineated, executed exactly within the lines . . . this isn't a sloppy job. He's taken his time here. And if you multiply that by twenty-five hundred squares, you've got a lot of time invested in this piece. But that's not all. He's using acrylic diluted with water—almost like painting with watercolor."

"How can you tell?" John asked.

"For one thing he couldn't get the control of line with full-thickness acrylic, straight from the tube. For another, the colors are too translucent.

"Now look at the blues and greens and the medium browns: they're more translucent than the other colors, so he's started painting them a second time to get a more intense hue. You see? He's painting this thing twice!

"OK. Rhea picked it up on Sunday, noonish, right? If Simon is innocent, the first time he could have seen the image, the pyramid, was Saturday morning. And his first opportunity to paint it would have been late Saturday afternoon. That means, if he stayed up all night and did nothing else, he would have had, at tops, eighteen hours to do this. The point is this: I couldn't do this kind of meticulous work in eighteen straight hours. My fingers, my back, my eyes would give out . . . I don't care how obsessed I was. Besides, Simon told Rhea that he'd been working on it for a couple of weeks. This is premeditation in living color."

"You have been thinking about it," Rhea observed.

John grumbled, "I think you're both suffering from hyperactive imaginations."

"Oh come on, John," Rhea objected. "It's right in front of your face!"

"Even if I did agree with you, which I don't, I couldn't act upon a triangle and a slash on a piece of canvas."

"Why not?"

"Because all Simon has to do is say it's upside-down, a coincidence. Period. No court is going to convict him on this. And convict him of what? We've still got the missing owner of the fingerprints to deal with. I can't bring him in on this. If he's acting in collusion with someone . . . I told Rhea and I'll tell you . . . as far as Simon's concerned, all we can do is wait and watch."

Rhea, Al, Jack, and Crunch went to the gallery a little after nine. The place was a mess from the night before. Plastic cups, cigarette butts, In Memoriam cards and assorted debris were strewn in all directions. Rhea despaired at the sight but ever-economical Al had a simple solution. He dislodged the leaning broom from the pyramid and swept all the garbage up to and around the bases of the two piles.

"There!" he said, with obvious satisfaction. "One more veil to the installation. What do you think?"

"It's fine," Rhea said, flaring her nostrils, "except for the odor. It already smells like an all-nighter in here and there's another three weeks before the show closes.

"So what?" Al smiled. "It's a malodorous event in the first place. All we're doing is enhancing the essence of the installation—guiding it, as it takes on a life of its own, to its logical conclusion."

"I know, Al, but—three weeks! What's it going to be

like, coming to work each morning to a stinking cemetery?"

"You're not sorry you're showing it, are you?"

"No. It's a valid statement. A brilliant one. I'll stand by it. I just don't particularly want to *smell* it."

"You're sick of it."

"I guess so. Aren't you?"

"Why do you think I'm getting ready to leave?"

"Right now?"

"I've got to get back to work. Two commissions from last night. Not bad. And now that you want me to do the April show . . ."

"When will I see you?"

"Why don't you come out for Sunday and Monday? The gallery will be closed."

"Maybe."

"Cheer up," he said with a smile, and took her in his arms. "We pulled off a big one."

She had to agree, but the embrace was nothing if not desolate—an ending of a kind. Al's levity made Rhea realize that the concentrated efficiency at the core of his talent was something that neither she, nor anyone else, would ever be invited to share. It was totally self-sufficient, self-fulfilling and willing to accept the consequences. At that secret point, from which all of his motivation emanated, he needed no one, not even Jack. His career was on a dramatic upswing. Did anything else really matter?

When they left, Crunch came up as if to console Rhea or, more likely, to be consoled. Crunch would miss the kid.

And she? They hadn't hugged. They had concluded a deal.

So what? Deep down inside, wasn't she just as protective of herself as he was? Wasn't she just as stingy? What had she given *him* besides the stage for a good business venture?

She climbed the stairs in JAN, sat down at Catherine's desk, booted up the computer, and typed into the terminal the heading: POTENTIAL MURDERERS.

Al Kheel's name went at the top of the list.

She smoked a Lucky Strike and stared at the screen. It was sort of like killing the goose that laid the golden egg.

"You're a businesswoman," she reminded herself.

Whatever was a boon to Al's celebrity was also boon to her business. She was now in a position to ask at least double the money for one of his boxes . . . not to mention all the free publicity . . .

We pulled off a big one.

A big internecine one?

All along, she had been sidetracked by the business potential of the installation. Now that the opening was over, now that he had got what he wanted and was gone . . . she had dismissed the possibility of his guilt from the beginning and she had stuck to that dismissal. So why was she having second thoughts now?

Al had said that there were too many details, that—like Simon's painting—the crimes had been overworked. And yet when he had told Tennyson, in detail, why Simon's painting was incriminating, hadn't it struck her that his explanation was, in itself, excessive?

Or was she just pissed off because she was suddenly burdened with the joyless task of adding one more weekend lover to her already crumpled collection? This line of questioning was getting her nowhere, but at the same time she couldn't afford to let go of it.

She typed in Simon Golden's name below Al's. Below that, she typed in Catherine Miller's name. Having fired Catherine—she could now see the enormity of that mistake. Maybe her biggest so far. You kept your enemies closest to you, anybody knew that. She had cut off her access to Catherine, and Catherine was an essential slice of the pie.

Why? Why had she been so willing to disbelieve that Catherine could have been having an affair with Emil?

Because her underfed appearance was physically repulsive to Rhea? The appearance of many a cocaine addict. Was Catherine the drug connection? And if so, how could Rhea prove it, now that she had stupidly burned the bridge?

Jesus, now that she looked back, it appeared that she had done everything in her power to sabotage her own search. Didn't she want to know?

She tried a different approach. She typed in the heading:

COLLUSION.

Al and who?
Simon and who?
Catherine and who?
Al and Simon and who?
Al and Catherine and who?
Simon and Catherine and who?
Al and Simon and Catherine and who?

Great. Another pyramid.

The telephone rang. It was Tennyson. "Jamie Kheel is clean," he said. "She and her boyfriend have spent the last week in Montauk in a big house on the beach with lots of friends. They didn't get back until late Sunday night. It's all verified."

"I guess you can't always pick who you want to be the demon."

"No. Can I speak to Al? There's something I'd like to ask him."

"He's gone back to Redding."

"Oh. What are you doing?"

"Watching and waiting like a good little girl."

"Something the matter?"

"No." She punched a button and erased the pyramid from the screen. "I'm glad you called. I meant to tell you something about the guest book but I forgot. Inez's family—"

"I know," John said, laughing. "They weren't fingerprinted. Simon complained to me when I first came in."

"It was my fault. I'm sorry."

"Don't worry about it. I took care of it."

"How?"

"I appealed to her sense of self-importance. I told her that that guest book was going to be a collector's item, that she was passing up a social opportunity of sorts. She herded up her clan and booked them. They're clean too."

"What about you? Were you fingerprinted?"

"No."

"Why not? You're the creepiest thing about this case."

"You want me fingerprinted? You'll have to do it yourself."

"No thanks."

"Might be fun. When you were talking to Joan McCabe last night," he continued, "you suggested that the key to the mystery was Emil's drug dealer. Why did you say that?"

"I'm not sure I know. It just sort of popped out. And then after I said it, I believed it. All along, I've been going back and forth about what was the weakest link in this whole mess and I guess that it suddenly occurred to me that the weakest link was Emil's dependency on drugs. The image of that disgusting enema bag . . . why? Do you think it was off the mark?"

"No, no. It could be dead center. I was just wondering out loud."

"Do you still suspect Al?"

"I haven't discounted any one."

"Including me. Am I still being followed?"

"Yes, but at this point it's more to protect you than anything else."

"Do you think I'm in danger?"

"I don't know. It depends on how much you know, or . . ."

"Or what?"

"Or how much someone *thinks* you know."

As she listened, she typed onto the clean screen:

MYSTERIOUS FINGERPRINTS.

"I don't know anything, John. Less each day. But I would bet my bottom dollar that the person who belongs to the unidentified fingerprints is no stranger to me. It's just a feeling but it's a very strong one. Emil just didn't have that many secrets from me. The only reason I didn't know his drug connection was because I didn't *want* to know. But I must have seen him . . . or her . . . at one time or another—"

"I agree. That's why I'm begging you to wait and watch and not do anything rash or without my knowing."

"When will I see you?"

It was the second time today that she had asked a man that clinging question and it secretly shamed her.

"How about dinner?"

"What time?"

"You tell me."

"The sooner the better. I'll be home right after six."

"Mm, I like the urgency in your voice."

"Don't joke."

Someone was knocking on the street door. She looked at her watch: 10:40. One of her staff. "Someone's trying to get in. I've got to go."

She hurried to the door and opened it. It was Felix. She could have kissed him, so relieved she was that it wasn't Simon. The idea of being in the gallery alone with Simon, even for a few minutes . . .

Felix passed by her in amazement. "You've already cleaned up?"

"Everything but the bar. It needs to be dismantled. You can start with that, if you want to. But don't throw away the bottles. Al wants you to stack them against the pyramids."

"Why?"

"He's into scents."

The telephone rang. She went into JAN and picked it up.

The muffled voice assaulted her ear with the "fire into gold" message. The man hung up before she could react.

Felix walked in, bringing a folded newspaper. "Have you seen what the *News* wrote about the reopening?"

"No," she said, swallowing the emotion working its way up into her voice. "Just the *Times*. Thanks. Felix, I don't want to be disturbed unless it's necessary. Tell Anne, when she comes in, that I'm not taking calls except for Tennyson."

She went into her office and closed the door. It was going to be a warm September day. Already her office was stuffy. She turned on the overhead fan. She flopped down on the couch.

Emil: what an enterprising fool. So what did that make her? She was different. She'd been an enterprising *royal* fool; traipsing through her insular world with a new love interest and with an invisible cash register strapped to her back, a publicity papoose, when what she should have been concentrating on was . . .

She opened the newspaper. On page five the headline read:

"Kheeled Over."

She read the lurid description of the events of the night before. She stared at the wheeling fan.

Now the man was calling her at the gallery. What kind of shift did that indicate?

Al would get half the insurance money, not to mention overnight fame after a tedious career. *Fire into gold.*

Crunch jumped up on her lap. Emil wanted Crunch stuffed. Who wanted her stuffed?

She pictured Al in his van, driving back to Connecticut. Was he humming a tune as he went through the toll gates? Crunch licked at her receding blisters.

"Stop that."

The fan turned slowly. All of these fragments! She couldn't allow herself to be worn down by them. That was the most important thing. She mustn't let go. She must dwell on them. Live with them. Night and day. Eat with them. Sleep with them.

She fell asleep.

Twenty

Eleven thirty.

Rhea woke up with an added dimension. She would have been hard-pressed to say what that dimension was, but it was there all the same and she paid silent tribute to her constitution for being capable of taking naps—even in the morning, when necessary. Naps were gifts.

She made a call to a publicist who owed her a long-standing favor. She asked him how one went about collecting all the press coverage. He told her not to worry, that he would personally see to it and forward it to her as it came into his office.

She went out to JAN. She nodded to Anne, who was on the phone. She peeked into the gallery and made a quick head count. Not yet noon and there were twenty-five or more people milling about. Felix and Simon would have their hands full with crowds.

Anne got off the phone and handed her a list of people wishing to speak to her—it read like a veritable proclamation of success.

"What did George Cavre want?"

"He's doing a box show in December," Anne explained.

"Who does he have in it?"

"It's to be centered around a core of a half dozen boxes by Joseph Cornell, and he wants a couple of pieces by Al. He didn't say who else was in it."

"The problem is, lack of inventory. Call Tennyson . . . no, call Gazelle Shears's office and ask what the quarantine situation is on Emil's apartment."

"Why?"

"Well, Emil had two of Al's boxes brought over to his living room for the opening night. Find out if we can take them out of the loft, on loan from the estate, for local shows. Don't say it's a private gallery that wants them. Say it's a museum that's interested."

"I can't lie to the police!"

"Well," Rhea said with a shrug, "then imply. After you're finished with that, call everyone who's purchased a Kheel through this gallery and ask them if they're interested in loaning their work. Tell them we'll handle all crating, shipping, insurance, et cetera, and emphasize how it will increase the value of their pieces."

"Rhea, I'm swamped already. I'm not going to be able to man JAN all by myself."

"I know. I've been thinking about that. Do you know anybody that we could get?"

"Not with experience."

Rhea's eyes widened. "Why don't we call Catherine?"

"Ha, ha."

"I'm serious. Tell her we've buried the hatchet, she can have a raise, we love her, we know that deep down inside she still loves us . . ."

"*You* tell her we know that deep down inside, she still loves us," Anne suggested, shifting in her seat.

"All right, I will. As soon as I get back."

"Where are you going?"

"Uptown. I won't be long."

"But Rhea, there are a thousand things I need to talk to you about."

"I'm sorry, they'll have to wait."

She walked to West Broadway and hailed a cab.

"Madison, between sixth-sixth and sixty-eighth," she told the driver, looking askance through the rear window. "I'll let you know when we get up there." She was being tailed.

She tipped the driver and got out at sixty-eighth, and walked into Giorgio Armani's. The ground floor was the women's boutique. She didn't stop there but took the side stairs to the second floor, where the men's couture was on display. It was a long, narrow, mirrored room . . . not unlike the interior of one of Al's boxes, really. A handsome black youth approached as if he were on a designer's runway and, in a heavy Italian accent, asked if he could help her. She replied, in Italian, that she was interesting in buying a dark suit.

"For your husband?" he asked.

"For myself."

"The ladies' suits are on the first—"

"I'm not interested in a lady's suit. I want the real thing. May I ask how long you've been working here?"

"Nearly three years."

"Then you will have known my business partner, Emil Orloff."

"But of course! He was one of our best customers. We read about it in the paper. We're so sorry—"

"Yes, it was dreadful. That's why I want a suit of my own: for sentimental reasons, you understand. The problem is . . . I need it by tomorrow night."

"Oh. I see. I would have to ask the tailor—"

"I'm prepared to pay whatever is necessary for the inconvenience. It's my way of paying homage to Emil. I don't know my size, of course, but I'm five-nine in my bare feet . . . which reminds me, I'll need some men's shoes as well. In fact, I'll need everything, from the bottom up, including a hat. Do you think I could get away without too many alterations? I have broad shoulders."

The young man put a pensive finger to his lips:

"With your coloring . . . how about something in a deep monastic gray?"

Thirty minutes later she was standing before a full-length mirror in men's shoes, with a tailor at her feet (chalking the cuffs) and three bemused salesmen milling in the background with ties, belts, and shirts.

The tailor was disgruntled. "With fabric like this, you should honor it with a second fitting."

"There's simply no time. You're sure you can have it by tomorrow?"

"Yes, madam. As you wish."

She was perspiring heavily when she returned to the Avenue. It was a warm and sunny day and the fumes from the barreling buses were nauseating. She hadn't had anything to eat, she reminded herself.

She hailed another cab.

The gallery, when she got back downtown, was crowded. To judge by the predominance of expensive black shoes and T-shirts, it was primarily made up of SoHo people. The rest of the town would come later.

A fresh plethora of phone messages awaited her. She waved them off, went into her office and called Catherine.

"Before you hang up on me, I would just like you to know that I have come to terms with your estimation of me. I understand that you think me a monster and I'm willing to live with that. Some of us have to have feelings and some of us have to be macho girls. That's the way of the world. The fact remains that you are an able-bodied assistant—when you're not weeping—and this gallery finds you quite irreplaceable. I think I can speak for Anne and Simon and Felix, as well as for myself and Crunch."

Catherine went into a nasty spasm of coughing.

"Catherine? Are you all right?"

Catherine cleared her throat. "Let me get this straight. Are you offering me a job?"

"At a twenty percent wage hike, on a temporary basis.

I have no illusions that you would want to stay here. Just until we can find someone to replace you and until we can get you a suitable position elsewhere. With my recommendation I believe that I am in a better position to find you a job than you are yourself."

"You're out of your mind."

"Maybe."

"What is this really, Rhea, a bribe? You want me to back out of the *Manhattanite* story?"

"I don't give a flying fuck about the *Manhattanite* story. Yellow journalism, to my knowledge, has never hurt an art gallery. In any case, whatever damage is accrued can't hold a candle to Emil's unconscionable method of entering the next world. You don't have to answer me now. In fact, I would prefer that you didn't. You have made a stand on behalf of your lover. Fine. I can appreciate that and it has gone on record. But it's time to move on. It's time to reinvest in what, up until now, has been a very productive relationship. Just think of the waste."

"Why are you doing this?"

"I thought I explained: You're sorely missed. We need you and we want you back. Believe me, I would never call you if I didn't think that you, upon reflection, could see that I am innocent of any foul play. That's the first thing I want you to consider. The second thing is this: whatever affection there may have been between you and Emil was not evidenced by his will. The man used you just like he used me, like he used everybody. It's time to recognize that and move on. The third thing is this: I have swallowed my considerable pride in order to mend things. It is not a daily occurrence. How hard could it really be for you to reciprocate? The fourth thing is this: you are twice as valuable to Joan McCabe as a *present* employee of the Orloff Gallery.

"Just think about it. And do me the kindness of getting back to me as soon as possible." She looked up to see Anne slack-jawed in the doorway. "I've got to go now. Anne sends her love. Bye-bye."

The phone rang almost the moment she hung up. Anne started back to her desk but Rhea stopped her.

"I'll help with the phones for a while," she said, grinning. "I'm on a roll. Besides, I've got something else for you to do. I'd like a printout of last night's guest list. I'd also like a printout of our mailing list."

"Mailing list!" Anne exclaimed. "That's nearly three thousand names."

"I know. You better get busy."

She picked up the phone. "Good afternoon," she said. "Emil V. Orloff. May I help you?"

It was an editor from *Art in America*.

Wait and watch, my ass, she thought.

Al called around three-thirty.

"Are you using the Shostakovich?" he asked.

She pushed back her chair with a sigh. "It's easy for you to want the music. You don't have to be here to listen to it all day long. You want everybody on my staff to quit?"

"No, but . . . it is part of the installation, Rhea. It's already been reported in the paper. People will expect it."

"Well, I'll defer to you on this but the volume's going to be way down." In a softer voice she added, "About this weekend. I don't know if I'll be able to come up or not."

"Don't worry about it. There's something else I wanted to mention to you. It's about Monday morning—while you were at the lawyer's for the reading of the will. It may be nothing but when the locksmith was finished, he gave the two new keys to Simon."

"I know that. So?"

"I was just wondering . . . when did Simon hand them over to you?"

"Let's see. They were on my desk when I returned from lunch with Véra."

"Right. And in the interim, Simon spent a long time away from the gallery on errands. One of the places he visited was the hardware store—"

"Where he could have had copies made," she finished the sentence for him in a rapidly expanding sense of bewilderment. "But why would he want his own copy?"

"I don't know. I just thought you might want to think it over, maybe mention it to Tennyson."

She hung up and dialed the local hardware store. She asked for the clerk, an artist, whom she knew personally.

"Do you remember when Simon came in the day before yesterday?" she asked. He did. Simon had purchased some paint and had a copy of a key made. Was there a problem?

"Not really," she lied. "But we've mislaid the receipt. I was wondering if you could send us a copy." She hung up.

Anne came in with papers to be signed. Felix came in with a question. "Matt just called and wanted to know what we had decided about next month's show. The catalog: do you want to cut the introduction or not? He's got to know by Friday."

"Leave it in," she snapped while furiously signing the papers. She noticed Felix and Anne exchanging glances. Next month's show, she groaned to herself. She wasn't suicidal, but, at this moment, she wouldn't have minded retracting her life for a decade or two.

"One more thing," Felix added hesitantly. "The Johnsons from Palm Beach are in town. They want to see some of Peter Halley's new work."

"When?"

"Tomorrow, around noon."

"Good. How many pieces do we have?"

"Two new ones. Both very big canvases. The problem is that we can't take the Johnsons downstairs. It's still a mess from Saturday."

"How big are the paintings?"

"One is nine by seven and the other is nine by twelve."

"OK. We'll take down these two big pieces in my office and put up the Halleys. They can view them here."

The overhead clearance of the stairs leading down into the storeroom wouldn't allow for the moving of such large paintings. As you walked out from JAN, just inside the larger gallery was a trapdoor on the floor, twelve feet long and ten inches wide. No hinges; it looked like a giant slot-shaped plug. It had been carefully designed so that it continued the plank pattern of the floor and no one ever noticed it. It took two people to lift it.

Rhea helped Felix pull it up. Carefully they set down the plug, several inches to the back. Brushing the dust off of her palms, she looked down into the opening. Twelve feet below, Simon was standing in the storeroom, looking back up at her. The sight unnerved her.

He disappeared, only to return with one of the big canvases. He lifted it up through the slot. Rhea and Felix brought it up through the floor and leaned it against the wall. They did the same with the second canvas.

She stared through the slot, down into the storeroom. Every time Simon passed beneath her, her pulse quickened. She felt queazy—like people who are afraid of heights.

What was she seeing that she had never seen before? Or was it just the opposite? What was she *not* seeing that she *had* seen before?

And then it struck her.

Saturday morning, the morning after the murder, when she had walked down in pursuit of Crunch, she had noticed a bottle of Remy Martin on the floor. Its placement had been directly below this trapdoor. Did it mean anything or was it just a coincidence?

She suddenly imagined Emil sitting on the floor, hugging his brandy and looking up through the slot at . . . at whom? Was he having a conversation with someone? Was there arguing? Were there wisecracks?

Were Emil and the person with the mysterious fingerprints engaged in an activity of mutual consent?

They put the trapdoor back into the slot but it didn't erase the troubling, vertiginous image of Simon in her mind. Rhea went into JAN.

The phones were ringing. The printing machine was whirring out the mailing list. Anne was doing her best to keep the lid on but she looked frazzled, dead on her feet. Rhea spied an open bottle of aspirin on Anne's desk and helped herself to a handful while answering the phone. She put two people on hold. She relished the pungent power of the aspirins dissolving in her mouth. Silently, the phone lights blinked off and on.

Think! Why would Simon want his own key? And why had Tennyson refused to see the pile of boxes in Simon's painting? Was he biased against any suspect who *wasn't* Al?

Assessing Simon's guilt continued to make her feel like she was shortchanging herself. Deplorable. She'd worked with him on a daily basis for the last two years, and yet what she *didn't* know about him would fill a library. Think! She'd read his résumé before hiring him. Where was he from? Somewhere around New York. Where had he gone to school? NYU? The New School? Who could she talk to, how could she find out about him without casting undue suspicion? As she tried to recapture details, something flickered in her consciousness—or rather, someone. Bill Whitehead. Bill had gone to school with him! Of course. Simon was Bill's connection to the gallery . . .

She pounced on Anne's Roladex and found Bill's number. She hesitated. To what extent was the calculating spirit of Emil dictating this proposed phone call? Emil had toyed with Bill's vulnerability, which she despised, and now she was about to utilize the same unfair leverage. Still . . . with the possibility of a show dangling over him, who knew what Bill could and would be willing to tell her about Simon?

Guilt overruled by determination. She picked up the phone and dialed his number. Ring, ring. He answered.

"Hi, it's Rhea. I've got a sudden impulse to see your work. The real stuff, not just the slides. You busy? I was wondering," she said, ignoring the murderous glare from Anne's direction, "if you would mind me paying a visit."

"You, you mean here? Now?" Bill sputtered. "Would I mind? Do you know where I live? That's right, the Bowery. You can walk it if you want. On the west side of the street, across from the Salvation Army. There's no buzzer but I'll be watching for you."

That was disgustingly easy. "Give me fifteen minutes," she said, and hung up.

Leaving Anne in the lurch for the second time today would be more difficult. The gallery was packed. The phone was ringing off the hook. Anne remained motionless, breathing through her teeth, silently daring Rhea to come up with a nonreproachable explanation.

Fuck it, it was her gallery. Rhea opted for the less-than-brave approach of leaving with *no* explanation. She backed up, smiling, to the exit of JAN. She pivoted, cautiously stepped over the trapdoor (bad luck to step on people's graves), and abandoned ship.

Twenty-one

It wasn't that much of a walk to Bill's but Rhea hailed a taxi. She saw an unmarked beige Ford with puny hubcaps pull away from the curb. It was following her cab. The impossibility of unburdening herself, of escaping even for a moment . . .

As she neared the Bowery, the desuetude of the surrounding buildings matched the shambles of her disposition.

Against her will, the strictly business context of her phone conversation with Al played back in her mind.

About this weekend . . .

Don't worry about it.

Glaring was what they *hadn't* said to each other. What weekend? There never would be another weekend together, would there? He'd had no problem dropping the subject, and she'd been all too willing to follow suit. The simple truth, she guessed, was that they were mutually scrubbing their intimacy. Ignited quickly, consumed quickly—they had pulled each other up from out of the heap and now that the show was off and running, they found their relationship secondary, if not intrusive.

Christ, she grumbled to herself. You see Romance planted and watch disinterestedly when it doesn't take to the soil. You fire one employee and hope you can nail another one, Simon, for a hideous crime. And now you're on your way to the Lower East Side to exploit a guy's hopes for a show in your gallery, knowing full well that you'll have to snuff those hopes. All the nonfelonious, untitled murders that you've committed in the last few days . . .

The cab pulled over in front of the Salvation Army, and she got out. The Bowery reeked of urine. Two bums, slumped together against a stoop, looked up for a moment and then returned to their perfect torpor. Across the street was a row of derelict buildings. She saw Bill motioning eagerly from a fourth-story window.

"I'll be right down," he yelled.

Not exactly the lap of luxury. Still, Bill was better off than a lot of artists she knew. At least he was still in town. The rent was so high, even for a dump on the Bowery, that many artists had been forced to move to Brooklyn, Hoboken, or beyond, living hand to mouth, waiting for the big break and a better view of the Manhattan skyline.

Working her way around a colony of broken wine bottles, she crossed the street. The metal door opened. Bill's face was flushed, his bulging forehead fairly throbbing with anticipation.

"It's a mess," he apologized, sliding an orange-juice carton away from the threshold with his foot. "Watch your step, it's kind of dark going up."

Understatement. Her eyes couldn't adjust. A light bulb of minimum wattage, entrapped by cobwebs, glowed begrudgingly at the top of each flight of stairs, punctuating the surrounding darkness but not illuminating it. The steps creaked. The acoustics were echoic. It was almost comically spooky.

"Christ, Bill. Why don't you get a black cape and candelabrum?"

"That's a joke, right?" His voice lingered over his shoulder. "Just one more flight."

"Other artists live here?"

"Nope. I'm the only one. The bottom three floors are still warehouse."

They entered at the back of his loft. A perfunctory kitchen, a bathroom and a daybed were crowded up against one another in the corner closest to her. The rest of the loft was work space, and it was large. There must have been sixty feet separating her from the large grubby windows at the far end overlooking the Bowery.

Asbestos flooring strewn with metal shavings. Heavy compressors, fuel and oxygen tanks connected to blowtorches, storage bins laden with sheet metal, swages and swage blocks, great spools of heavy-gauge wire, a table drill, rotary file, anvil, oversize hammers and other unidentified devices—all implying weight and industry. Dangerously so. How long before the floor buckled from the mass?

The high ceiling looked equally precarious. In between the numerous skylights and suspended from beams by ropes and pulleys were Bill's highly polished sculptures of steel. Anacondas in the sky. They looked as if they could crash down at any moment.

"How much do those things weigh?" she asked.

"Three, four hundred pounds. You want to look at them now or would you like a drink first?"

"Drink first. What do you have?

He smiled at her for the first time. "Dewar's," he said.

Why was it so hard to look at him? It wasn't just that big double-cliff forehead, it was also his eyes. They were so small and so close-set (yet not unkind) that every facial expression, even the most well intended, was reduced to humorless intensity. She had the scratchiest desire to mock his solemnity, and yet . . .

As she watched him exact a new bottle of scotch from a paper bag, she suddenly understood that he had bought the booze specifically for her. Dewar's White Label was practically her trademark. How long had he been waiting for this moment? He searched rather nervously for glasses and said he would have to wash some. Embarrassed and slightly ashamed of herself, she made for the diversion of the windows at the front of the loft. Across the street the shadows crawled up the buildings as the sun made its descent. The bums and their fiesta . . . except for the beige car with black sidewalls, all was blatant aimlessness.

"Ice or straight up?" he called from the back.

"Straight."

She stepped back. She noticed, framed between two of the windows, a 1981 review from the *Village Voice*. A group show. She scanned down through the names (several of which were now fairly well known) and stopped at Bill's name. His work was described as "intense" and "promising."

Two crummy adjectives on yellowing newsprint. Was that Bill's take-home pay after all these years? Barbarous, the power she held over him. If she'd come to exploit Bill, she now realized she wouldn't pull it off so easily. Her heart wasn't in it. She'd come to get information about Simon and she would succeed. But somehow she'd also have to come clean about the April show, and she wasn't looking forward to it.

Deep down, she'd never really sympathized with artistic deprivation. No use denying it. It was too masochistic for her highly motivated sense of gain. Anyway, she'd never had to. Emil had always been there to take up the slack. Emil had operated with a fundamental (albeit hypocritical) understanding of the plight of artists. He talked their language and they knew it. For the artists, Emil had been a kind of cynical soul mate. What did she represent to the artists? Business acumen? That was no longer enough. A serious deficiency. If she was to remain in this business, now that Emil was gone, she would have to cultivate a rapport.

Bill came up from behind her with two glasses and the bottle. She held the glass while he poured. His hand was trembling. Her throat accepted the scotch like fuel.

One of the bums suddenly stood up and exploded into a violent conversation with a hallucinatory foe.

"Great windows to get drunk by," she commented.

"Been done many times," he agreed. "You can forget just about everything here."

She didn't believe him. Bill's loft was a prison of unfulfilled dreams, and he looked anything but relaxed.

She took a big drink, trying hard not to pity him.

"Hope you don't mind me asking but . . . this is a big space. You've got a lot of expensive equipment. Where do you get the money?"

"Anywhere I can. Right now, I've got a job making light fixtures for an architectural firm uptown, which pays pretty good. Sometimes I've been forced to take roommates. Simon was here a few years back."

Bill brought up Simon! It was in this fortuitous (and not unnatural) way that she extracted a thumbnail sketch of Simon's past.

Both Bill and Simon had grown up in a small, bucolic town on Staten Island—a working-class town not particularly nurturing for boys who dreamed of becoming great artists in the Big Apple. So close, so far away. Their mutually felt isolation increased their intimacy. When they were old enough, against their parents' wishes they enrolled at Pratt to study art. In order to pay for tuition and room and board, they worked part time in a cracker factory in Brooklyn.

"Simon used to tell everybody that we were the ones who punched the little holes in the saltines, but, in truth, it wasn't that interesting. Anyway, after two years, I switched to NYU and took a few courses . . . met a different group of artists. Simon stayed with Pratt and managed to get his degree."

"But you've remained close?" Rhea asked hopefully.

"Yeah, I guess so. We don't spend a lot of time together. We're both too busy working. We keep bumping into each other. It's a small town if you're searching for the same thing . . ."

"Which is?"

Without the slightest trace of irony, Bill answered: "A pensive photograph of myself on the cover of *ARTnews*."

She nodded and took another drink. On the street, a well-heeled pedestrian hurried through the mire. Was he lost? He stepped quickly, dodged a bloated palm held out for small change and passed from view. Rhea changed the subject.

"What do you think about Simon's paintings?"

He cast a protective glance at his *own* work dangling in the background. "Simon's problem is that he's shy. And it shows in his work. It's meek. Lacks force, guts, virility. You know what I'm saying? Critics expect to see sperm on the canvas."

"Tough going if you're a woman artist," she said, making a face.

"Yes. It is."

"I was kidding, Bill. Sperm on the canvas? Sounds like something Emil would say."

"It was," he answered with a finality that made her shudder. She poured herself another drink.

"Emil didn't like Simon's work," he added.

"So I heard. Do you think Simon held a grudge against Emil?"

"No. His reaction to criticism is as meek as his work. That's what's so pathetic about him, and I've told him this, too: just because someone says your work is shit doesn't mean that it *is* shit. He just doesn't fight back . . ." Bill suddenly knitted his brow. "Why do you ask me that, anyway? You don't think that Simon had anything to do with . . ."

"Don't get huffy. I'm just playing devil's advocate. As far as the police are concerned, anybody remotely connected to the gallery is a suspect. I'm certainly high on the list. Look, I'm just trying to narrow the field."

Bill placed his glass on the windowsill. "Simon did not kill Emil."

"You're sure."

"Simon did not kill Emil," he repeated with increasing conviction.

Against her will, she realized that she believed him—in spite of Simon's painting.

The conversation had played itself out. She refilled her glass. She needed the fortification. The unhappy business of discussing Bill's sculptures remained ahead. He kept glancing back to them as if to call attention to them. If she ignored them much longer, he'd suspect . . .

"Enough of this gloomy talk," she said, forcing a smile. "Let's have a look at your work."

"I'll lower them," he said, nodding eagerly, "so that you can have a better look."

"You don't have to." She glanced at her watch. 5:15. She needed to get back before the gallery closed.

"It'll only take a second. They're meant to be exhibited on the floor. I just have them hanging to make room."

One by one, she watched him lower the steel snake sculptures. She dutifully studied them. The truth was that she preferred them overhead. The implied danger of being under all that weight was kind of alluring. Up close, though, they lost their sense of fun and left her feeling flat. Instinct warned her that *fun* was not a part of Bill's vocabulary. No use approaching his work from that direction.

"So what do you think?" he finally asked.

"Um," she murmured vaguely, keeping the brim of

the glass tight against her lips. She was stuck. She simply couldn't bring herself to lie about them.

"You don't like them," he guessed.

"It's not a matter of liking or disliking," she hedged. "It's just that . . . sales-wise, I'm not sure how I'd go about approaching it. We need to test the water."

"Well, what do you mean by testing the water?"

"I was thinking about the group show in June."

"I don't need a group show, Rhea. I need the solo in April."

She drained her glass. Dishonesty obstinately refused to come out of her mouth. "I've given the show to Al Kheel."

His face went through a sort of mental upheaval. "That son of a bitch."

"If you're going to get mad at someone," she warned, "get mad at me. It was my idea."

"What bullshit!"

"It's true—"

"Everybody knows he's hitting on you! Why else would you give him another show so soon? He's got a show right now!"

Taking the full brunt of the insult, she answered as calmly as she could: "That's not a show. It's a statement. He deserves a chance to have his work seen as it was intended. And anyway, what goes on between me and Al—"

"Intended!" he laughed derisively. "God, if I could bring myself to tell you what he intended!

"I think you already have."

She was shocked. She'd expected disappointment but not open-faced anger. "Emil may have promised you a show in April. I didn't. I came here to try to compensate for any injustice he may have . . . to be honest with you, I think a spot in a group show is fairly generous. I am running a business, Bill. I have a certain clientele. And I have to keep them in mind, I have to evaluate their tastes and—"

"Evaluate!" he pounced on the word. "In this town, a really good dealer *dictates* tastes."

"That's right, but not because some would-be artist dictates to the dealer."

"I don't know," he said, seething. "Al Kheel seems to be doing a pretty good job."

"'This is ridiculous," she said, setting the glass on a tabletop and picking up her purse. "I'm leaving. You know, you really amaze me. I've been giving you the benefit of the doubt. What proof do I have that Emil gave you a show?"

"Al heard him."

"Al heard him bad-mouthing your work, that's what Al heard! And it's not just Al. Anne was given explicit instructions by Emil that your slides were not to be construed as a part of the Orloff stable—"

"Al's turned you against me, hasn't he?"

She started to go, but he blocked her path.

"Let me tell you something about your precious Al."

"Get out of my way," she ordered.

"No, goddamn it," he grabbed her arm, "Not 'till you've heard me out."

But for a moment he said nothing. He studied her face as if trying to recapture some lost train of thought. The violence with which he had suddenly grabbed her arm and the proximity of his face to hers was unnerving. His breath smelled like iron.

"It was on Monday," he began. "While I was painting the walls. Now I remember. Al and I got into the message he was painting on the wall. I told him I thought the installation was better off without it. I told him the 'fire into gold' was too corny and he turned around to me and, as cool as ice, he said, 'This is how Emil and I planned it.' I just stood there for a minute. At first I thought he was joking. But he wasn't. He was dead serious and . . . so preoccupied with himself that I'm sure he had no idea what his statement implied. Don't you get it? He was saying that he and Emil . . ."

He let go of her arm. She didn't move.

"Why didn't you say something about this before?"

"To who? To you? Al's main squeeze? That would have done a lot of good!"

"Then why not the police?"

"I thought of that, believe me. But it's not exactly prima facie evidence, is it? And his word against mine. All he had to do was to say it was a bad joke."

"Maybe it was."

"Maybe it wasn't. Not that you'll ever believe that."

"I've got to go."

"What are you going to do?"

"I don't know. I . . ."

The last ray of hope drained from her face. She just stood there, helpless and mute. Her head was spinning from too much booze without any food and the shock of his sudden outburst.

"I'll tell you what you're going to do," he sneered. "Nothing. Nothing at all."

He turned away from her in disgust. Reaching for a rope hanging from the rafters, he started to hoist up one end of a sculpture. Watching the retreat of the silver snake made her feel inexplicably sad.

"You still have a spot in the June show if you want."

"I don't need handouts." He stopped and laughed. "You hear that? Bill Whitehead doesn't need handouts. Pretty funny. Maybe I should go back to school. Maybe they have a course on how to fuck gallery owners . . ."

She ran down the blackened stairwell as fast as she could.

Twenty-two

It was 5:55.

Like the night before, the gallery was far too crowded for the people to actually see the installation. It didn't seem to matter. It was a scene in which people felt moved to linger in spite of (or perhaps partly because of) the violent interlacing of the Shostokovich string quartet.

Rhea stormed into JAN. The phones were on hold, blinking off and on like warning signals. Anne, short fuse incarnate, was rifling through a stack of papers, brushing a damp strand of hair away from her forehead.

"Is the mailing list printed out?" Rhea asked.

"It's on your desk," Anne snapped without bothering to look up.

Felix came rushing in. "Rhea! thank God you're back. It's like a circus out there."

"It doesn't seem to be getting you down. Do you know some of these people?"

"I'd like to. Lots of good-looking women on the floor."

"I'm so relieved that your job keeps you close to the action. So what's the general consensus out there?"

"That it's scandalously legit. Though lots of people

are disappointed Kheel's not here. I think they would like to see him in a loincloth, nailed to a cross, martyr fashion—"

"That might be arranged. Turn off that goddamn music. It's five minutes to closing time."

Rhea thundered back into the throng, pushed her way through to the opposite end, grabbed the main light switch and flipped it off and on as if she were raiding the place. Reluctantly, people got the message and began to funnel out onto the sidewalk. When the last group, her staff, had been driven out, she closed the door.

She went to the bathroom, drained the dregs of the coffee machine into a mug and retreated to her office. The mailing list on top of her desk was as thick as a phone book. Shored up with the bitter coffee, she set to work— poring through the names, hoping against hope that one name would magically pop out from the page, announcing itself as the owner of the missing fingerprints.

After twenty minutes of nonproductive searching, she felt her will breaking down. She stopped and lit a cigarette. Kheel the martyr? Or murderer in mixed media? How was she going to confront Al with Bill Whitehead's accusation?

Suddenly . . .

She looked up, she gasped, her body, in an involuntary reflex, nearly jerked off the seat. Standing in the doorway was a figure quietly watching her.

"Jesus Christ, Emil! You nearly scared me to death! How did you get in here anyway. I thought I'd locked the door."

"You must have forgotten," he said, laughing.

"What's so funny?"

"You called me Emil."

She gulped. "No I didn't."

"Yes," Tennyson insisted, "you did."

She rummaged through her head and folded under the weight of the truth. No satirical comebacks left in the arsenal. She returned her attention to the mailing list, fighting back tears.

"You were supposed to meet me at your place at six-thirty, remember? We had a date."

"Was I? I forgot," she said, turning a page.

"What are you pretending to read?"

"I've somehow missed a name, a name that's got to be here, a name I know. John, I *know* the owner of the missing fingerprints. I just can't bring it up into the light. There's all these clues rushing around, clamoring for my attention. But if I stop to pay attention, the clues suddenly go mute. It's maddening. And your looks don't help matters. It's only natural that I would . . . if you didn't look so much like Emil . . ."

"Oh, it's my fault, is it? Would plastic surgery make you happy?"

"Maybe if I went away for a few days . . ."

"No way." The humor had left his voice.

"But don't you see, I'm too close to all of it. If I removed myself from . . . went somewhere that was completely different . . . anywhere . . ."

"You're still officially a suspect," he reminded her.

"Wait and watch . . . myself go crazy. That's your prescription."

"It's not a bad one, either. This is no time to do anything foolish. You've got to promise me that you won't try to get away. It could only hurt your position."

"My position is a joke anyway." She lit another cigarette. "Have you ever read how they catch pythons in India? They drive stakes into the ground, about eight inches apart, to form a large circle. In the middle of the circle they drive another stake, to which they tether a kid goat. The python slithers in, gulps the kid, and the swallowed protrusion prevents the snake from getting back out. Very safe maneuver, unless you happen to be the kid. *That's* my vaulted position."

She took a deep breath and laughed.

"It's odd. I really am beginning to feel like the victim. I think the anonymous phone calls are getting to me. I'm beginning to think defensively. And it seems to me that the best defense is to take action, to flush out the son of a bitch before he gets me. Do you think that's paranoid?"

"You've got to promise me that you won't do anything rash."

"Goddamn it, I *am* rash. That's who I am."

"My ex likes to say that, once a person defines himself, he becomes a parody of himself."

"And I like to say that, in real life, philosophical application is not particularly cost-effective. In any case, all afternoon I've been as rash as I could possibly be and it's led to some very interesting information. Make yourself comfortable and I'll tell you about it."

She informed him that Simon had had his own key made, that she had verified it with the hardware store. Then she related how her curiosity had led her to Simon's only known friend, Bill Whitehead, which had led to her dousing Bill's hopes for a show in April, which, in turn, had led to Bill pointing the finger at Al.

"Is that a busy afternoon or what?" she concluded. "Oh, and there's one other thing."

She ushered him out to the trap door and, with his help, lifted the slot out of the hole.

"Right down there," she said, pointing, "was where I found the bottle of cognac."

Tennyson shook his head in astonishment. "It's amazing that none of my people noticed this."

"No one ever does," Rhea said. "It was designed *not* to be noticed. I don't know what it means, but . . . it makes Friday night somehow more real. Don't you agree?"

"Yes, I do." he answered, still peering down the hole. "Did Emil always have brandy around?"

"Always."

"Where did he keep it?"

"Usually in the cabinet under the sink in the bathroom. Occasionally in a desk drawer."

"Is there any brandy in the cabinet now?"

"Yes."

"Stay right here," he said.

He went into the bathroom and came back out with a bottle in his hand. He turned toward the coffin and disappeared down the steps. Lights went on downstairs, and a few seconds later he was staring up at her from the storeroom.

"Now," he called up. "Where was the bottle?"

"Over this way a little, right next to that bin. There."

He put the bottle on the floor, looked up at her and then looked all around the storeroom.

"I can tell you right now, John," she said, "there is no reason in the world for Emil to have been loitering where you're standing . . . unless this slot was opened."

He looked up and smiled. "Most interesting."

She shuddered. She begged the Emil look-alike to come back up.

They replaced the false floor.

"So what can you conclude from this? It's creepy, we know that. But what's the point that we're missing?"

He shrugged. "It's too . . . tenuous to call even circumstantial, but . . . I go for it. Something was going on here that included a bit of teamwork. The bottle on the floor: it makes me think that everything was going as planned, almost methodical, casual even."

"Casual," Rhea echoed. She turned pale and felt overcome by dizziness. She grabbed Tennyson's arm.

"What's wrong?"

"There's nothing in my stomach. I haven't eaten anything all day." She sank to the floor. "And there's this new development about Al's involvement."

"Unverified involvement," he corrected her.

"I thought you'd be elated at such news," she complained. "Bill has clearly pointed the finger at Al. Isn't that what you've been waiting for?"

He made a noncommittal gesture and sat down beside her.

"Let me get this straight. Al told Bill that he and Emil had planned the trashing of the show?"

"That's right."

"And Bill claims Emil promised him a show next April?"

"Yes, and, unfortunately, it's probably true."

"Why, if Emil had no intention of making good on the promise?"

"For the sheer cruelty of it. Toward the end Emil was so wretched he was capable of—"

"Let me ask you this," John interrupted. "At what point did Bill tell you this?"

"I don't follow."

"Well, this April show he was hoping for—you told him that he wasn't going to get it, that you'd given the slot to Al, right?"

"Right."

"So . . . did he accuse Al before you broke the bad news to him or after?"

"After. That's why he got so mad. Otherwise, I doubt that he would have mentioned it at all."

"That Al had pulled the rug, so to speak, from under him."

"Yes, but I explained to him that it wasn't Al's idea. It was mine."

Tennyson seemed unimpressed. "Bill's an artist. He's not in competition with Rhea Buerklin. He's in competition with other artists. From what you tell me, Bill's floundering with a career that's never quite taken off. At last his big break comes into view. He's had enough of painting walls for *other* artists' shows. Now he's going to get his own show. Then, suddenly, he finds out that Al Kheel has nudged him out of the picture. He explodes. On the spur of the moment, he concocts a story that implicates his enemy. What could be more plausible?"

"You're defending Al?" she cried.

"You're accusing him? That's just as surprising," he retorted. "Look, all I'm saying is that jealousy can make a man do desperate things. You've got to see it from Bill's standpoint. Al gets everything he wants from the beautiful woman: the show, the publicity, the career and the beautiful woman. And what's Bill get? A double kick in the ass by Al and the beautiful woman."

"What's all this 'beautiful' crap. Let's get something straight. I'm not Al's woman, if that's what you're implying, I'm not beautiful and—"

"Behind all the fucks and shits and pisses, there's a *very* beautiful woman."

"Irrelevant," she said overruling the compliment. "Bill's interested in me because of what I can do for his career."

"And now you fear that Al has used you like Bill would like to use you, is that it? Is that why you're now denouncing Al?"

"I'm not denouncing anyone. I'm just relating to you what Bill told me."

"With a complete lack of remorse," John observed. "Tell me the truth, Rhea. What do you feel for Al?"

"I . . . don't know. It's like I don't feel anything at this moment. Like I've deployed all my sensations to the task of finding Emil's murderer."

"You're objectivity is remarkable."

"In other words, I'm a coldhearted bitch. What do you care?"

Tennyson sighed and stood up. "The fact remains that it's Bill's word against Al's. And Bill had every reason to want to strike out at Al. There's no way I can move on this except to wait and watch, which is exactly what you're going to do. If you had any notion of confronting Al with Bill's accusation, get it out of your head. Promise me."

"I promise."

Tennyson looked skeptical. She'd promised a little too quickly. He changed the subject. "I've been doing a little research on Véra Vertbois. Last month, she and her husband filed for bankruptcy."

"That doesn't surprise me. She told me she was having problems."

"The possibility of fratricide can't be excluded."

"You mean you think she hired someone?"

"Well, when I questioned her at the Carlyle she didn't give the impression of being bereaved."

Rhea shook her head. "Véra's capable of murder. But she's not capable of thinking up the trashing of the show. Damn it, let's narrow down the list."

"Impossible, as long as there's a question of unidentified fingerprints. And why would Simon want a key?"

"I don't know."

"And why did the murderer take Emil's keys but not his billfold?"

"I don't know," she repeated miserably. "In fact, I'd forgotten all about that. The enema bag."

Tennyson stopped for a moment before asking: "What about the enema bag?"

"Something just struck me. If Emil contributed anything to the trashing of the show, it would have been that enema bag. The gesture is so unnecessarily repulsive, so gratuitous. It would be just like him to show off how depraved he could be."

Tennyson's eyes widened. "Are you suggesting that Emil envisioned his own murder as part of the installation?"

"Am I? Oh god, I don't know, I don't know. No, John. That's getting way out there—even for Emil." Then she laughed. *"Nature morte."*

"What's that mean?"

"It's the French phrase for 'still life.' *Mort* means 'dead person,' 'corpse.' Emil almost died from drugs . . .

what *about* the drug connection, John? You said you thought it was important."

He nodded. "Narcotics is working on that right now. It may be our best lead so far. There were three dime bags of heroin found on the body. That indicates a street dealer. He wasn't buying in large quantities."

"How does that help us?"

"Dealers who peddle small quantities use the same kind of wax paper packets, but most of them have trademarks stamped on the outside. It's a kind of underground advertising used all over town. One popular brand right now is called Dinosaur because it has a dinosaur stamped on it. In Emil's case, the packets had Air Mail stamped on them. If you go to Avenue A to score, you don't ask for a pusher's name, you ask for Air Mail. If we can find the dealer who pushes Air Mail—and we can, we will—we've either got Emil's connection or someone who knows Emil's connection."

"Do you think that person could be Al?"

"It's more likely to be someone who lives in New York."

She agreed. "Is the pusher also the owner of the mysterious fingerprints?"

"Possibly. I would like to think probably."

"And the anonymous phone caller—are they all the same guy?"

"I would like to think so."

"And if Al is at the bottom of all this," she continued, "then isn't it likely that Al and our mysterious personage are friends?"

John nodded thoughtfully. "There's a definite hook to that question. The caller, at least the first time when I answered, thought I was Al. I'd bet my life on it. The question is, why would this guy have an ax to grind with Al if he didn't know him? So who are Al's friends?"

"That shouldn't be too difficult to figure out. Hell, Jamie, his wife, left because he wasn't social enough. He thrives in isolation. There's his son. There's his ghost-father, HoHo, who is assumed to be dead. The only other person that I've seen him friendly with was that guy Sachetti."

"Who's Sachetti?" John asked with an eager look.

"You met him. He was that cop up in Redding."

"Great," John said with a smirk. "I'll check up on him. Of course, if he's a cop, his fingerprints would be on record. So he couldn't be the man who was here the night of Emil's murder."

"Let's get out of here," Rhea said, sighing. "I'm starved."

"One more question before we go," he said as he stopped her. "Why did you buy a man's suit this afternoon?"

Rhea laughed. "So your men checked up on that, did they? Halloween is just around the corner. I'm going as a businessman."

John stared at the floor and sighed.

"Don't buy that, hunh? OK." She walked back into JAN and turned off lights. When she returned she said, "What if I told you I don't know why? Maybe it was just an instinctive purchase. Maybe I literally want to be in Emil's shoes for a while. Or maybe I just like dressing up like a man."

"A parody of yourself?"

Dinner, at a local restaurant, was a glum affair. She was all talked out. She refused a drink although she would have killed for one. People kept coming over to the table and congratulating her on the installation, which only worsened her mood. When the plates had been removed, she insisted upon paying for her half of the check. If she intended to alienate him, she was doing a good job.

John walked her home in silence. He didn't seem to expect to be invited up. He didn't ask.

"Don't say anything to Al about your visit to Bill's loft," he reminded her and walked off.

When she opened her apartment door, the telephone was ringing. It was Catherine saying that she would come back to work, starting tomorrow morning. Rhea didn't know whether to weep or to rub her palms together. In any case it helped to lift her mood. She picked up Crunch's bowl. "Quit whining. I didn't have anything to eat all day either."

She looked at her watch. At least she hadn't missed all of the ball game.

She propped Simon's painting on top of the TV and turned on the set. Where was all this anger toward John coming from? Because he called her beautiful? Because he looked like Emil? She was too old, too experienced to be jittery around a fucking man.

To hell with good intentions: she got up and fixed herself a drink. She returned to the TV and tried to catch up with the game.

Why couldn't everybody be smooth between the legs . . . like Kewpie-dolls?

As she watched the Mets (who smashed the Montreal Expos 10 to 0) and drank her scotch, her anger mellowed into a benumbed feeling of recklessness. The case was going everywhere and nowhere at the same time. What difference did it really make what she did or didn't do? Parody of herself, indeed. She laughed out loud. Men or no men, after a six-day submersion into murky waters, she was about to flee the mud. Tennyson would be pissed.

God, what a great game!

The St. Louis Cardinals held onto a one-and-a-half-game lead in the division but, by God, the Mets were still playing ball. And so was she. She'd lost a key team player but now, miraculously, Catherine was coming back to the dugout.

She switched off the set. She picked up the mailing

list and reread the names. But this time with a newly arrived concentration. Methodical, casual . . .

If she had to *memorize* the mailing list, she would. If it took a thousand readings, she wouldn't care. She would inundate her every thought with those names until the missing one popped (compressed and perfectly round) out of the pitcher's glove over to her bat and bam! Out of the ball park.

She went through the apartment turning off lights. She took her dog and her mysterious fingerprints and climbed into bed. She fell asleep with the soothing, vengeful thought that her new suit would be ready by tomorrow afternoon.

Twenty-three

Thursday morning, September 17. Rhea woke up to a cloudy day. She looked over to her phone. The man with the hoarse ghost voice hadn't called her. Why? She felt slightly disappointed. Was he interested only in spooking Al?

She reached over and pulled open the drawer of her bedside table. She riffled through the contents until she located her passport. She patted it for a moment, then put it back in the drawer. She got up and cooked breakfast.

Ideas persisted.

The strongest link was Emil's drug connection. Mysterious fingerprints, mysterious pusher . . . events were wheeling into an ever tighter circle of probability that the pusher *was* the owner of the fingerprints.

Problem: the fingerprints hadn't been found in Emil's apartment. Emil's pusher didn't do house calls. And if he didn't do house calls, where did he connect with Emil? The obvious location would be the gallery.

Deeper problem: what was the connection between the drugs and the devastation of Al's show?

She emerged on the slatternly sidewalk of Greene

Street. She looked up at the sky. Gray and glowering. The weather could definitely work to her advantage, she thought to herself.

She picked up the morning paper before she went to the gallery. When she got into her office, the first thing she checked in the *Times* was the weather report. The forecast was for rain, becoming heavy by tomorrow. She carefully studied the temperatures and precipitation (in the last twenty-four hours) of foreign cities.

Catherine came in at eleven. Rhea put down the paper, shook her hand, closed the door to her office and asked Catherine to sit down. Without any preamble, Rhea told Catherine everything she and the police had discovered about the case— except for Bill's allegations. The imparted information, Rhea realized, helped to downgrade the tension between them. With each additional detail, their mutual embarrassment decreased.

"There's several reasons why I've told you all of this. First, you deserve to know it. Second, there has to be absolute openness if our renewed proximity is going to be profitable. Third, and most important, I want you to understand how crucial it is that we find out who was supplying Emil with drugs. Catherine, if we can't get to the bottom of it, this case will never be resolved."

"You've suspected me of knowing something," Catherine said simply.

"About the drugs, yes," Rhea answered. "Though I have never suspected you of any intentional wrongdoing . . . it seems likely that you would have been in a position to . . . damn it, Catherine, I wouldn't be sitting here talking to you if I didn't believe you wanted to know what happened to Emil as much, if not more, as anyone else. It's clear that you loved him."

"Did you love Emil?"
"No, I didn't."
"Never?"
"Never."

"But you knew he loved you, didn't you, Rhea?"

Rhea took a deep breath. "When it come to men, I'm shit. Does that answer your question?"

Catherine nodded vigorously as if to shake away the tears that suddenly flooded her eyes.

"Now come on Catherine, don't start this again. It's just too late for personal regret or guilt or any of the rest of it. The only thing that's relevant is . . . who killed Emil?"

Catherine sniffed and brushed away her tears. Finally she said: "You'd better call your detective friend and tell him to come by. There's no need to repeat myself, is there?"

Thirty minutes later Tennyson, Rhea, and Catherine were enconced in her office with the door shut. The room was blue with smoke.

"Emil first started coming on last winter," Catherine began. "I wasn't doing coke all the time or anything like that. But whenever I had some money, I'd spend it on a gram. One evening around closing time . . . it was in February, I remember because it was snowing outside . . . I was in the bathroom, making a line of coke by the sink and I'd forgotten to lock the door. Emil came in, saw what I was doing, smiled, closed the door, locked it and said, 'Let me try it.' I drew him up a line. I was very nervous. Anyway, he snorted it and made a horrible face . . . said it was the worse stuff he'd ever put up his nose. Then he reached into the side pocket of his coat and said, 'Try mine.'

"That was the beginning. After work, we went over to his loft and stayed up all night doing his coke. I was thrilled. He'd barely even looked at me before that night and suddenly . . . he was very funny, and he made me feel like I was the only person in the world. I was in heaven. He was so attractive . . . anyway, that was the beginning. I wasn't supplying him. He was supplying me."

"That's when you became lovers," Tennyson said.

"Yes. I mean, I never fooled myself into believing that it was any kind of grand passion or anything."

"You said he was supplying you. Did there come a point in time when that changed?"

"In a way, yes. You have to understand that I'd never been heavy into coke before. For one thing, I'd never had the money. But after a month or two . . . he had this endless supply and he was very generous.

"One night he and Rhea had a dinner to go to uptown—"

"When was this?" Tennyson interrupted.

"Oh . . . early spring. April sometime."

"Go on."

"He was just about out of coke, he said, and he asked me to do him a favor and hang out at his apartment that night. He said that there would be a man coming with a package and all I would have to do would be to hand the man an envelope of money."

"And you did it for him."

"I would have done anything for him."

"Who was the man?"

"His drug dealer."

"Yes, but what was his name?"

"Wilson. Teddy Wilson."

"Do you know where he lives?"

Catherine closed her eyes and nodded. "Riker's Island," she said.

"He's in prison. Now?"

She nodded again. "He got busted in May. It was in another part of town. Emil wasn't in any way incriminated but he was suddenly without a connection."

"You say this Teddy Wilson is on Riker's. His trial couldn't have come up this soon. He didn't get out on bail?"

"He did but they caught him trying to leave the country, so they put him back in without bail."

"I see. So what did Emil do then?"

"He started making trips to Avenue A on his own. I didn't like it and by that time I was pretty shook up about everything anyway . . . Wilson getting busted, and I was getting pretty strung out myself. I thought it was a good time to put on the brakes, you know? It was stupid for a man in his position to be jeopardizing everything he had by going over to Avenue A. We started arguing about it.

"And then one night he scored some heroin and . . . I blew up. I told him I'd had enough and that he'd have to choose between the drugs and me."

"And what did he say."

"He said, 'That's easy . . . I'll take the drugs.'"

"Sounds like Emil," Rhea interjected.

Tennyson admonished Rhea with a look. He turned back to Catherine. "What happened after that?"

"I saw him a few times after that. But it was over."

"Was he still going down to Avenue A?"

"No. He'd made another connection by then."

"Who?"

"I don't know who. He wouldn't tell me."

"Then how do you know?"

"The last night I was with him . . . that was in May . . . we were at his apartment and he got a phone call. 'No, not here,' I heard him say. 'I'll meet you at the gallery in twenty minutes.' He hung up and kind of leered at me. He put his finger to one nostril and played like he was sniffing up, you know? Then he told me he had to go attend to some very important business. I walked down with him. He asked me if I wanted to go to the gallery with him and I said no. And that was it."

"You never went over to the apartment again?"

"He never asked me. Summer was coming on. In June and July, he spent most of his time at his place in the Hamptons. And then the gallery was closed for the month of August and the first of September. And a few weeks ago, when we reopened the gallery, I was shocked by his appearance. He'd obviously been doing a lot, way too much, he looked ten years older. A few days before Al Kheel's opening I tried to talk to him privately, just for a minute. He told me to fuck off."

Tennyson took a deep breath. He turned to Rhea. "This change for the worse in Emil's appearance: didn't you notice?"

"Yeah, I noticed," Rhea said, shrugging. "Who couldn't notice?"

"You didn't say anything to him?"

"It would have been a waste of time. I'd long since resigned myself to the fact that he would do whatever he wanted to do and that harping would only make him worse. I had a business to attend to. I didn't have time for Emil. My only hope was that he would stay away and . . . at least on that level, he was very accommodating."

"So who was his new connection?" He turned back to Catherine. "Did you ever see him take anybody into the gallery, Felix or Simon or Anne? Do you remember him having any private conversations with any of the staff?"

"You mean, since we've reopened this month? No. He was only here that I know of two or three times—"

"And those were the briefest of appearances," Rhea interrupted.

After Catherine returned to JAN, Tennyson closed the door and asked Rhea about the summer vacation.

"Did you ever go out there?"

"Yes, the first weekend of August. I spent the night out there. There were some papers to be signed."

"How was he then?"

"Normal . . . that is to say fucked up. We were supposed to go to a party that night, some important clients who had a house out there. Emil passed out around eight and I ended up going to the party without him."

"What did you do for the rest of the holidays?"

"I rented a chalet in Villiers, Switzerland, for three weeks. It's just above Montreux. I didn't do anything. I read, visited a few friends . . . John, what about Inez? She was out there in the Hamptons all that time with him. Did she talk about any visitors?"

Tennyson shook his head. "He didn't have any overnight guests, according to her. Some day visitors from people who have places out there. She said he came into the city twice. I've checked the dates. Both times he withdrew twenty-five hundred dollars from his bank."

"Drugs."

"I would imagine so."

"Al could have been supplying him."

He nodded. "I talked to Bill," he said. "Why didn't you tell me he and Simon went to Pratt?"

"Is that important?"

"Well, that's where Gabby, my ex, teaches. She remembers Bill quite clearly. She wasn't crazy about his work. She called him a one-idea artist, but she said he was diligent and that he never missed a class. As for Simon . . ."

"Yes?"

"She says she remembers him precisely because he was so forgettable, so *invisible*, I think was her word."

Rhea spent the afternoon going over the mailing list. She wasn't making any headway and yet she wouldn't let go of the names. More than ever, she was certain the name was hiding.

Anne came in around four with the package from Giorgio Armani's and a stack of checks to sign. Going through the checks, Rhea was reminded of how much it cost to maintain the gallery on a monthly basis and how little her present show was going to reap, at least in the short term.

As she was signing the employees' paychecks she asked Anne, "How's Catherine doing?"

"Happy to be back at work, I think."

After Anne left, Rhea opened the large package, took out the clothes and placed them in a plain brown shopping bag she had brought to the gallery that morning for this specific purpose. As she was bending over, stuffing in the last item, she had a sharp physical pain in her midriff. It was as if someone inside her had grabbed hold of her stomach and had squeezed it with all his might.

Emil, no doubt. He was trying to tell her something.

The name she had been searching for . . . it had come right by her and, once again, she'd failed to recognize it.

Twenty-four

It was past ten, Thursday night, and so intent had she been poring over the mailing and guest lists, she'd missed most of the Mets game. She'd just turned on the TV when the phone rang.

"Hello?"

"Did you know that there is an exchange for all things, just as there are goods into—"

"You require a lot of attention, don't you? Still pushing the Air Mail heroin?"

The caller hung up.

She looked out the window. It was beginning to rain again. The phone rang.

"Hello?"

"Did you know that—"

"Change the record, would you? Look, can I get back to you on this?"

Rhea slammed the receiver into the cradle of the phone. Ten minutes later it rang again.

"Listen, motherfucker—"

"It's me." Tennyson laughed. "I thought we agreed that you would try to *keep* him on the phone."

"I did try."

"That's not the way my men reported it."

"I couldn't help it. He's a pest. He broke my concentration. I'll try to do better next time."

"So will he, I'd imagine," Tennyson responded. "He's not likely to enjoy being swatted like a cockroach. And I think you'd do well to remember he's not just a pest."

"Yes, Your Inspectorship. I get the message. You know, I'm getting so close to figuring out who it is, John. I feel it in my bones. I've been close all day to coming up with a name. This afternoon especially."

"What were you doing this afternoon?"

"Paying bills, writing checks. I almost had it and then . . ."

"Did you go back over the checks? Try to retrace your steps?"

"Yes, but I'd already lost it. How about on your end? Any new developments?"

"Catherine called Joan McCabe tonight and backed out of the whole deal."

"I'll be damned. How do you know?"

"Just do. Want some company?"

"Now? No thanks."

"Well, if he calls again—"

"Yeah, yeah, I know. I'll listen with rapt attention. Good night, John."

"Good night."

She watched the end of the Mets game, which was no less aggravating than her futile attempt to find the missing name. They lost 4 to 1.

She looked out her window. The gutters down on the corner of Greene and Spring were filling with rain. She promised herself that, come morning, she would read the lists one more time and, if nothing came of it, she would go ahead with her plan.

The next morning Rhea got up at six and read the lists with no success.

She showered and dressed as usual. Then she made a thorough search of her closet. She went through every coat pocket, every purse. She came up with $121.38. In an old shoe box, she found assorted foreign currency. In French francs, she came up with the equivalent of around forty dollars. She stuffed this into her valise along with her passport, her lists, a change of underwear and essential toiletries. She grabbed her umbrella and went out into the pouring rain.

She walked to the corner of Spring and West Broadway and stopped at a public telephone. She pulled a piece of paper out of her pocket. She dialed the number for Air France reservations and got a seat on the Concorde leaving Kennedy at one that afternoon. She went to the bank and withdrew four hundred dollars—not as much as she needed but she was afraid of drawing attention to herself—if need be, she could get more at the Paris branch of American Express.

She opened the gallery at 10:00. Felix arrived at 10:30. She gave him one of the keys to the gallery. "Don't let this out of your possession. When Simon gets here, I'd like you two to concentrate on cleaning the downstairs. It's a mess and we need the space."

"What about the people coming in?"

"I'll keep an eye on things up here . . . at least until noon. It shouldn't be crowded until then."

By 11:15, she had everyone busy. Simon and Felix were downstairs. Anne and Catherine were catching up on overdue paperwork. The gallery itself had a moderate number of people tracking in water, shaking their umbrellas and milling about.

She slipped into the bathroom, locked the door, opened the cabinet under the sink, and pulled out her bag of men's clothing. It took her ten minutes to get dressed—longer than she had expected. She made a proper mess of the tie and had particular trouble with the men's buttons, which buttoned from the wrong side.

She dumped the contents of her purse and the lists into her briefcase, threw her purse and sloughed women's clothes back into the cabinet, and peeked out the door. None of her staff was to be seen. She opened up her umbrella, keeping it close down to her head, and walked out the front door.

It was raining even harder than before. She turned right and ducked into Fanelli's. She swept past the bar and stepped into the old-fashioned telephone booth. She called the gallery. Catherine answered.

"Hi, it's me. I just stepped out for some cigarettes but I think I'm going to go uptown from here. Tell the guys to come back up from the basement."

"When will you be back?"

"It depends. Probably by three but don't worry if I don't get back at all today. I've got a million things to take care of uptown. I'll call you later."

"You're the boss."

You're goddamn right I am, she thought as she hung up. She darted back outside, half ran to the corner of Broadway and caught a cab heading downtown.

"Kennedy," she called from the back seat. "Air France, and as quickly as you can."

It wasn't until after she had her boarding pass that she took the time to look at herself in the windows overlooking the airfield, which, due to the leaden sky, worked as translucent mirrors. Up close she didn't pass as a man but the suit was a good fit, and with an umbrella . . .

She boarded the Concorde, worked her way back to the smoking section, and took her window seat. She could never get used to how cramped the Concorde was. Her window wasn't much bigger than a postcard.

She closed her eyes and smiled. Never had she felt such exhilaration. It was like being a character in a spy novel. In spite of the rain, the Concorde left on schedule: 1:00 straight up. It roared down the runway with an intoxicating velocity that threw her back against her seat.

Tennyson didn't want her to set off any alarms around Al and Simon. What better way to ensure that than to put on ocean between them?

The jet landed at De Gaulle Airport at 10:30 P.M. local time, fifteen minutes ahead of schedule. Since she had no luggage, it didn't take her long to get through customs.

She called the gallery. It would be just about closing time there. Catherine answered. "Where are you?" she asked. "You sound like you're in a tin can."

"Must be a bad connection. Listen, something's come up. I'm not going to get back today. Is everything all right?"

"The gallery's been packed all day. Mr. Tennyson has been asking for you."

"Tell him I'll be back Sunday."

"Sunday! Where are you?"

"Someplace where I hope to get my thoughts together. I trust you guys can hold down the fort for that long. Felix has a key now. He can open up for you guys."

"What about Crunch?"

Rhea had forgotten about the dog. "Christ . . ."

"I could take him home with me," Catherine offered.

"Catherine, I am so glad you're back."

"Me too."

By 11:00 she was in a black taxi, whizzing through the industrial wasteland that surrounds Paris.

One weak point in her getaway was that she hadn't been able to secure a hotel reservation—never an easy last-minute thing to do in Paris in the fall. But she wouldn't worry about it. It was a beautiful warm September night, the outdoor café would be packed . . .

She got out at rue de Seine and sat down at a tiny table perched in front of La Palette, a favorite outdoor café for artists, French and expatriate alike. Jean-François, the maître d'hôtel, immediately recognized her, came over and bussed her on both cheeks.

"Madame Buerklin! What a wonderful surprise. What brings you to town?"

She picked up her briefcase and, thinking of the lists within, answered, "Just came to catch up on my reading."

"*Superbe*. Francine-Marie! A whiskey for Madame, quickly! And how's everything in New York?"

Good, she thought. No one knows about it over here. She made several pleasantries without alluding to Emil and asked, "Is Peter still the concierge at the Hôtel Pont Royal? The fact is, I just got in and I don't have a place to stay."

"Of course he is! He'll be delighted. I'll see to it immediately."

The girl brought her scotch and she relaxed a little. She made a quick search of the surrounding tables to see if she knew anyone. Some tables away, she thought she recognized Francis Bacon's profile but she couldn't be sure. He'd met her once but it was highly unlikely that he would remember her. She relaxed. The streets were alive with people promenading down the narrow sidewalks. On the other side of the street a fire-breather was performing. In the distance an accordion could be heard—the whole Parisian nine yards—and to be suddenly transported smack-dab into the middle of it was a magical elixir.

An odd but plausible possibility suddenly punctured the lilting surroundings. All along, she'd been castigating *herself* for failing to identify the missing name. Perhaps that was the wrong approach. What made her think that the police were any more capable than she? What if they, too, were guilty of an obvious oversight?

By nine-thirty the next morning she had had breakfast in her room, and was back in her man's suit.

She went down to the lobby. Peter, behind the tall concierge's desk, beamed as she approached. For years she had meant to ask him why he was called Peter instead of Pierre, but she always checked her impulse. For some reason, his genuine delight at seeing her made her forget to ask.

"Good morning, Peter. Is everything ready?"

"But of course!"

He produced a knapsack, patted it, and rattled off the contents: "Two bottles of Pouilly-Fumé, a corkscrew, apples, bleu de Bresse, Camembert and bread, just as Madame ordered. Do you wish a taxi?"

"Thank you, that won't be necessary."

She stuffed her lists in the side pocket of her knapsack, put her arms through the loops and hefted it up on her back. She went through the revolving doors of the Hôtel Pont Royal into a glorious morning. She walked up the rue de Bac, turned left at the river, bypassed the Musée D'Orsay and went down the steps to the train station. Five minutes later she was on a train headed for Versailles.

The tour buses and crowds were already very much in evidence by the time she got to the palace. She avoided all of this by darting through the right entrance and heading straight for the gardens in the back. With the palace now behind her, and most of the people as well, she breathed more easily. She paused for a moment at the top of the park and took in the spectacular view of the Grandes Eaux and the Grand Canal, which almost disappeared into the horizon.

She skipped down the right flight of crescentic stairs and then continued her descent, her new shoes crunching over the finely raked gravel.

To the right of Neptune's fountain, she rented a bicycle. It was an old-fashioned one, vaguely blue with a beaten-up wire basket attached to the front of the handlebars. But she was enchanted with it, especially with the silver bell she could ring by flipping her thumb against the lever. She lowered her knapsack into the basket and started pedaling around the Grand Canal.

Heading away from the palace the breeze was behind her, but as she rounded the far end some fifteen minutes later, the wind blowing in her face reminded her how out of shape she had become in the last week. She didn't stop to rest. She pedaled on, rejoicing in her heavy breathing.

You'd make a good midwife, Tennyson had told her. But she didn't feel like a midwife. *She* was the one in labor, and the time had almost arrived.

Having circumvented the Grand Canal, she pedaled to the right—passed both Trianons, passed the Temple of Venus, rode around the vicinity of Marie Antoinette's bogus but charming "hamlet" and pulled over to the base of an ancient plane tree. There was a thick carpet of grass. She half fell off her bike and landed in the grass, trying to catch her breath. She was sweating through her shirt. She peeled off her jacket. Minutes passed. She began to breathe with a slower regularity. The vast quiet all around her began to dominate and soothe her exhaustion.

She uncorked a bottle of wine and took a deep drink, savoring its smoky-spicy flavor.

She extracted her lists. With her back against the plane trunk, her legs wide apart, her knees up so that she could use her thighs as a kind of lap desk, she read the lists.

She finished the first bottle of wine and opened the second one. She gazed at the deep foliage above her, rustling against the sky. Even though she had caught her breath, the wine was making her perspire more than ever. The hair around her temples was soaking wet.

She put the lists over to the side in the grass. She

rubbed her kneecaps and closed her eyes. Think! Make it come. Someone who, because of some fluke of omission, the police had failed to fingerprint. Someone whose name, not unlike the concierge's, was questionable but continually overlooked.

She imagined a long-ago Rhea, a faraway Rhea (could it have only been yesterday?) sequestered behind a desk, entrenched in the confusion of an unsolved murder, in the heart of an ugly city, paying bills, signing checks . . .

Think, goddamn it, push! Someone who, for some reason, she and the police had regarded as a second-rate suspect and therefore had failed to take seriously.

Anne's paycheck, Simon's check, Felix's check, Catherine's check, Bill's check for helping with the installation . . .

Push! It's coming out . . . Someone who, although hidden from view, didn't mind risking fingerprints . . . who perhaps had an uncontrollable *need* to call attention to himself. Someone who felt the need to boast, whose vanity and wounded pride would provoke further destruction, like the trashing of Al's studio . . . someone whose frustrated attempts to assert himself, to get attention could propel him into a series of anonymous phone calls . . .

Someone who, for some reason, the police had failed to fingerprint.

Bill Whitehead: Simon's friend.

He'd painted the gallery walls two days *after* the fingerprinting. The police had overlooked him just as she had. He hadn't been invited to the reopening, so he couldn't be fingerprinted there. He was an ambitious but humiliated artist. He lived on the Lower East Side, which would have made him a handy drug connection for Emil. The gallery used him as an extra employee three, maybe four times a year, so it wouldn't have been difficult for Emil to make the connection, especially if he dangled a show over his head.

Her eyes widened. They filled with tears. The blood

rushed to her head. The bottle went slack in her lap leaked out into the grass.

She remembered the abject sadness of her visit to his loft: the yellowing *Village Voice* review, his trembling hands when he poured the drinks, his resentment of Al, and his sudden outburst when she told him Al was going to get the April show.

Intended! God, if I could bring myself to tell you what Al intended!

"Oh!" Her cry hung in the trees, animal-like and primiparous. She tucked her chin. A tear dripped down onto her lap. She stared myopically at the spilled wine between her legs.

Those vain, mysterious fingerprints that begged for attention . . . "It's a boy," she whispered. "What have you done, Bill?"

Twenty-five

If, in the bucolic park of Versailles, her mind had undergone a kind of metamorphosis by engendering the identity of the unknown fingerprints, her relief was short-lived. By the time she arrived back in Paris, by the time she returned to her hotel, Rhea was thoroughly depressed.

She wasn't having second thoughts about Bill. They were his fingerprints, all right. She would have sworn on a stack of Monets that they were his. Who else could the police and she have overlooked?

No, it wasn't his identity that tormented her. It was what his identity might or might *not* prove. So they were his fingerprints. So what? That demonstrated that Bill was in on the trashing of the show, but it didn't prove that he was the murderer. True, his fingerprints were on the branding iron. But so were Al's and so were Simon's and so were Felix's and so, for that matter, were hers.

One thing was for sure: Bill hadn't acted alone.

Felix: she suddenly felt perturbed about him. Almost from the beginning, she had discarded him as a suspect. Why? Because he was German? Someone to talk to when the English language became too tedious? Because of his healthy, good looks? Because his boyish, unflagging quest for girls seemed to preclude any other interests?

Still, Felix remained the least likely of suspects. And the fact that she, at this late date, after having realized that Bill was the only one who hadn't been fingerprinted, was capable of trumping up a charge against Felix proved conclusively how muddy her thinking remained. Why was she still casting stones in all directions? Why didn't Bill's involvement make that brutal night at the gallery any easier to visualize?

Because Emil's murder hadn't happened in a vacuum, that was why. Because Bill's *sole* involvement simply didn't explain enough.

While she called room service for a bottle of whiskey, something out of the corner of her eye attracted her attention: a copy of the Friday *New York Times* peeked out from under her briefcase.

The day before, at Kennedy Airport, she had picked up the paper and, during the flight, had discovered that there was a review of Al's installation. The article had excited her not so much because it was sensational publicity as because the reviewer had used several key words that she found compelling in terms of her own ongoing investigation. Words that she had circled somewhere across the Atlantic Ocean. She snatched the paper and reread the article with heightened attention.

The reviewer's slant was that Al's show was a statement on the newest trend of art, neo-geo, a.k.a. simulationism. The tone of the reviewer was sniffy but he did concede that the installation raised several issues pertinent to the current surge of "Art as Opportunism," as he called it.

> *The only new art that has been perfected in the last year or so is the art of Idea-Slumming. Wandering through galleries these days is like ransacking a used-car lot. About the only thing one can do to test the*

> *product is to kick the tires, pay the tacky car dealer, and cling to the hope that it will get one at least as far as one's driveway.*
>
> *When an artist (such as we saw last year and who shall remain unnamed) can make casts of bunny balloons and Bob Hope statuettes and call them art, when the press targets this with all the hype of an ad campaign, and when the public is willing to wait in line for the privilege of paying $50,000 or more for a stainless-steel statement of cynicism—what else could follow but the elegy now on view at the Emil V. Orloff Gallery?*

The article went on to suggest that the "fire into gold" message was nothing more than an "ancient Greek aphorism *recycled* to define simulationism. Indeed, it would almost be heretical *not* to use a plagiarism to define this dubious art form."

Could be, she thought.

But if that was the real intention of the message (which would, once and for all, put an end to the Al-Ghost-HoHo theory), it also identified the only person in her life who had the convoluted intellectual equipment and the perversity to conjure it up in the first place: Emil.

She reread the article, this time writing down on hotel stationery the words she had circled:

ambition
cynicism
greed
unrequited vanity
second-hand passion
despair hyped as wit

The more she looked at the list—God, she was obsessed with lists—the more it looked like an exact recipe for Emil's demise. The question was, who had added which ingredients? There was a knock on the door.

"Entrez!" she growled.

It was room service with her scotch. She tipped the man and returned to the stationery, doubly fortified.

She wrote:

> BILL WHITEHEAD: *ambition, unrequited vanity*
> SIMON GOLDEN: *ambition (sort of)? unrequited vanity (sort of)?*
> AL KHEEL: *ambition, cynicism, greed, unrequited vanity, second-hand passion, you name it*
> CATHERINE: *second-hand passion*
> FELIX: *perpetual erection*
> EMIL ORLOFF: *cynicism, second-hand passion, despair hyped as wit.*

Too many cooks in the kitchen. They couldn't all be responsible, though unintentionally they may all have contributed.

She opened the French doors and looked out over rue de Bac. In the distance she could see a sliver of the Seine and, towering above it, the Mansard roof of the Louvre. Directly below her workers were going home for the day, heading for the *Métro* and queuing in bus lines. Did she envy them their homes from her rented window, or was it just their tidy routines she coveted?

She looked up at the sky. It would be a beautiful Saturday evening in Paris. A shame to waste it. There was a score of friends in Paris she might call for company . . . She closed the French doors and pulled the full-length curtains shut. She took a shower and ordered up dinner.

She called Tennyson in New York.

"Goddamn it, Rhea, you promised me you wouldn't do anything rash."

"I haven't. Extravagant, maybe, Arbitrary, maybe, but not rash. I've identified the fingerprints. John, are you there?"

"Yes, I'm here. Who do you think it is?"

"Not think. Know."

"Well are you going to tell me or not?"

"What will you do if I tell you?"
"I'll nab whoever it is and verify it."
"Then I won't tell."
"Why the fuck not?"
"Because this is my . . ." She almost said *baby* but checked the impulse with a sour smile. "This is my discovery. And I deserve to be in on it. Just call it unfinished business between Emil Orloff and Rhea Buerklin."
"Is this all bullshit or what?"
"You'll see when I get back."
"And when will that be?"
"I can catch the Concorde tomorrow morning at eleven. That'll put me at Kennedy at 8:45 A.M., New York time."
"I'll be there to pick you up. I'll be easy to pick out. I'll be the one pointing a gun at your head."
"Good night to you too, John."
Her dinner came but she ignored it.
She drank scotch and watched a TV show, a singularly mirthless American sitcom dubbed into French. It was better than a barbiturate.
She passed out around nine.

Sunday morning.
Kennedy Airport clamored and roared under bright blue skies. In blatant contrast were the dark circles under her eyes, her dirty three-day-old suit, and the thunderous scowl with which Tennyson greeted her at the gate.
She held out her arms as if to be handcuffed. He didn't think it was funny. "Who is it?" he asked.
"Bill Whitehead. You guys fucked up. You fingerprinted everybody that first day but when Bill came to work on Monday . . ."
Tennyson said nothing. Was he unconvinced or just angry with himself for the oversight? When they got to his

unmarked car, she watched him stick a flashing light onto the top. She got in on the other side. He turned on the siren. He peeled out. He veered around a congestion of taxis and limos.

"Put on your seat belt," he ordered.

"Where are we going?"

"To the Bowery, naturally."

"So you admit that you didn't fingerprint him."

"Would I be going to the Bowery if we had?"

"Gee whiz, what a sore loser. Are you pissed off because I figured it out or because I slipped through the fingers of your bozo tail? It wasn't very difficult, by the way."

"The man's suit," he grumbled. "I should have figured that out. Have you been wearing it the whole time?"

"I like it."

"You look like a bum. Jesus Christ, Rhea, there was a possibility that you were dead. Do you have any idea what I've been through?"

She shrugged. He changed the subject. "When you disappeared, I brought in Simon and Al for questioning."

"Together?"

"No, separately."

"On what charges?"

"No charges, just questioning."

"And?"

"Simon's a weeper. He denied everything and about every two minutes begged us not to hit him."

"You roughed him up?"

"No. He was just scared out of his wits. Please don't hit me. Please don't hit me. You can't get anywhere as long as they keep that up."

"The painting in my loft? How did he explain that?"

"He says it's absurd . . . that we've turned the painting upside down just to frame him. I felt like a damn fool even bringing it up."

"What about the extra key he had made up?"

Tennyson looked at her for a moment. "He says Al told him to do that, that you had asked Al to have a copy made."

"Not true."

"Yes," John sneered, "but who's lying? Simon or Al or you?"

Rhea turned toward him. "Me!"

"Yes, you. I thought your position with Al had shifted. Cooled."

"It has. I haven't seen him since Wednesday, the day after the reopening."

"But you've talked to him."

"Several times."

Rhea punched in the cigarette lighter and offered Tennyson a Gitane. He shook his head. "Those French cigarettes smell. Al said . . . no, he *bragged* that you're paying the bills until his April show."

"Just trying to cover my losses."

They traveled several miles in silence. Rhea exhaled in his direction as much as possible without being too obvious. Finally she said, "Did you ask Al about the keys?"

"Of course. You know what he said? He said, 'Why would I tell Rhea that Simon might have had a copy made if *I* had told Simon to have the copy made in the first place!'"

"Good point."

"I suppose so. He says that Simon must have been mistaken."

"And how does he explain Bill's accusation—that he and Emil had planned the destruction of the show?"

"He denies it, of course. He said that Bill was just jealous because he, not Bill, was getting the April show. He denies, Simon denies . . . everybody and their mother in this case have plausible deniability." John added, "Al's lying through his teeth."

"About what?"

"About a lot of things. The question is, how do we get him to tell the truth?"

"You still think he killed Emil?"

"If he didn't, he sure as hell knows who did."

"Bill Whitehead?"

"We'll soon find out, won't we?"

"John . . . what if Simon's painting really *is* a coincidence?"

"God forbid that I should be right on that point! In any case, at this point both Simon and Al are ACD."

"What's ACD?"

"Adjournment in Contemplation of Dismissal. In street terms, a criminal too smart to be held."

The car went speeding up over the apex of the Fifty-ninth Street Bridge. The skyline of Manhattan gleamed optimistically in the morning sun. It seemed to mock her, and suddenly it stabbed her with self-doubt. What if Bill was innocent? What if the unidentified fingerprints belonged to someone completely unknown to anyone involved with the gallery?

The Sunday morning traffic on the FDR was minimal. Tennyson turned off the siren. The car jerked from one lane to the next in an effort to miss the potholes.

"I won't pull up in front of Bill's place," he said.

The speed of the car, the sudden absence of the wailing siren, the idea of once again facing Bill Whitehead in his gloomy inner world—all of it filled her weary body with a churning mixture of anticipation and dread. Tennyson took the Houston exit.

"We'll find a telephone booth so that you can call him first, make sure he's there."

Two blocks away from Bill's loft, Tennyson pulled over to a public telephone.

"What if he doesn't want to see me?" she asked.

"If he's as ambitious as you say he is . . ."

"Got a quarter? I'm broke."

He handed her the coin. She got out of the car and made the call. "Did I wake you up? I'm two blocks away and I'd like to talk to you."

"What about?"

"Everything. Bill? Are you still there?"

"OK, I'll be downstairs."

She walked back to the car. "It's all set. He'll have the door open. Now what do we do?"

Tennyson gave her some rudimentary logistics. At the corner of Bill's block, Rhea walked on ahead. She clutched at her unlatched valise with one hand and knocked at Bill's metal door with the other. The door opened immediately.

The crevice in Bill's forehead deepened. His mouth dropped open. "Rhea? My God, I thought you were one of the local winos. What have you done to yourself? And what's with the man's suit?"

She loosened her grip on the valise. The lid flopped down and the entire contents scattered at their feet. Bill was bent over at the waist when Tennyson hurried up and grabbed him by the forearm.

"What the . . ." Bill turned on Rhea. "You . . . you lousy bitch."

"There, there," Tennyson maintained his grip. "Just want to ask a few questions. We can do it at my office or you can invite us upstairs. Whichever you prefer."

"I don't have anything to say to either of you! You don't have any right to—"

"You're going to be fingerprinted, Bill," Rhea said.

He stopped struggling. His eyes glazed over. His chin dropped down. For a moment he seemed to be staring at the palms of his hands as if he'd never seen them before. All the tension drained from his body and a strange calmness took its place. He nodded his head.

"I wondered how long it would take. I mean it was just a matter of time, wasn't it?"

"Just a matter of time," Tennyson agreed.

"Come on up," he said.

Rhea could have sworn that he was trying to suppress a smile.

Twenty-six

Bill flipped on the lights when they entered his loft. Rhea gasped.

"Well," Bill asked her, "what do you think of my new installation?"

As before, the sculptures were suspended from the ceiling. The difference this time was that, hanging from the sculptures were countless nooses made of heavy rope.

"I call it 'Mass Suicide,' the title referring to the mass, the weight of the work. Makes a heady display, don't you think?" he laughed. "A good picture for the *Post*. I've been thinking a lot about publicity lately." He walked over to a storage bin and made as if to open a drawer.

"Hold it right there!" Tennyson commanded, grabbing for and extracting his gun with a rapidity that made Rhea jump, but seemed to leave Bill unimpressed.

"You open it, then," Bill said.

"Stand back," Tennyson ordered.

He opened the drawer, which rattled with tools. He looked up, brows knitted. "What am I supposed to see?"

"Under the bits box," Bill said. He seemed almost amused.

Tennyson pulled out a wad of dime bags of heroin stamped Air Mail and a clump of keys. He tossed the keys to Rhea.

"They're Emil's," she said. "I recognize the key ring. It's from Cartier's."

They both looked at Bill. He seemed impatient with their lack of reaction. "Well? Isn't this where you read me my rights? Don't I get some handcuffs? Maybe I'm not playing the part right. I wish I could break down and blubber for you . . . I snorted some heroin just before you came, I . . . feel so good."

He meandered through the maze of nooses, fingering and admiring them as he passed each one, setting them into a gentle swaying motion. "It's odd," he continued. "Every since that night I've envisioned this moment. It's not at all as I had imagined it. Where's the drama? Where's the press?"

Tennyson read him his rights. Whitehead nodded and suggested that they be seated.

They moved away from the colony of nooses. The only chairs were in front of the large windows overlooking the street. Rhea noticed that the bottle of Dewar's was still on the windowsill. Absentmindedly, she opened it and took a slug. She offered it to the men but they shook their heads.

"Heroin and whiskey together make me nauseous," Bill apologized, scratching his neck and arms. "And who would clean up the mess? My mother would. I wonder what my parents will say when the reporters interview them? I wonder what embarrassing details they'll give of my childhood?"

He turned toward Rhea. "I lied to you the other day. I told you that Al *said* that Emil had planned the trashing of the show. That's not true. Al didn't say anything about Emil. Are you relieved?" He laughed.

"Why did you lie?"

"Why do you think? You told me that you were giving Al the April slot, my show. I lost my head, that's all. I was angry and sorry for myself and jealous. I wanted to strike back at him *and* you. No, the truth is quite the opposite. Last Monday, at the gallery, while I was painting the walls, several times that day I tried to get Al to talk about Emil but he wouldn't. He didn't want to talk to me about Emil. He didn't want to talk to me at all. I was just the intruding hired hand." Whitehead stared out the window with a blank expression. He could have been watching a TV program of no particular interest.

"Where was I?"

"You said that Emil promised you a show last spring," Tennyson said. "Was that a lie, too?"

"What?" Bill resumed his scratching. "Oh . . . no. That wasn't a lie. It happened just like I told Rhea it happened. I was helping out at the gallery. Al came into town with some new work. I helped him bring it in. I showed Al and Emil my work and Emil liked it. No, Al's the one who's lying. He heard Emil praise my slides. He praised them then and he praised them later, at Fanelli's, and Al was a witness."

Rhea and Tennyson exchanged a glance.

"I know what you're thinking," Bill said. There was a slight hint of emotion in his voice. "You're thinking that Emil was bullshitting me. It's true, he didn't offer me a show right then and there but . . . he kept indicating his interest . . . and Al was a witness. It's so mean of Al to deny that. Doesn't he have success enough to allow me . . . of course, at Fanelli's, he was so full of himself that maybe he didn't really hear."

Tennyson sighed. Rhea could see him fighting his own impatience with Whitehead's rambling.

"Bill," he said, "You keep mentioning Fanelli's. Why was Fanelli's so important?"

"Because that's when it all began. That's when the seed of the idea . . ."

"Emil invited you and Al to Fanelli's for drinks?"

"What's so hard to believe about that?" Bill straightened up slightly. "I'm an artist—just as good as Al Kheel—and Emil was an art dealer."

"And that's when he proposed the idea of giving you a show?"

"No, quit putting words in my mouth, would you? In the first place, getting Emil to talk about anything for more than thirty seconds at a time was like pulling teeth. He jumped around from one subject to the next. That was part of his charm, I suppose. That night, he was worse than usual. He was very agitated. When I pressed him on the subject, he said that he would be more in the mood if—"

"If?"

"If he felt a little better. He said his connection had just been busted—"

"Teddy Wilson. Did you know him?"

"I'd seen him around. He supplied quite a few people down here. Anyway, Emil was complaining that he was in need of a do-right."

"Do-right?" Rhea asked.

"Slang," John explained, "for a reliable drug dealer." He turned back to Whitehead. "In other words, Emil was asking you to score for him. And did you?"

Bill shrugged. "He would have got it from someone else, if I wouldn't have."

"And he was dangling a show in front of your face to make it easier for you."

"He liked my work."

"OK, he liked your work. So you left Fanelli's and scored for him. And then you came back? And was Al still there?"

"Yeah. They must have been drinking pretty hard while I was gone. I couldn't have been gone more than thirty minutes. When I got back they were pretty drunk. Emil and Al were joking about doing a box show made out of detonators, you know, dynamite boxes. It was just a joke but . . . I don't know. I didn't see what was so funny. I mean, here was an artist who was represented by a good gallery making fun of his own work."

"You were jealous? Shocked?"

"No. Just turned off by it."

"You didn't feel excluded? What happened then?"

"Al expanded on the idea. After a while, Al's idea of a show, an installation presented as a kind of detonation, an examination of destruction, became more general and far less joking in tone."

"What was Emil doing?" Rhea asked. "What was his reaction?"

"He didn't say anything. He just sat back and let Al expand. But there was something in his silence . . . you could tell he loved the idea. His eyes were gleaming. Anyway, after a while, the idea kind of wore itself down. Emil was getting itchy. Al said he had to get back to Connecticut. He left. Emil paid the bill and we left."

"He didn't go into the bathroom at the bar?"

"You mean to toot up? No. That struck me as funny, too. He said he had scruples when it came to Fanelli's, that it was practically an institution of higher drinking, one of the oldest bars in New York and that he wouldn't sully it by—"

"So where did you go from there?"

"To the gallery. He got out the heavy artillery—a syringe, a spoon—and hit up."

"We're talking about heroin, right?"

"Right."

"And what were you doing?"

"I tooted some. I don't mainline. We got fucked up. He kept laughing about Al's trash installation. And he started expounded on what he would *really* like to do for an installation before . . ."

"Before what?"

Bill shrugged. "It was just a figure of speech . . . before it was all over."

"And that's when he came up with the idea of Al's boxes thrown in a heap?"

"Not Al's boxes. Just a show. Anybody's work thrown in a heap, exhibited like junk. He was kind of ranting. Even if he was serious about the idea, I just assumed that nothing would ever come of it, you know? As drugged as he was, he might not even remember it the next day. I really didn't take it seriously. It was just fantasy."

"Oh, I see. You were patronizing him," Tennyson intoned sarcastically. "Lending a sympathetic ear to a junkie who was in a position to help you. In fact, you became his pusher that night, isn't that right?"

"I didn't think of it that way. Up until then, I'd never scored for anybody but myself."

"But Emil Orloff wasn't just anybody, was he? He owned an art gallery that advertised in national magazines and you were under the impression that you were an artist worthy of his attention."

Bill stiffened but didn't say anything.

"All right. Let's go on. You began scoring for him on a regular basis, is that right? And when was the next time he talked to you about a junked show?"

"It was early summer. He was out on Long Island by then but he came into town to score. I pressed him about my work but all he said was 'in good time' or some such bullshit. He said he had an idea cooking that, if he could swing it, and if I would be willing to help, would make him very happy."

"Did he give you details?"

"Some. I didn't want to know. It sounded too hallucinogenic. Besides, I was getting impatient about my own show. I told him I was tired of going over to Alphabet City for him, risking my neck to get him drugs, that there was nothing in it for me. He told me to be patient. The next time he came into town—"

"When was that?"

"I don't know . . . mid-July, I guess."

"For more dope?"

Bill nodded his head.

"You scored for him?"

"Yes. He handed me five hundred dollars apart from the dope money. He said it was a bonus for my patience. Then he started talking about the box show in detail. All the details had been worked out by then."

"Including the message?" Rhea asked.

"Everything," Bill repeated. "I told him he was crazy. I told him I wasn't going to go to jail for . . . and then he laughed at me. He said what I was *already* doing for him was a damn sight more illegal than smashing a few boxes. I refused to be a part of it . . . God! This smack makes me itch. Good stuff."

"So you refused to be a part of it," Tennyson said. "What happened next?"

"That's when he offered me my show, the April show. He gave me dates and everything so I knew he was serious. He committed himself. It was all set."

"And you agreed?"

"What do you think?" Bill laughed.

"I was referring to the trashing of Al's show. Did you accept his conditions? Did you agree to trash Al's show?"

"No, I didn't." Whitehead bristled. "Believe it or not, I actually had some consideration for Al Kheel."

"Did you like Al?"

"I don't know. I could take him or leave him . . . no, that's not true. I hated the son of a bitch. He was so fucking cocky. But that's not the point. It wasn't a matter of liking him or disliking. It was just the idea of destroying another artist's work. It was too demeaning."

"And what made you," Tennyson sniffed, "get over your distaste? Apart from getting your own show?"

"Emil told me that it would make Kheel a star." He turned toward Rhea. "He was right, wasn't he? Kheel's the man of the hour, isn't he? Even then, I could see that Emil was right. I didn't know then that . . ."

"That what?"

"Nothing. Skip it." Bill laughed. "Christ, I told him, if I've got to trash a show, why don't I trash my own work? Make *me* the star. Emil looked at me kind of funny. 'How do you smash steel sculpture?' he asked me. End of argument. We had a big laugh over that. You see, by then we'd become good friends."

All of this time Rhea had watched, spellbound, as Bill had warmed to his own confession. The ease with which he related the story was no doubt facilitated by his intake of heroin. But there was something else. It must have been an enormous relief to be able to confess, to get it off his chest. She could understand that. What she couldn't understand was the pride, the vanity that grew in him with every additional detail. He was stage center at last. He was like an actor savoring every word that came out of his mouth. He was listening very carefully to every intonation of his own voice—apparently oblivious to the consequences of his confession.

"John, I'd like to ask Bill something," she said.

"Go ahead."

"Bill, what was Simon's role in all of this?"

"I told you before. Simon wasn't in on this. Emil wouldn't have trusted him. Simon's meekness . . . Emil didn't trust it or like it. He said Simon was *your* lackey. He also said his painting was shit. What are you dressed up like a man for, anyway?"

"So you agreed to his plan," Tennyson continued.

"In the end, yes. After the opening-night party, I was to meet him at the gallery."

"What time was that?"

"The plan was for two o'clock. Naturally, he didn't show up until two-thirty. He was always late. Still, I was nervous. I was beginning to wonder if he'd gotten cold feet."

"Why didn't you go to his apartment?"

"I never went to his apartment. That was part of the plan."

"I see. You were great friends with Emil but he never invited you to his house, is that it?"

"I wasn't invited because he didn't want to arouse any suspicion."

"Right. So he showed up at two-thirty. Then what?"

"I could see, as he crossed the sidewalk, that he was totally fucked up. He could barely walk. He was carrying an enema bag over his arm, you know, like a waiter carries a napkin? I was really pissed off. I told him this was no time to be fucked up."

"This was in the street? And nobody saw you?"

"It was two-thirty in the morning."

"Yes," Tennyson said incredulously. "On a Friday night in SoHo. Nobody saw you? I can't believe that."

"Maybe someone did see us." Bill shrugged. "If they did, they didn't pay any attention."

"To an enema bag?"

"Look. There are weirder things on the streets of SoHo than enema bags."

Rhea laughed in spite of herself. Tennyson shot her a look.

"Anyway," Bill continued, pleased with the success of his observation, "we weren't out there for very long. Thirty seconds, tops. He gave me the keys, I unlocked the gallery door, he turned off the security system and we went to work . . . that is, *I* went to work."

"You started destroying the boxes," John said.

"That's right."

"That couldn't have taken you long."

"It *shouldn't* have. It did. Emil kept getting in the way. First he couldn't manage the filter for the coffee machine and I helped him with that."

"Coffee?"

"For the enema bag. Then after I took care of that, while the coffee was brewing, he started waltzing around as if he were some kind of fucking choreographer or conductor or something. The way he was waving his hands! Then he got this brainstorm of bringing up a big painting from downstairs."

"The trapdoor," Rhea blurted.

Whitehead looked confused over her excitement.

"Why a big painting?" Tennyson asked, again signaling Rhea to keep still.

"To add to the confusion," Bill said, smiling. "That's what was so brilliant about the installation. Everything was calculated to confuse. Anyway, we lifted aside the trapdoor, he went downstairs and handed up a big painting. His idea was to prop it against any old wall, it didn't matter. He came back upstairs . . . the painting was an abstract, I've forgotten whose . . . and he shook his head. He didn't like it. He fixed his enema bag and went back down. I dropped the painting to him and he handed me a different one. He didn't like that one either. I dropped that one back down and talked him into forgetting about that idea. Let's just stick to the original plan, I said. He agreed and I got back to work."

"Did he come back upstairs?"

"No, and I was glad of it. I took one last look down the hole. He was squatting with his stupid enema bag and a bottle of something, brandy, I think, just shaking his head and mumbling to himself. I think that's when he began to nod out. I knew he'd done a lot of smack. I didn't know how much. I didn't really care at that point. I had to get to my work, you know? I was nervous. I didn't want to make this an all-night party and Emil . . . nodding out on me didn't help. Anyway, I wrecked all the boxes. I piled them up into two piles like we had decided. It was a lot of work. I swept up all the glass and shit around the piles. I put the note—"

"The 'fire into gold' message? That was your handwriting?"

"A warped version of my handwriting. I perched it on

top of the larger pile. I wiped down the broom with a rag—"

"Why did you do that when your fingerprints were everywhere else in the room?"

"I told you. That was the beauty of the plan: confusion. So anyway, this maybe took me a half hour or so. When I was finished, I went over to the slot and called down for him. 'Emil,' I yelled. 'Come take a look. It's finished!' There was no answer. I called again. Still no answer. I went downstairs. I looked all over the place. I couldn't find him. Finally I heard a kind of mumbling. I found him in the very back of the storeroom, sort of under that work table, with his pants down, that disgusting enema bag up his . . . the rig next to him. He was shaking, not convulsions, really, but almost. I got scared . . . I got down next to him . . . his face was all gray. I've never seen that color on a man's face before, and there was spittle coming out of the corner of his mouth and his eyes were glassy. I shook him and he suddenly came to, pushed me away with one hand. It was if he'd been playacting all along, though I knew he couldn't have been. He was pissed off. 'What are you waking me up for?' he said. 'Let me be,' he said.

"'Fuck you, man!' I said. 'What we're doing is crazy enough without you nodding off on me with a fucking enema bag up your ass. I can't believe this shit!'

"He looked up at me with this smile, cool as cucumber, he smiled and said, 'Does it disgust you?'

"'Fuckin' A, it disgusts me!' I said.

"That's when he picked up the syringe. He tried to find a vein. He was just poking away at his arm. It was impossible to look at him.

"'Haven't you had enough of that?' I said.

"And he looked up at me and said, 'I've had enough of you. You're a fool, Bill,' he said. 'You think I'm disgusting. *You're* disgusting. You are one of a million mediocre artists on this pathetic planet who thinks he has genius. I have genius. You have nothing. In any case, I wouldn't give you a show if you were the last artist on earth. Your work in my gallery?' He laughed. 'Over my dead body.'"

Bill looked up at Rhea. The faint beginnings of smile curled around his lips, and then disappeared. He turned to Tennyson. "I saw Al's branding iron nearby. I grabbed it. I smashed his fucking smiling head in. I went back upstairs. I looked at the place. I didn't know what to do. What could I do? I tooted up some smack. I just sat there for a while. I mean, all of this for nothing. I just sat there trying to understand what had happened. It was like he was begging me to kill him. I had to think what to do next. Trying to get up the nerve to move . . . I was too scared. I was shaking all over. Had he planned for me to kill him? And then I got angry all over again. I went back downstairs, I picked up the branding iron and hit the son of a bitch all over again."

Bill looked up. "He asked for it. He knew I would . . . he . . ."

For several moments no one said anything. Rhea looked to Tennyson for some kind of reaction. He gave none. She looked back at Bill, who sat smiling and trembling at the same time.

Finally, John cleared his throat and said, "On Sunday, Rhea asked Simon to call you. When he called you . . . why did you accept the job for Monday? Weren't you afraid to come back to the gallery? When Rhea signed your paycheck—that's when . . . do you realize that you might never have been discovered if you hadn't accepted that job?"

Bill shrugged. "I was more afraid *not* to. I was afraid that someone might get suspicious if I didn't take the job. Simon told me how everybody had been fingerprinted on Saturday, so I thought that maybe the coast was clear. The one thing that Emil had done right was to keep me in the closet, so to speak. Nobody suspected me. There was no reason to suspect me. Besides, it was a good way for me to find out, firsthand, what was going on. There was one other reason. I had to talk to Al."

"You were going to confess to Al?"

Bill looked at Tennyson as if he didn't understand. Then he let out a high-pitched laugh. "Confess? Confess? Why, you dumb shit!" He wiped the tears from his eyes. "I was going to make him help me get that show in April."

"Why did you think he would help you?"

"I don't believe this! You don't get it, do you? I'd taken all the risks for him, I'd furthered his career. I deserved my show. That show belonged to me. I'd earned it. The least he could do was to help me to get it, to persuade Rhea to give it to me, and what does Al do? He acts like he doesn't know what I'm talking about. 'I killed Emil. I wrecked your show. You owe me,' I told him. He looked at me like I was crazy. 'Maybe you should stay away from the paint,' he told me, 'I think the fumes have gone to your head,' he said. And then he walked off."

"Are you implying," Rhea suddenly stood up, "that Al was in on this?"

"Implying!" Whitehead giggled. "Give the lady in drag a cigar! Not only does Al walk out of this a free man, he collects the insurance money, he gets a great boost in his career and the piece of ass as well!"

Tennyson's first slammed into Whitehead's bared teeth. He seized him by the collar and pulled him to his feet. He gouged one thumb up under Whitehead's Adam's apple.

"I'll have you breaking out in assholes if you don't answer me and answer me straight. What was Al's part in this?"

They had to wait for Whitehead to stop coughing. His lip was split open and he kept spitting out blood. "I told you!" he cried. "Al Kheel planned the whole thing!"

"And on Monday, when you came to work for the gallery, you actually told him that you had killed Emil?"

"Of course I told him. Not that I had too. He knew, but he was playing innocent. Right to my face."

"Accessory to murder," John said.

"Accessory to fuck! You think he'll ever admit to that? He'll go to his grave denying it. I only wish . . . if I had it to do over again, it would be his brains I'd splatter. To my face, he said he didn't know what I was talking about. The fucking audacity . . . and then to deny to Rhea that he ever remembered Emil offering me a show!"

"And so you drove up to Connecticut. Is that why you trashed his place?"

"That's right. It was a kind of poetic warning. Since he wouldn't talk to me, I had to do something . . . he could have still set things right with Rhea since he was . . ."

Bill felt his lip. "Since he and Rhea were intimately involved, I figured he could get her to do anything."

"How did you know where he lived?"

"In August, I helped him with a job up there. I drove up there every day for two weeks. He was going crazy. He had a kitchen to finish for someone, his show was right around the corner. He needed some help so he called me up."

"And the phone calls. That was you, too, wasn't it?"

"I had to talk to him, I had to talk to someone about it. It was eating me up inside and he acted like he didn't know what I was talking about and . . . he wasn't going to get away with that. It was like he was trying to drive me crazy. Well, two people can play that game, right? At first the phone calls were meant to be a warning to him. But then they became a warning to me."

"What do you mean by that?"

"I don't know exactly. But it's true."

Carefully, he put a finger to his mouth. His eyes widened in shock. "You've broken one of my teeth," he said.

"So what were you going to do next? If we hadn't come, what was your plan?"

"I don't know. There was always the nooses." He giggled.

Tennyson called the station. Two patrolmen arrived a few minutes later. Bill finally got his handcuffs. "Do me a favor," he said to Rhea. "See if you can get the press to take a picture of my place. You know, the ropes and everything . . ."

They led him away. John offered to take Rhea home but she shook her head. "I need some fresh air. It's only a ten-minute walk from here. What are you going to do about Al?"

"Bring him in." Tennyson shrugged. "Arrest him as accessory to murder, conspiracy to defraud the insurance company . . . I can come up with at least a half dozen charges. I'll just have to hope that he talks."

"But it's his word against Bill's."

"Basically, that's about the size of it."

Twenty-seven

She left Bill's loft around noon and walked the short distance to SoHo. It was a bright, warm afternoon and the usual Sunday tourists were circumnavigating the heart of the art district. She must have been a spectacle in her crumpled man's suit, her hair pointing in all directions. It wouldn't take much imagination to view her as a precocious bag lady. She certainly felt like one.

She went to a pay telephone and dialed Al's number.
"Hello?"
"It's Rhea. Is Jack with you?"
"Of course."
"Good. Don't ask any questions. Just do as I say. Put him in the van and drive to a pay telephone and call this number."
"But—"
"There's no time to explain. The cops are probably on their way to your place right now. Got a pencil? Here's the number of my pay phone . . ."

She paced back and forth in front of the phone. At one point two Scandinavian backpackers approached the phone but she growled at them menacingly—slaver and all—which sent them in the other direction posthaste.

The phone rang about five minutes later.

"Rhea? What's all this about?"

"Did you get away from your place?" she asked.

"Yes. Now what's the big deal? What am I running from?"

"The police. They got Whitehead."

There was a pause on the other end.

"What for?" Al finally said.

"They interrogated him. He was fucked up on heroin and told them everything. I know. I was there. He said you were in on the whole thing from the very beginning, that you knew he killed Emil, and that you were planning to collect the insurance money."

"That's ridiculous. I don't know what he's talking about."

"There's no time for explanations. It's your word against Bill's but I just thought you might want the benefit of knowing Bill's statement before the police catch up with you."

"Where are you?" he asked.

"A couple of blocks from my place. Drive into town, park the van somewhere else and grab a taxi to my place."

"What makes you think they won't be watching your place?"

"They've got their hands full with Bill, haven't they? I'm off the hook. I'm no longer a suspect, if I ever really was. Besides, Tennyson told me he was sending his men to get you. He's not looking for you here. Your odds are better with me than they are in Connecticut."

"We're on our way."

She rushed home trying not to think of Jack's arms around her neck.

Her apartment was hot and stuffy. She took a quick shower, put on some blue jeans and a T-shirt, and limped into the kitchen to make coffee. (The men's shoes had given her blisters, which had long since burst. She had somehow managed to ignore the pain until now. When the coffee was brewed, she poured herself half a mug and filled the other half with brandy.

She went into the living room, dragged a chair over to the corner windows and stared out, down on the milling crowd below. She tried not to compare it with her last window view, the one in Paris, but in vain. She tried to shut out all the noise and conversations in the background. She tried to feel like she was alone. She tried to concentrate on what she would say to Al, how she would handle it.

At 2:20, Al and Jack buzzed up. She gave them both perfunctory hugs, sent Jack into the living room to watch TV and asked Al if he wanted a drink.

"Do I need one?" he asked.

"I do."

Jack came into the kitchen.

"Where's Crunch?" he asked.

"Crunch is on vacation with Catherine. He'll be back tomorrow. Listen, Jack. There's something very important I have to discuss with your dad. We're going to go in my bedroom for a while. And I'd really rather we weren't disturbed. When we're finished talking, I'll give you a big bowl of ice cream, how's that?"

"OK," he said, and wandered aimlessly down the hall.

Al and Rhea grabbed their drinks, walked back to the bedroom and closed the door. "Where the hell have you been, Rhea? The cops pulled me in Saturday, asking about you. They asked me about the key Simon had copied . . . all hell's broken loose."

"You're telling me! I went to Paris—"

"Paris!"

"I don't have time to explain. I got back this morning, John was at the airport waiting for me and, quite by chance, I got in on Bill Whitehead's confession."

"Confession of what?"

Rhea set her drink down. "There's no time for this shit, Al. I've been straight with you all along, haven't I? I'll do anything to help you get out from under the law . . . I mean, basically, as far as I can see, all you have to do at this point is to deny your ass off. But I deserve the dignity to be told the truth. And I want it now."

Al slumped down on the edge of the bed. He stared at his glass and then up at her. His eye was still discolored, though the swelling had gone down.

"Now," she repeated.

"If I didn't tell you before now, it was because I didn't want you to be involved. There was no reason for you to get caught up in the fraud. You're not that good a liar, anyway. Are you angry with me?"

"With you? No. I'm angry with Emil. A lot of good it will do me now. It was yours and Emil's idea, wasn't it? Right from the very beginning."

He nodded. She sat down beside him, trying not to touch him though he kept moving his leg over. She capsulized Bill Whitehead's confession. When she was finished, Al kicked off his boots and lay back on the bed.

"Well?" she said.

"Well, that's pretty much it except for a few details. That first night at Fanelli's—while Bill had gone to score for Emil—and by the way, Bill was gone for a hell of a lot longer than thirty minutes, I was drunk. I told Emil about HoHo. He didn't really comment about it then. But a month or two later, I can't remember when exactly, he hit me with the whole idea all over again, including the message, which could be construed as a message from my father. All of it was planned out . . . it was the most amazing thing I'd ever heard . . . to realize that Emil was really intent on doing it. It was exciting. It was beautiful from all directions. I won't lie to you, I didn't back away for long. The insurance money, the publicity, all of that helped of course but, beyond that, it was beautiful in itself. You have to believe that *I* believed in the beauty of it."

"Emil's death was not beautiful," she said.

"No," he agreed, "that was not beautiful. But there wasn't much I could do about that, was there? The day after he was killed when I came to the gallery and found out he was dead, what could I do but continue as if he were still alive? The plan was only as good as the showing of the *re*installation . . . that was the greatness of my plan, the reinstallation. You can't deny it. You saw it immediately. There was no turning back.

"Whitehead was the problem. He'd been promised that fucking show. When he showed up on Monday, he kept coming up to me, trying to confess . . . right there in the gallery, for Christ's sake. So he'd killed Emil—what was I supposed to do about it? Felix and Simon in the same room . . . I was afraid he was going to call attention to himself. The fact that he was there, period, was horrifying enough, never mind confessions! I didn't know what to do. I just refused to talk to him."

"Is that why you denied that Emil had promised him a show?"

"Of course! What was the idiot doing, talking about that, drawing attention to himself at a time like that? It was only later that I realized how much I'd pissed him off.

"When we drove to Redding that night and I found my place . . . I knew it was Whitehead and that my problems were just beginning. The scariest part about it was that he didn't wreck the whole house, just the studio. It was the belligerence of it, as if, now that he'd got a taste for destroying my work, he would go on and on. I knew what he had in his mind: he thought I could talk you into giving him a show after all. But there was something else going on. He was obviously out of control or at least I didn't have any control over him. He wanted something more than a show out of me. He wanted to erase my success."

"That's why when he called here," Rhea said, "and talked to Tennyson, thinking it was you . . ."

"He didn't call here to talk to you. Christ, he was like

a machine that had been programmed for a certain function that couldn't be switched off. I'm glad they've caught him. And I *will* deny the whole thing to my grave. Why should I admit any involvement? I never intended for Emil to be killed. The police will soon figure out that Whitehead's not sound. I don't think anyone will believe him against me, do you?"

"No." She got up. "I wouldn't think so. And if Emil hadn't been killed?"

"What do you mean?"

"If Emil hadn't died, you two would have gone on with your plan . . . collecting the insurance money, everything. I don't suppose it was ever intended for me to find out. You and Emil would have acted as if the reinstallation were a sudden stroke of genius. Emil would have appealed to my love of economy, or irony . . . he would have convinced me of its publicity value and I would have gone along with the idea, never knowing that it had all been a conspiracy."

"I guess so. There was no point in getting you involved."

"Oh no! Just because it was half my gallery . . . there was no reason to let me in on it."

"All of this was planned before I . . . I knew you. You can't be mad at me for—"

"Oh, so you're saying that if you had known me before, things would have been different. There would have been no trashing because of your affection for me."

"Come on now—"

"I was beginning to suspect something before I heard Bill's confession. Things didn't quite add up. I kept thinking, who is Al Kheel? He's ambitious, he's cynical, he's greedy. He's a good roll in the hay. He overexplains Simon's painting . . . that bothered me. He uses his kid to assuage a sore spot in my past—"

"Now wait a minute," Al objected, suddenly sitting up.

"He's way too resourceful in a time of disaster, even for my taste," she continued, pacing up and down the room, her voice growing louder. "He destroyed his father's work when he was a little boy and was perfectly capable of appreciating the sour irony of destroying his own work. He was perfectly capable of making love to me, or anyone else for that matter, for personal gain—"

"Rhea—"

"He's capable of exploiting the memory of his father with all that ghost-HoHo business—"

"Now hold on."

"No, you hold on, cowboy!" She picked up one of his boots and threw it at him as hard as she could. "I can stomach all of it. It's a crummy world out there and I've seen enough of it to more or less expect it. I'm no better than the next person. But the one thing I can't stomach is . . . when I suspected Simon of being involved and I showed you his painting turned upside-down . . . oh God, Al, why didn't you try to make me think that I was crazy? Why did you allow me to point the finger at Simon? You didn't just allow me—you jumped at the chance, you came up with all sorts of reasons why that painting *was* incriminating. If I'd only listened to John. The one thing I'll never forgive you for is your willingness to pin the whole thing on him."

She walked away, and then turned back around again. "I take that back. I can forgive you about Simon. I can forgive you even that. What I can't forgive you is allowing Jack, your own son, to be terrorized day and night by the ghost of HoHo. You used him just like you used everybody else."

She walked over to the walk-in closet and put her hand on the doorknob. She started to turn it but then stopped. "I understand why Bill killed Emil," she said. "I can picture the exact moment when he became a killer. It was a moment when all the humiliation that came with being second rate, something that had plagued him all his life, rose up and rebelled and struck out at the disgusting symbol Emil had become. It was submissiveness turning in on itself and erupting into passion. I probably would have done the same thing. But you . . . your crimes have nothing to do with passion, do they, Al? It's just common greed that rules you. Greed and the lust for fame."

She opened the closet door.

"Did your tape recorder get everything he said?" she asked.

John Tennyson and Sergeant Lipski walked out of the closet. Al jumped to his feet.

"Crystal clear," John said. "How you doing, Al?"

The assistant DA came out of the closet too.

"What do you think, Shears?" Rhea called. "Do you think you've got enough on him to put this slime away for a few years?"

"I think so."

"Rhea!" Al cried, "You've set me up? After what we've—"

"Don't you say that to me!"

"But—"

A low-throated scream came barreling out from the deepest recesses of Rhea's soul. She tore into Al with a power that caught him off guard and threw him to the ground. It was the one time in her life that she wished she had long fingernails. She jumped on top of him and clawed his face. He screamed in pain. It took all three of them—Lipski, Tennyson and Shears—to finally pull her off of him.

But not before she'd had a satisfying dig into his lying eyes.

Twenty-eight

The Italian approached with the appetizers and Gazelle Shears broke off in mid sentence.

She and Rhea were served salads. Véra Vertbois had ordered the Blue Points. After a flickering display of long fingernails, she secured the tiny fork in a rather prodigious manner and stabbed a hapless oyster. The waiter poured the champagne and backed away.

"Wouldn't mind having a side order of him," Véra murmured, once he was out of hearing distance.

"He's a third your age," Rhea observed, without any particular reproach.

"Do you think so?" Véra asked hopefully. "Ooh, just ripe for a few educational romps with the old governess. Now, dear," she turned to Shears, "do continue. You were at the most thrilling point of the story. Absolutely seat-shifting. Rhea was on top of the cowboy, scratching his eyes out, yes, go on."

Shears, not accustomed to delivering seat-shifting narratives, fiddled with her rope of lilac beads before continuing. "Al came this close to being blinded."

"Marvelous!"

"He still hasn't fully recovered the use of his left eye. Rhea is lucky that we didn't arrest her for assault and battery."

"Assault and battery?" Rhea protested. "It was a clear case of attempted murder on my part. If it weren't for Jack, I would have killed the bastard. Poor kid. That's the saddest part about this whole thing. I hate to think what will happen to him, now that the court has handed him over to Jamie. Claiming that she needs to be with him *now* is such a vile ruse. There's not a motherly bone in her body."

"Who's Jamie?" asked Véra.

"An aging art groupie who also happened to give birth to Jack. There's no justice."

"Very little justice, at any rate," Shears agreed. "Take Bill Whitehead: he's been charged with drug-related second-degree murder, held without bail pending psychiatric analysis and saddled with a mediocre court-appointed lawyer—he doesn't have a chance. He'll be locked away, forgotten, and that will be the end of him."

"Shouldn't he be?" Véra asked, sipping her champagne.

"Of course, but . . . well, I was about to compare his situation to Al Kheel's. We'll get Al, probably, on the insurance-fraud charge but I'm not so sure about the murder conspiracy. Even with the tape of his confession, a conspiracy charge is always difficult to prove. And now, with this new development . . ."

"Yesterday," Rhea explained with a sigh, "an uptown art dealer, John Hansen, announced that he was taking on Al as a member of his stable. It's a damned good gallery."

"Good lord," Véra said, shaking her head. "You mean Al fucks male gallery owners too?"

"The point is," Rhea said, ignoring the insult, "Hansen's also putting up the money for Al's attorney fees."

"More precisely," Shears inserted, "Hansen has hired

George Breckenridge, one of the best criminal lawyers in the country."

Rhea asked Shears, "Do you think Al will walk?"

"I don't know about that, though given Breckenridge's record it's possible. In any case, Breckenridge will postpone the case as long as he can. It could be months before Al's case actually come up, maybe longer."

"How horrible." Véra's expression paled. "Shears, dear, this doesn't have any bearing on the release of my inheritance, does it?"

"What's horrible," Rhea cut in, "is the way the press persists in glorifying Al's role—as if he were some sort of folk hero, as if his misdeeds were excusable in light of the sordid realities of the art world. It's such crap. And what's worse, they've got him saying things that I know came from Emil's mouth. He's stealing Emil's thunder. Emil would be rolling in his grave if, that is, Véra hadn't been too cheap to buy him one."

Véra put down her champagne glass and smiled at Shears. "Rhea is alluding to the fact that Emil's ashes have been relegated to a kind of crematory clearing house." She turned to Rhea. "But I don't see what that has to do with being cheap. He hardly deserves a memorial chapel, does he? And I'm warning you, Rhea, if you start saying nice things about my brother, I really will have to leave."

In fact Véra did get up and leave, but only in order to reach, in a rather woozy fashion, the rest room.

"She's smooth," Shears said, smiling and arching an eyebrow. "I'll give her that."

"Yeah," Rhea growled. "Like the edge of knife is smooth. Still, once she gets her inheritance, she'll be harmless enough. She'll take her bag of gold back to Paris, pay off her debts, make peace with her dressmakers, resume her little rentals of love with gigolos, and stave off old age as long as she can . . . I don't know . . . sometimes it's hard to imagine why anyone would pursue a loftier life-style. You, for instance. You say there's very little justice . . . so what makes you stay in the law business?"

"What makes you stay in the art business?" Shears retorted.

"It's my life." Rhea shrugged. "Maybe I should get out. This would be the time to do it. A lot of things have changed in the five weeks since Al was arrested."

Rhea was referring to Black Monday, which, one week earlier, had not only caught Wall Street with its pants down, but the art world as well. Some of her best clients, especially the young investment bankers, had evaporated overnight. There was burn-out all over town, the consequences of which were still anyone's guess.

She sipped her wine knowing full well, of course, that she wouldn't quit the business. She'd be the last to give up, although her life at the gallery would never be quite as cut and dried as it had been in the past. A picture of artists, in general, was forming that had never been there before. Induced by her inadvertent plunge into Bill's and Al's and even Simon's private worlds of grievances and ambitions, she could no longer afford the luxury of regarding them as mere commodities. Still, the gallery had got back to a more or less routine schedule. (The period of mourning these days was about five minutes. Different, newer headlines had all but buried the scandal of Emil's death.)

"Emil was burned out," she said out loud.

"I'm sorry?"

"Oh, I was just wondering . . . I think I'll always wonder if Emil didn't set up Bill to murder him. God knows he'd reached that kind of dead end."

She would go on, just as the world around her had gone on, in its complicated avoidance of burnout.

The Mets had lost the division championship. Becker, her lawyer, had assured her that she could get Emil's bequest without Crunch having to visit a taxidermist. And John . . .

John Tennyson had become a necessary fixture in her life, which puzzled her, comforted her, and—why was it so hard to admit it? Excited her as well.

"Uh, oh," Rhea warned Shears, draining her glass and readjusting, metaphorically, her shoulder pads. "Here she comes: Miss France, 1946."

Véra emerged from the rest room, renewed by and convinced of the powers of newly applied lipstick. She sat down, replaced her napkin on her lap, looked up at Shears and said, "Gazelle, shouldn't we have a little talk, just man to man?"

"About what?" Shears asked, instinctively grabbing for her wineglass as if for protection.

"Well, dear," Véra said, smiling, "It's about your . . . wardrobe—"

"Véra," Rhea interrupted. "I think it's only fair to warn you that, once you've been given a taste of the indescribable joy of gouging someone's eyes out, you can never get enough."

"Oh yes, I see," Véra backed off. "Very self-destructive, isn't it?"

"In the same way that Italian waiters are destructive, yes."

"Or our dearly departed Emil, for that matter." Véra presented a dainty face of commiseration. "In spite of his beastly nature, one was rather amused by him, wasn't one? I mean, he did know how to stir one's kettle."

"Véra, you've never been within walking distance of a kettle."

"Perhaps I should have said cauldron. In any case . . ."

It would be a long lunch.